To contact the author or other inquiries:

lemonadestandbook@gmail.com

For Lena, Kayla and Alex

God has truly blessed me with them

THE LEMONADE STAND

A Story of How Freedom is Lost

"But no one can enter a strong man's house and plunder his goods, unless he first binds the strong man. Then indeed he may plunder his house."

– Holy Gospel Mark 3:27

"It is impossible to introduce into society a greater change and a greater evil than this: the conversion of the law into an instrument of plunder.

–The Law by Frédéric Bastiat

The Beginning

It was the night before Election Day in Jefferson Township.

On the evening news, the local meteorologist predicted a warmer than usual Election Day, so everyone could pull their shorts back out of the closet!

Kayla Alexander, a smart young lady with a curious mind, compassionate soul and a desire to help others, was sitting on her front porch with her Mom and Dad enjoying the warm night air. In the distance she heard the music playing from an ice cream truck as it went around trying to make a few last dollars before the cooler weather set in for good. Some of the neighborhood kids were out playing basketball, shooting balls into the hoop they had set near the curb. The sounds of their chatter and laughter drifted over to where Kayla was sitting. The night was clear with the stars and moon shining brightly in the sky.

Kayla was a good kid by anyone's definition. She was smart, pretty, and polite and had a kind heart. All her teachers in high school thought very highly of her and usually wrote great things about her on her report card every semester. She always made the honor roll, was a singer in the chorus, and loved to play around with computers. She was an only child who lived at home with her parents.

Her dad was a businessman and her mom didn't work but was very involved in the community.

Her home life was a good one. Nice and normal by anyone's definition. Her family lived in a modest, ranch style home on a quiet tree lined street. Her father loved to read, mostly books on history, economics, and current events, and the house had a small library filled with volumes on the topics her father liked best. Kayla's mom kept trying to get her father to only buy digital books, "They take up less space and don't collect dust!" she would say, but Kayla's father just loved real books made from real paper. Every so often, Kayla would find him in the Library; book in hand, with his nose literally buried in the pages.

"Smell it!" he would say to her, holding the book out. "Best smell in the world!"

With a big smile, Kayla would tell him he was crazy. But he knew better. He knew she agreed! And agree she did. Kayla loved books as much as he did. Except her tastes tended more towards books about science and nature, and fictional stories about wizards, rather than the history books her father loved.

On the weekends, Kayla and her family would visit, or be visited by, friends and relatives. Her family tried to go to church as often as possible and usually felt unfulfilled when they couldn't make it for whatever reason. Faith was an important part of their lives.

In the nice weather, they played horseshoes, went swimming, and rode bikes. In the winter, they would play board games inside or maybe even go to the shooting range to shoot some of the rifles and pistols Kayla's dad owned. That was one of Kayla's favorite things to do with her dad.

At the range, they would talk about lots of things like school, family, the weather...and history. Her father loved to talk about history. He would often tell Kayla why it is so important to know about events that have occurred in the past. "Things change," he would say. "But basic human nature doesn't." His philosophy of life was a simple one, there is good and evil in the world, right and wrong, and we have to work hard at keeping the good ahead of the evil, the right ahead of the wrong.

"Look back in time", he would say. "If it happened once before, it can happen again. No matter when and where you lived, there have been people who have sought to oppress others, sometimes for nothing more than their own gain, and for their own power. They have done so under the banner of many different philosophies, movements or politics. They have done it for many different reasons, most of the time saying it was 'for your own good', they did this all with the same goal in mind...to take from others what was not theirs."

He would go on, "Whether its material things like money or property, or immaterial things like freedom or dignity, it doesn't matter. Because the takers just want to take; and although the takers sometimes use violence, they usually don't have to because sometimes...many times, people will give up their freedom willingly. The unscrupulous takers will make the people feel afraid, unsure, and unsafe by manipulating their fears and concerns and then the takers use that against them!

" The takers would also try to make takers out of everyone else. They would get them hooked on relying on others for money, food...and the things they need to live. They would crush others spirit of freedom and self-reliance on purpose. Again, all for their own gain. Once a society becomes a majority of takers, that society has probably been lost.[1] Keep in mind though Kayla, takers aren't just poor people, they are rich people too. They can be rich people who get things like tax breaks and subsidies, which are taken from others as well, from a government that should hardly be involved in the economy in the first place.[2]

"Thank God we live in a place like Jefferson Township where we have a very small government and a society based on the principles of Life, Liberty and Property!"[3]

He would also say, "Freedom loving people must always stand guard against those who would take their freedom away. They especially must always stand guard against a creeping tyranny, for a creeping tyranny is insidious. Mainly because people willingly let it in and before they know it, it has choked the life out of their Liberty. And then it's usually too late to do anything about it. Their freedom is dead."

At the range they would also talk about guns, "We have guns not only because they are fun to shoot, or because we can use them to hunt. We also have them for protection. Protection from

---

[1] Eberstadt, Nicholas. *A Nation of Takers: America's Entitlement Epidemic.* West Conshohocken, Pennsylvania: Templeton Press, 2012. Print.

[2] Kristoff, Nicholas. "A Nation of Takers?" *The New York Times.* https://www.nytimes.com/2014/03/27/opinion/kristof-a-nation-of-takers.html Posted March 26, 2014. (Retrieved June 14, 2018)

[3] "Most scholars today believe that Jefferson derived the most famous ideas in the Declaration of Independence from the writings of English philosopher John Locke. Locke wrote his Second Treatise of Government in 1689 at the time of England's Glorious Revolution, which overthrew the rule of James II.
Locke wrote that all individuals are equal in the sense that they are born with certain "inalienable" natural rights. That is, rights that are God-given and can never be taken or even given away. Among these fundamental natural rights, Locke said, are "life, liberty, and property."
"The Declaration of Independence and Natural Rights." Constitutional Rights Foundation. http://www.crf-usa.org/foundations-of-our-constitution/natural-rights.html (Retrieved June 20, 2018)

those who would do us harm, even the government. A government that is trying to control and oppress its people usually starts by disarming them. When only government has the guns, Liberty is dead."

Kayla loved talking with her dad because he loved talking with her. Talks like this made Kayla feel very fortunate to live where she did, where individual Freedom and Liberty flourished. She knew it was not as it was in Jefferson Township everywhere, and she was grateful she had been blessed to have been born here.

As they usually did in the evening, Kayla and her parents were chatting about what went on in each of their days. Earlier in the day Kayla had an idea and she was waiting for the right moment to speak to her parents about it. When there was a lull in the conversation she spoke up.

"I know Christmas will be right around the corner, do you think if I set up a lemonade stand outside of City Hall I could make some money to buy Christmas presents?" she asked them.

Throughout the day Kayla had been thinking about the previous summer when her mother had taught her the old family lemonade recipe. The recipe was in her family for a very long time and everyone who tried it seemed to love it. So, Kayla figured she could put that knowledge to good use and make some money with it.

The recipe was quite simple...

Fresh lemons, pure spring water, ice cubes made from spring water, and real sugar. That is all that went into each pitcher, and it had to be stirred by a wooden spoon for some reason. Kayla didn't know why, but really didn't care. The lemonade tasted great and she didn't want to mess it up.

She thought of all the people in town who would be coming to City Hall to vote and knew it would be a good place to sell her lemonade. *I hope that the unusually warm weather makes them thirsty!* She thought to herself.

Her parents looked at each other. Kayla tried to see if they had that skeptical look that parents sometimes got when they think their kids propose a crazy idea.

To her surprise Kayla's dad said, "That sounds like a great idea!"

"Thank you!" Kayla exclaimed and gave each of her parents a big hug. She ran into the house and went straight to bed because she knew she had a big day ahead of her tomorrow!

On her way in she yelled, "I'll need a ride!" and before her parents could answer she was gone!

The next morning, Election Day, Kayla woke up early, got dressed, brushed her hair, and talked her mother into taking her to City Hall with her. Kayla's mother was going to be working in the polling place all day as a poll watcher and Kayla needed the ride because she only had her learners permit right now. It would be a few months before she would be able to get her full driver's license.

Kayla's mother said she would be happy to drive her so Kayla packed up the car with a small folding table, a folding chair, sugar, a whole bunch of paper cups, a glass pitcher, a cooler full of ice, which she had loaded up from her father's big ice making machine in the garage, and, of course, a wooden spoon. She also brought a small cutting board and a knife to cut the lemons as well as a small plastic juicer. Her mom had to help her load the big, five-gallon jugs of spring water into the car. When it was all done she felt like something was missing. Then it hit her...Duh! She needed lemons! She asked her mom if they could stop at the grocery store along the way to buy lemons and she said sure.

She then took out a big piece of oak tag paper, the kind they used for projects in school, and made up a sign that said, *"Grandma's Old-Fashioned Lemonade. 50 cents a Cup"*. She decorated it with stickers and pictures of fireworks they had left over from a party they had the past summer. She carefully put the sign into the car on top of the other things and then her and her mother headed off to City Hall.

City Hall was a big, old, brick building in the central square of town. It had a large central building with a big, white spire on top that had a big clock on the front. Kayla liked the clock because it had Roman Numerals on it and looked like it was from a hundred years ago, which, in fact, it was. Built off on either side of the main central building were two smaller side wings where offices and such were located.

When they arrived, Kayla's mom parked the car in the lot next to City Hall. They got out and walked up the big, wide steps to the huge double doors that led into the central main hall. When they walked in the sound of the door closing behind them echoed off the cool marbled walls. It was somewhat dark inside and had the smell of an old library. They walked down the hallway that was on the right until they came to the Town Clerk's office. Kayla's mom knocked on the frosted glass of the door and a voice from inside cheerily said, "Come in!"

They walked into a small office that was lined on every wall with bookshelves, except the wall behind the desk which had a big window in it that looked out towards the street in front of the building. Every space on every shelf seemed to be taken up with books and stacks of papers. Behind the desk, which was in the middle of the room, sat a somewhat plump woman who had a big smile on her face. That was Mrs. Adams, the Clerk. Kayla's mom said "Hello" to her and then asked if it would be OK if Kayla set up her stand outside.

Mrs. Adams, said, "Sure thing sweetie! Just don't set it up along any of the paths or the driveway where people need to get by." Looking around for a second or two Kayla said to Mrs. Adams, "How about over there?" She was pointing out the window at the big red, white and blue sign perched on the lawn of City Hall. The sign read, "City Hall-Jefferson Township-The Freest Place on Earth!"

Mrs. Adams said, "That would be a great spot sweetie! It's away from the walkway but close enough to the sidewalk that you should get a lot of people walking by."

Kayla liked Mrs. Adams... especially because she called her "sweetie". Now she liked her even more because she was going to let her set up her lemonade stand that would, hopefully, sell enough lemonade to help Kayla make some money.

Thinking she shouldn't wait around lest Mrs. Adams change her mind, Kayla said, "Thank you," as she turned around and ran out to her mother's car to get her stuff.

After a few minutes, Kayla was in business. She made her first batch of lemonade, hung her sign on the table, and sat down in her chair with it leaning back against the big City Hall sign.

She looked around and noticed there was not much foot traffic yet. It was still somewhat early. She turned around and looked up at the big sign behind her. "The Freest Place on Earth" she read and smiled. She loved living in Jefferson Township. Everyone in town always seemed to be so happy! The streets were clean, people were friendly, and everyone just seemed to get along.

And the town did have a lot of freedom. Kayla's dad talked to her a lot about how lucky they were to live in a place that had so much freedom because it was a rare thing in the world. Why was the town so free? Because it was based on the principle that the most sacred things a society could have was respect for Life, Liberty and Property. That principle permeated everything in the town from the type of government it had, to the legal system and right down to how people treated each other. It was *the* main characteristic of the town's culture.

Soon enough, people started to show up to vote. First, it was a trickle, and then a steady stream as the day went by. Kayla was so busy! She kept making pitcher after pitcher of lemonade. People loved it! *Grandma's Old-Fashioned Lemonade* was a big hit!

The meteorologist on the news the night before was right. It was a somewhat warm day so people were extra thirsty it seemed and Kayla was selling a lot of lemonade. Late in the afternoon when Kayla went to make yet another pitcher of lemonade, she opened the ice chest and her eyes grew wide in panic.

Oh no! She thought to herself, *I'm almost out of ice!*

She knew if she ran out of ice, she would have to fold up her table and go home. Think of all the money she would lose! There were still a few hours of voting in the day and more people would be heading over to City Hall to vote. There would be a big rush as people started to come home from work.

The place where she could buy more ice was far away and she did not have any way to get there and then carry the heavy bags of ice back to her lemonade stand. She was not worried about leaving her stand unattended, she was just concerned about all the business she would lose!

Just before Kayla had a full-fledged panic set in, a kid pulled up next to the lemonade stand on his bike.

"Whattcha doing Kayla?" he asked.

Kayla looked up from her ice chest. Hank, a boy she knew from school, was straddling his bike in front of her lemonade stand.

Hank was somewhat plain in a pasty-faced sort of way. He always wore tan pants, a polo shirt always buttoned up to the top button, and, for some strange reason, Sperry Topsider boat shoes that always seemed to have one of the laces untied. She could not remember him ever wearing sneakers outside of gym class.

He was one of the smartest kids in school, very good at science and math. Whenever there was a project, or a lab partner needed, he was always a good person to have on your side. Kayla had a couple of classes with him over the years but they were never really friends. She always thought he seemed a little bossy. A little like a know it all. He also loved to follow the rules and Kayla was not like that at all. She wasn't a troublemaker or anything. But she liked to have fun. Hank followed the rules no matter what, no questions asked, and Kayla liked to question things. Especially if things did not seem right.

"Hi Hank," Kayla said. "I've been selling lemonade all day but I'm about to run out of...."

Before Kayla could finish her sentence, she looked at the back of Hank's bike and saw that he had one of those kiddie trailers hooked up to it. The kind parents use to tow little kids around in when they are out riding their bicycles.

"What's that?" She burst out, pointing at the trailer.

Hank looked confused for a second and turned to look at where she was pointing.

"Huh? Oh that? It's the trailer for my kid sister. My mom made me take her for a ride today. She said it was such a nice day we should get out of ..."

"Hank! You've got to help me!" Kayla said. She ran out from behind the stand and grabbed Hank by the upper arms giving him a little shake.

Hank blushed. He had never been this close to a girl before. *And boy!* He thought to himself, *she's pretty!*

"Help...what..." he was confused.

"I am almost out of ice! Please, please can you ride to the store and get me more ice?" She pleaded. "I wouldn't be able to carry all that ice back...but your bike...the trailer! You could fit it in there!" Sensing that Hank was still confused Kayla said, "I'll pay you!"

"Ice...store?" Hank said, "Sure I would help you but what about my sister? She's in the trailer! I couldn't pile all of that ice on top of her!"

Kayla thought quick, "I'll watch her! Just leave her with me. I've baby sat before! Never had a problem! I'll watch your sister and you go get me the ice. I'll even pay you!" she said again in case he did not hear the first time.

"I don't know if my mom..." Hank started to say. But before he could finish he saw the disappointed look start to take hold on Kayla's face.

"Ahh what the heck!" he said as he got off his bike. "I'll do it!"

Kayla grabbed Hank and gave him a big hug. "Thank you!" she said. Hank turned an even darker shade of red!

Hank walked to the back of his bike and unzipped the canopy to the bike trailer. He helped his little sister Jennie out of the trailer and walked her over to Kayla.

"Jennie this is Kayla. She's a friend of mine. Kayla, this is Jennie. She's 6 years old."

She was a cute little kid, gave Kayla a big smile, and said, "Hello Kayla!"

"Hi Jennie!" Kayla said. She stooped down to Jennie's height so she could look her right in the eyes. "Can you do me favor and help me sell some lemonade for a little while?"

"Sure!" Jennie exclaimed.

Kayla took Jennie behind the stand and sat her down on the ice chest. She then pulled out a bunch of money from her pocket and walked back over to Hank.

"Thank you so much for this Hank!" she said. She pushed some bills into Hank's hands and said, "This should be enough for the ice, and here's extra for you for helping me!" She handed him a ten-dollar bill.

"I'll do it because I want to help you Kayla," Hank said, "You don't have to pay me." He tried to give the ten back to Kayla.

"Oh no no no!" she said. "I want to pay you! You're doing a job for me and it's only right I pay you for it! It's worth every penny to me to give you money for doing it. You are helping my business and deserve to be paid!"

Hank looked at the money in his hand. *I could use the money...*, he thought. After all, he was saving for a new video game. With a twinge of jealousy that Hank did not realize had occurred, he also thought to himself, *...besides, did you see that wad of money she had? She can spare it!*

Hank shrugged his shoulders and said, "Ok. "

He got on his bike and started to pedal away. "I'll be back as soon as I can," he said over his shoulder and then he was off.

As Hank rode away Kayla felt a tug at her pants. She looked down and saw Jennie staring up at her.

"Kayla?" she asked.

"Yes Jennie?"

"What does 'sell' mean?"

Kayla started laughing and grabbed Jennie by the hand. "Come on! I'll show you!"

Eventually Hank made it back with the ice and Kayla was able to keep selling lemonade right up until when the polls closed.

Turns out Hank still felt guilty about taking the money from Kayla so he asked if he could stay and help. Kayla said OK and they actually wound up having some fun. Little Jennie was a big hit with the customers! She would say, "Thanks for coming!" every time someone bought a cup of lemonade. People loved how cute she sounded and would buy an extra cup just to hear her say it again!

Soon enough the day was over. Kayla's mom came out from inside City Hall and told Kayla it was time to go home. Kayla tried to give Hank more money but he would not take it. Kayla instead gave some money to little Jennie and told her to tell her mom that the money was for her and her brother for helping out at the lemonade stand. Hank packed little Jennie back in the trailer and headed home.

Kayla did not think of it at the time but Hank and Jennie were her first employees! Because her business of selling lemonade was doing well she needed help to keep it going. She "hired" Hank and Jennie to help her out. They worked for a wage that was acceptable to all of them and everyone was happy with the arrangement. No one else had to be involved.

Kayla was happy because she was able to stay in business all day. Her customers were happy because they could keep buying lemonade, and Hank was happy because he was paid a wage that would help him buy the video game he wanted, and Jennie was just...happy!

Kayla's mom helped her pack everything up and put it back into the car.

"How did you do?" she asked.

"Really good!" Kayla said.

She told her mom about the "ice scare" and how Hank showed up and helped her out. She told her mom it felt good to be able to pay Hank for what he did because he had told her he was saving for a new video game. Kayla said it was a nice feeling knowing she helped him get something he wanted.

"Ahhh..." her mom said, "your first employee!"

Kayla thought about that for a second and said, "Does that mean I'm the boss?"

"It sure does," her mom said.

Kayla liked that! *Maybe*, she thought to herself, *I could keep being the boss somehow.*

That night Kayla and her dad were watching the election returns on TV in her living room. It seemed like Mayor Ronald was reelected and that made Kayla's dad happy. Kayla's dad liked Mayor Ronald because he believed in a town government that would leave people alone as much as possible and would only bother with people when they bothered with others. Kayla's dad also believed in a free market based on people freely exchanging goods and services and Mayor Ronald did as well. Her dad thought that the free market was the best way for people to be happy, free, and prosperous.

Jefferson Township had a minimal amount of government, and the government that existed; the people gave very specific powers to. The whole system was set up based on the underlying philosophy that aggression against another's Life, Liberty, or Property is wrong and could even be a crime. The people of Jefferson Township were traditionally very suspicious of any kind of government, because they knew history proves that over time, if people let it, a government tends to grow so powerful that it takes away people's Freedom and Liberty. Therefore, in Jefferson Township, the people set up a system where they granted their government very limited powers.

As they sat together on the comfortable brown couch in their living room, where the only light came from the flickering of the TV set, Kayla waited for a commercial break. When it finally came, she looked up at her father and said, "Daddy?"

"Yes dear?"

"I did pretty good selling my lemonade today." She said.

"That's great Kayla! Did you make a lot of money?" he asked.

"Yes, I did! I also hired my first employee!" she said.

"First employee?" her father asked.

Kayla told him about Hank.

"Wow!" he said. "That's great Kayla! Being a boss is a big responsibility, especially when you own your own business. People count on you to make the right decisions so the company keeps making money. If the company keeps making money, the company will be able to keep paying employees their wages. The more employees you have the bigger the responsibility."

Kayla thought about that for a few seconds. She remembered how good it made her feel to know she was able to pay Hank. She wondered if it would be possible to keep doing that. That is, run her business and have people work for her so she can help them out too. Not to mention the fact that she made a lot of money for herself today as well! That was great too! Not only will she be able to buy some nice things for her family for Christmas, she even had enough to buy some nice stuff for herself. *Why not?* She thought. *I worked hard for that money!*

Kayla was quiet for a few seconds.

"Hey dad," she said, "Do you think I could open a lemonade stand all the time?"

Kayla's dad smiled.

"What for dear?"

"Well the people loved my lemonade so much I thought that if I could sell it all the time that would make them happy and I could keep making money."

"Hmmm," her dad said.

"It would be a great way for me to make money to buy things I like, and, you know," she said", soon enough I'll be driving and this could help me save money to buy a car..."

She saw a worried look cross her father's face at that comment!

"...and save for college!" she recovered.

Kayla's dad seemed to be pondering this but did not say anything.

Kayla's dad was a good man. He worked hard at trying to provide for his family and was very thankful to be able to live in Jefferson Township where he and his family were able to live freely and pursue happiness in their lives. Taught to be independent and self-reliant by his parents, Kayla's dad took freedom seriously. He loved his family and he loved his town and felt truly blessed by God to have been able to live in such a free place where people had the opportunity to be as prosperous as they were able and where the government stayed out of his life as much as possible.

Because Kayla's dad was also a student of history, he knew that living in freedom was a rare thing in history. Sure, some people have always been freer than others, but never before had any place been as free as Jefferson Township. He loved it here and tried to protect what Jefferson Township stood for by being as active a citizen as he could, and by teaching his kids the same honor, respect, independence, self-reliance, and personal accountability his parents had taught him.

"I'll tell you what", Kayla's dad said, "I will buy everything you need to get started..." Kayla's face lit up..." on one condition..."

A big smile came across Kayla's face...

"I will get you started, but you have to promise that you will pay me back with a portion of any money you make until you have paid me back what I will loan to you, plus a small extra called interest. You will have one year to pay me back. Is that a deal?"

Kayla thought about this for a moment. She really believed she could make some money selling lemonade but she knew that she did not have enough money of her own to get started. Her dad was offering to give her money to get started, kind of like planting a seed, because he believed in her and her lemonade stand idea. All he wanted back was what he lent her, plus a little extra. Kayla thought for a second and realized that there was no guarantee that she would continue to sell lemonade and make money, so the little extra interest she would have to pay her father was fair because he was taking a risk of losing his money on her lemonade stand idea. She thought that was a fair and good arrangement. She had a good idea for a business that she felt would make money but she did not have any money to get started, he had money and believed in her idea. If her lemonade stand were a success they would both make out, if it failed, they would fail together.

With a big smile she said, "Deal!"

Her dad said, "OK, let's shake on it!" and held out his hand.

Kayla looked puzzled for a second and asked, "What does that mean?"

"That means you promise to stick to the agreement we just made…no matter what. By shaking hands, you give your word on your honor that you will stick to this deal as we have agreed and that you will pay me back on our original terms no matter what. Even if your lemonade stand does not work out and doesn't make any money."

Kayla hesitated for a minute. This was a little different from what she thought the deal was. She thought that if the business did not work out she would not have to pay her father back. She thought the money she owed him would just disappear.

"But how do I pay you back if the stand goes out of business and doesn't make any money?" she asked.

"Well Kayla you have to understand." Her father said. "I am taking a chance by giving you my money. I believe in you and your idea, but I am still taking a chance because there is not any way for us to know for sure you will make money. I believe that you will, so I am willing to take a chance and give you money to get started. However, you have to give me a reason to want to take that chance on your idea. The money I give you could be used by me for something else so it is worth something to me. That is why you will pay me interest. Also, because I am lending you some of my own hard-earned money, I have to be sure that you will work very hard to make my investment in you pay off. By requiring you to pay me off on our contract no matter what, that will encourage you to work hard to make your lemonade stand a success."

Kayla asked, "But if I lose all of the money you lend me and have none saved from the lemonade stand, how am I going to pay you back?"

"With something called collateral", he answered.

"What's that?"

"It's something valuable you own. You use it to reassure me, as the person lending you money that you are serious about making this business work, and it shows me that you are willing to put something that you find valuable at risk in order to start this business. I am giving you something valuable to get started, my hard-earned money, you have to show me you are willing to risk something you have that you find value in as well."

"You mean like some of the jewelry grandma gave me?" she asked.

"Yup."

"Or my bicycle?" she asked again.

"Uh huh". He said, nodding his head.

Now Kayla wanted to understand very clearly what was happening here. She asked, "So if the lemonade stand doesn't work and I lose all of my money..."

"No...you will be losing the money I lent to you," her father cut in.

"Right...all of the money you lend me, I have to give you my jewelry?" she asked.

"That's right." He said.

"But what if I don't want that deal?"

"Then you don't get my money to start your lemonade stand." He said as a matter of fact.

Kayla believed her lemonade stand would make money, but she was not sure of how much it would make. That scared her because she loved her jewelry and did not want to lose it. She felt good that her dad seemed to think the business was a good enough idea that he was going to lend her the money to get it started, but boy oh boy, it was a big chance to take.

She started to think, she could sell her jewelry to get the money herself, without taking a loan from her father, but she probably would not be able to sell it for what it was worth. Besides, if she sold her jewelry, then she would not own it at all anymore.

Kayla thought her dad's proposal was fair because it seemed like a way that they both could make out. He will lend her the money for a small price in interest, she does not have to sell her jewelry for less than what it is worth..., and...she can keep wearing it. If the business works out her father gets to make some money and she gets to keep her jewelry and make some money as well. If the business fails, she will lose her jewelry, but she will lose it anyway if she does not put it up as collateral because she will have to sell it to get the money to buy the stuff to open her new lemonade stand business. Another option was to not open the lemonade stand, keep her jewelry, and forget the whole thing. However, she really thought the lemonade stand would do well. She did not want to miss this opportunity to start a business and make some money. It all seemed to make sense.

Kayla stuck out her hand and said, "Deal!"

They shook on it.

Kayla was very excited about starting her lemonade business and she could not wait to get started!

The next day Kayla and her dad went down to City Hall first thing in the morning to talk to Mrs. Adams, the Town Clerk. Kayla asked her dad why they had to speak to her.

"Everyone in Jefferson Township is free to set up whatever business it is they would like to start," he said, "but there are some rules that the townspeople want business owners to follow. There aren't many, but they are important. They are there to guard either against people doing things that intentionally hurt someone else, physically, or against their property."

Kayla thought that was strange and asked her dad, "Rules?"

Her dad said, "Yes. Rules. The rules are there to make sure that a business owner understands their business cannot hurt someone. The rules are also there to make sure a business owner knows they have to be honest about whatever goods or services they sell. After all, it wouldn't be right if you sold lemonade that made people sick or told people you were selling lemonade but didn't put any lemons in it, now would it?"

That seemed strange to Kayla. *Why would someone want to sell something that made someone sick, or was not what they said it was?* She asked her father exactly that.

"Because sometimes people will do anything to make money," he said. "People will hurt other people, steal, or lie just to make a few bucks and that is not right. It is OK to want to make money. It's OK to want to make a LOT of money," he said.

"In fact, that is what makes Jefferson Township such a good place to live," he continued, "because all of those people who are trying to make a lot of money for themselves and their family. They make things or provide things that people want to have and are willing to pay for. That helps to create jobs for other people. Then people work at those jobs to earn money. This makes those people

27

happy because now they are able to get the things they want or need. Remember how Hank was happy when you paid him for getting your ice?" he asked.

Kayla nodded.

"Why?" he asked.

"Because he was going to use the money to buy a video game," Kayla answered.

"See what I mean?" her father asked.

Kayla said, "I do!"

"On Election Day we vote for a Mayor and we also vote for who we want to represent us on the Town Council. The Town Council is the part time legislative body that writes laws for the Township. The people gave them that power. The laws they write should never go beyond the limits that the people set for them in the Town Charter. If they do," her father said, "the people have the right to remove the Council person or persons who violated the Town Charter."

Kayla was a little put-off by all of this. She could not believe that people would actually want to hurt each other on purpose just to make money, but it must be true because her dad would never lie to her. As she thought about it, a question popped into her head.

"Well what if someone does do some of those bad things? What happens then?"

Her dad said, "For one, the victim can sue the person in court. One of the limited functions of our government is a court system where disputes between people are settled. The people allow a court system in our Township to have the power to settle disputes between people based on the rule of law. An impartial Judge and Jury hear the case and come to decision based on the law. If someone thinks a business cheated them, lied to them, or in some other way aggressed against them, they can sue."

"Aggressed?"[4]

"Aggressed is when someone starts an attack or a fight against someone else. Or violates their property in some way." Her father said.

"That's just crazy," Kayla said. "I would never hurt someone on purpose."

Her dad looked at her and said, "I know you wouldn't, but other people do not know that."

"What do you mean dad? Do people think I want to hurt them on purpose?" Now she was getting excited.

Her dad smiled at her and said, "No, no, no Kayla! Not at all. Think about this; what if the lemonade you sell at your stand made someone sick by accident? What do you think should happen then?"

---

[4] "Aggressed: To initiate an attack, war, quarrel, or fight."
(http://www.thefreedictionary.com/aggressed)

Kayla though about this and said, "Well...I guess I should say I'm sorry and maybe pay their Doctor bills. I should also find out what made them sick so I can fix it."

"That's right Kayla. Sometimes accidents happen and if they do, you should make things right with the people who were affected."

"That sounds fair," Kayla said as her father pulled their car into City Hall's parking lot.

Her father parked the car. He turned to Kayla and asked her a question.

"But what if you didn't 'do the right thing'? What do you think would happen?"

Kayla thought for a few seconds. "I guess people would hear about what happened and stop buying my lemonade because it made someone sick. It could put me out of business."

"That's right," her father said. "As long as freedom of speech exists your business would suffer without the government ever getting involved because word would spread about what you and your product did to someone. Especially today with the internet and all of the social media sites that exist now. News travels fast! The beauty of the free market is that it can regulate itself without the government getting involved. A smart business owner will always naturally try to offer the best and highest quality good or service they can provide. This is how they ensure their business will grow and thrive. They don't need the government telling them how or what to sell. The market tells them. If you are going to open a lemonade stand, it is in your best interest to only sell the highest quality lemonade you are able too. That's what's going to keep people coming back to buy your lemonade!"

Kayla said, "I get it. My business will be successful if I offer a high-quality product to people. If I don't, for whatever reason, the market will judge me and I could even get judged in a court of law if someone decides to sue me because if a bad product that made someone sick, for example."

Her father smiled. 'That's right! Now let's go inside."

When they got inside City Hall, they found Mrs. Adams sitting in her little office. Kayla smiled when Mrs. Adams called her "Sweetie". Kayla and her dad explained what they wanted to do. Mrs. Adams said, "Oh sweetie! That is great! Let me get you something that can help you out."

Mrs. Adams spun around in her chair and started to open and close drawers in the big file cabinet behind her. She was talking to herself saying, "Now, where is it?" and "Where could I have put it?" Kayla smiled at her father and he smiled back.

Suddenly Mrs. Adams said aloud, "Here it is!" and spun back around in her chair at the same time she was pulling a folder out of a drawer. She was looking at Kayla and her dad with a big smile on her face. She said, "I'd lose my head if it wasn't attached, but here it is!" She laid a thin stack of stapled together papers on the desk in front of Kayla. It could not have been more than three or four pages.

"What is this?" Kayla asked.

"Why it is our Town Charter. These are the rules that we the people allow our government to enforce," Mrs. Adams said.

Kayla knew something about it because they learned a little bit about it in school. She said, "Oh, this is like our Constitution, right?"

"That's right sweetie," she said. "These are the rules that tell the town government *exactly* what their powers are. You see...back in the day when the town was called Londonville we had a bad Mayor, Mayor King, who used to just make up his own rules to run the town as he went along. Eventually the people got tired of this because they felt like Mayor King wasn't allowing them to be free and that he didn't respect them."

Kayla remembered some of this story.

"Didn't the townspeople eventually kick him out?" she asked.

"That's right," Mrs. Adams said. "They did it with the help of a big landowner in town named Mr. Vernon, who also didn't think Mayor King was governing the town correctly. Unfortunately, the Mayor did not want to leave and he started fighting with the townspeople. The people chose Mr. Vernon as their leader and he was able to rally the townspeople to fight back against Mayor King. After many years of fighting where many people died and got hurt, they finally succeeded in getting Mayor King to leave.

"Eventually, during the first free elections the town ever had, Mr. Vernon was elected Mayor. He and some of the town's other leaders created these new rules. They also changed the name of the town to Jefferson Township. This Charter tells us, or, more importantly, *tells the town government,* exactly what it is allowed to do. When the people decided it was time to be independent of Londonville they declared it so in a document that was read out loud to every citizen of the town. It was an exciting moment! This Declaration said that the people of Jefferson Township have certain rights that are unalienable. Do you know what that means?"

Kayla raised her eyebrows.

Mrs. Adams said, "That means these rights are ones that always belong to you no matter what. They are your natural rights that the government does not give to you. They are rights that you cannot take from someone else and that even you yourself cannot go against or give away."

"What do you mean by that?" Kayla asked.

"Let me see if I can explain," Mrs. Adams said. "In a free society there will be no such thing as slavery for example. Correct?"

"That's right," Kayla answered.

"Why?" Mrs. Adams asked.

"Because if a person is a slave they are not free to do with their life what they want," Kayla said. "Being a slave would mean you are in a state of involuntarily servitude to another. In a truly free society involuntary servitude cannot exist."

"That's right," Mrs. Adams said. "What else?"

"Well based on the other principles of Liberty and Property, in a truly free society a person cannot be the property of someone else, or a slave, because they will always have the liberty to leave," Kayla said.

"That's right!" Mrs. Adams said, "Our schools have been doing a good job I see!"

Kayla said, "Yeah! And my mom and dad too! We talk about things like this a lot!"

"So," Mrs. Adams said, "In a truly free society can a person sell themselves into slavery?"

Kayla thought about this for a second.

"Well...they might try to but it could never be binding," she finally answered.

"Why?"

"Because in a truly free society a person could not be held to an agreement like this. In a free society at any moment that person could simply say they don't want to be a slave anymore and walk away," Kayla said.

Mrs. Adams said, "Right! Their freedom, their life is a natural right that they possess. It is not granted to them by any government, law or even Constitution. It is always theirs no matter what! Now the 'slave owner' could sue the person for a breach of the deal, but the fact that the person who sold themselves into slavery could walk away, regardless of the repercussions of that action, by definition proves they are not and have never been a slave."

"So, if the 'slave owner' tries to force a person into staying as a 'slave' he could be arrested?" Kayla asked.

"That's right," Mrs. Adams said. "Because the so-called 'slave owner' is forcibly taking the so-called 'slaves' life, liberty and even property, in the form of his own person, away. One of the limited powers we have granted the government would be the ability to arrest that so-called 'slave owner.'"

"So how can there be slaves?" Kayla asked.

"Well...," Mrs. Adams said, "In this same situation we have been talking about if the government forces the person to lose their freedom to remain as property of the 'slave owner', if the government forces the person to remain in a state of involuntary servitude, the government has effectively made him a slave."

"So, slavery exists because the government gets involved and allows it?" Kayla asked.

"That's right sweetie," Mrs. Adams said. "If someone takes away someone else's life and liberty, and the government uses its power and force to allow that to happen, or to stop others from preventing that from happening, the government has enabled slavery to exist."

"Wow," Kayla said.

"That's right," Mrs. Adams said. "You could also be subjected to a form of slavery if the government forces you to join the military and then go off and fight and maybe even die fighting a war, for example."

"Like a military draft or conscription," Kayla said.

"Very good! You get it! You have a good grasp of what natural rights[5] are!" Mrs. Adams said.

Mrs. Adams said, "Many believe natural rights come from God. So, you see, our Town Charter is based on this and it is a very important document because it tells the government what their exact powers are and leaves the rest up to the people. Anything not in the Charter the people get to decide on. Pretty cool huh?"

Kayla said, "Oh yeah! But what if the people decide they want to change the Charter?"

"Well...," Mrs. Adams said, "there is a section that tells us how we can go about what is called *amending* the Charter if we want to. It has been amended before but it is not easy to do."

"But why?" Kayla asked. "Why did they make it so hard to change the Charter?"

---

[5] "Locke wrote that all individuals are equal in the sense that they are born with certain "inalienable" natural rights. That is, rights that are God-given and can never be taken or even given away. Among these fundamental natural rights, Locke said, are "life, liberty, and property."
"The Declaration of Independence and Natural Rights." *Constitutional Rights Foundation.* http://www.crf-usa.org/foundations-of-our-constitution/natural-rights.html (Retrieved June 20, 2018)

"Because Mayor Vernon and his friends knew that one of the worst things that could happen to a town is if the rules were changed too easily and too often because that would make it just the same kind of place that Mayor King had created. They made the Charter difficult, but not impossible, to change to force people to actually think about what they were doing or what they wanted to do.

"The founders wanted people to take their time if they wanted to change the Charter so that passions and emotions of the moment got a chance to cool down a little. They wanted to make sure that clear heads made well thought out decisions after ample time to discuss all of the positives and negatives of the proposed change. This also ensured that as many voices as possible from all sides were heard. They thought that if a proposed change made it through all of that, then it probably was something most people at that time were OK with."

"So, the Town Charter means what it says?" Kayla asked?

"Oh yes," Mrs. Adams said looking quite serious. "The Town Charter means what it says and is actually quite easy to read even though it was written a long time ago. It's a simple set of rules that has allowed Jefferson Township to be the freest and most prosperous place on earth because it limits what the Town Government is allowed to do and leaves most of the decisions up to the people."

Kayla knew a little bit about the Charter but Mrs. Adams seemed to know a lot more so she decided to trust what Mrs.

Adams said. Even still, she made a promise to herself to learn more about it.

Kayla picked up the Charter and thumbed through it. She saw things such as, "Right to keep and bear arms," and, "The Township shall have power to..." and decided that yes, she must learn more about it.

She put the paper down and asked Mrs. Adams, "But what about my lemonade stand? Can I open it?"

A big smile came back across Mrs. Adams' face. "Oh yes! Of course, you can sweetie!"

"Are there any rules I have to follow? My dad said that there might be some," Kayla asked.

"Yes, there are, "Mrs. Adams said. "Hold on..."

Mrs. Adams turned back around in her chair to her filing cabinet, opened a drawer, and pulled out a single piece of paper that she put on the desk in front of Kayla.

"Here you go," she said.

Kayla looked at the sheet that did not have much written on it. On top it said, *Jefferson Township Business Contract.* Underneath the title there were some simple sentences bulleted out.

A Citizen of Jefferson Township can create any business they desire. The business owner is able and free to make as much income and gather as much wealth as they are able from that business.

Jefferson Township views a person's wealth as their property and the protection of Life, Liberty, and Property is of utmost importance to maintain a free society.

The business owner agrees...

- *... to not lie about or misrepresent their goods or services.*
- *... that in the event of a dispute over a product or service provided by a business operating in Jefferson Township that cannot be resolved between the parties involved the matter will be brought before a Judge and Jury of Jefferson Township whose decision is binding and final.*
- *...to listen to the citizens of Jefferson Township when they voice any concerns about their business at a public town meeting and the business owner vows to make a good faith effort to address those concerns.*

At the bottom was a place for someone to write in their name and signature.

Kayla could not believe it. It all seemed so easy. She grabbed the pen that Mrs. Adams extended to her.

Mrs. Adams showed Kayla where to sign, which Kayla promptly did.

Mrs. Adams said, "Congratulations sweetie!"

Kayla said, "What happens next?"

Mrs. Adams said, "Once a week during the Town Council meeting the public is invited to comment on anything that is occurring within the town. This includes being able to voice any concerns or questions about any business in town. As a business owner you are expected to be there to answer any questions about your business."

Kayla asked, "Why do we do that?"

"Well," Mrs. Adams said, "let's say you want to start a business that involves making dynamite..."

"Dynamite!!!" Kayla said incredulously.

"Yes dynamite!" Mrs. Adams said. "I know it sounds extreme but just follow along. If you want to start a business making dynamite what could happen?"

"Well if I don't know what I am doing I could blow myself and the rest of the neighborhood up!" Kayla said.

"That's right!" Mrs. Adams said. "People who live near your proposed dynamite business could potentially have their Life, Liberty, or Property affected by it, especially if you don't know what you are doing. The public hearing gives people the forum to discuss concerns they have with your business of dynamite making. If they make a good enough case that what you are doing could have a negative impact on their Life, Liberty, or Property, the Town Council may stop you from continuing your business until a solution is worked out. This could involve you having to move your dynamite business to a secluded, safer area; asking you to prove your qualifications to be in the dynamite making business and so on."

"I get it." Kayla said.

Mrs. Adams said, "The people gave the Town Council and our court system the power to act as a mediator when disputes arise between people. If one of the parties does not agree with the decision of the Town Council, they have the right to challenge that decision in court. If the owner of the dynamite business does not like the fact that the Town Council says they cannot start their business near people's homes, for example, the dynamite business owner can challenge that decision in court. The business owner would then have to present a case as to why he or she thinks it would be OK to have a dynamite business in a residential neighborhood!"

"That would probably be a tough case to argue for the dynamite maker," Kayla said.

"That's right sweetie," Mrs. Adams said. "It's a process that allows common sense to have a part in decision making. It also allows the citizens of the community a forum to voice their concerns about things they feel may come in conflict with their Life, Liberty or Property. They could probably make a pretty good case that someone shouldn't be allowed to make dynamite in a residential neighborhood! To be fair to the dynamite maker no one is saying he can't make dynamite, just that he needs to make it somewhere away from people's homes. Now if the dynamite business had the potential to pollute the air or poison the environment around it the town may prevent the business from operating."

"Because that would be affecting other people's lives and property, right?" Kayla asked.

"That's right sweetie!" Mrs. Adams said. "Unless the business owner can show what he would do to ensure his dynamite business doesn't do those things he could be prevented from operating it. I know that's an extreme example but does it make sense? The principle behind it that is?"

"Yes." Kayla said. But she had another question.

"But should the guy even be able to make dynamite and sell it being it could be harmful to others?"

"Well of course he should!" Mrs. Adams said. "Just about any product could cause harm to someone if it is used inappropriately. A car could kill people, a kitchen knife could too. Even something as simple as a rope can be used to cause harm to others if someone wanted to. Do we ban all of those things? Of course not! If we followed the logic that we should ban things that *may* be harmful we would have to ban everything! And who wants to live in a society like that? In Jefferson Township we believe people in trusting people to respect each other's Life, Liberty and Property with appropriate powers granted to our minimal government to deal with those who don't."

"OK," Kayla said. "I agree to follow the rules!" She signed the document and handed it to Mrs. Adams.

"That's great sweetie! Make sure you come to the next Town Council meeting to make it official!"

Kayla was so happy she could not wait to get started.

As they were leaving City Hall, Kayla asked her father if they could look around for a spot where she could set up her lemonade stand permanently. She knew that she could not do it in the same spot on the City Hall lawn by the sign as she did on Election Day because that was just a onetime favor from Mrs. Adams, but she and her father did not have to look far.

Just near City Hall was an empty field that had once been a part of a much bigger *Henry Family Farm*. Mr. Henry was older now and did not do as much farming as he used to.

Kayla pointed to the lot and said, "Hey dad, how about over there? It's right near where I sold the lemonade last time so I know it's a good spot. You think Mr. Henry will let me do it there?"

"I don't know." Kayla's father said. "Let's go ask him."

They walked over to Mr. Henry's house. It was an old, white farm house that had a big front porch. As they climbed the wooden front steps Kayla could see into the house through the screen door. Inside was a huge portrait of who must have been Mr. Henry's parents hanging over the fireplace. To Kayla, it looked like a house someone's grandparents lived in.

The land Mr. Henry owned had been in his family for generations. Jefferson Township had once been a very big farming community. Over time most of the farms went away as people found they could make better, and easier, livings as business owners and shopkeepers. But the people who lived in town never lost the strong work ethic that their ancestors had as farmers. Working hard and being entrepreneurial were always a big part of what being a citizen of Jefferson Township was all about. Kayla was proud to be carrying on that heritage of hard work and entrepreneurship which was so ingrained in the culture of her town.

She knocked on Mr. Henry's front screen door. From somewhere inside the house Kayla heard Mr. Henry say, "Coming!" and he emerged from what looked like the kitchen area. He was wiping his hands on a dish towel as he came to the door.

Mr. Henry was an older man who only had a few wisps of gray hair left on his head. He said, "Oh hi Kayla! Hi Mr. Alexander!" as he opened the screen door and stepped onto the porch. "Is everything OK?"

Kayla then proceeded to explain to Mr. Henry what she wanted to do.

He said to her, "So you want to be an entrepreneur? That's great!"

He agreed to let her set up her lemonade stand in his empty lot on one condition…as "rent" she would need to pay him one dollar for every day she sets up the stand. Kayla thought he would just let her set it up out of the kindness of his heart so this was a new wrinkle in her plans. She remembered her father once told her, "Nothing is for free.", and realized he was right. After thinking for a few seconds, she actually felt guilty for expecting something for nothing.

"So, what do you think Kayla?" her father asked.

When he saw her hesitate Kayla's dad said, "You know, Mr. Henry paid money for that land...hard earned money. It is his to do with what he pleases. It is his right to make money with it if he can. You think this is a good spot for your lemonade stand, right?"

Kayla nodded yes.

"Nothing in the world is free. Nothing! There is a cost associated with everything that happens in life and everything that exists in life. Your time; your property; goods or services your business sells.

"Nothing...is ...free!

"You must decide. If you think what you want to do is worth the cost associated with what it is, then it is worth it to pay that cost. If you think this is a great spot to sell your lemonade, then the cost probably is worth it. If not, then you will have to keep looking until you do."

Kayla thought about this for a few seconds. Sure, the rent for Mr. Henry's land was another expense but she really thought it was great spot. She decided it was worth the cost to set up her lemonade stand there and pay rent to Mr. Henry for using his land.

Kayla looked at Mr. Henry and said, "Deal!" She stuck out her hand and they shook on it.

A lot of business deals got done in Jefferson Township by virtue of a handshake and without written contracts. A person's word meant something.

The day after Kayla and her father met with Mr. Henry, she set up her first lemonade stand on the piece of land she rented from Mr. Henry.

Her dad had some lumber laying around at home which he used to build the stand. It was as tall as a countertop and had space to fit about two or three people behind it. He built shelves underneath to hold her supplies and gave her a couple of old bar stools to sit on. He used the last bit of wood to build an awning of sorts to shade whoever was working behind the stand as well as any customer standing in front. Before her father put the awning up, Kayla painted *Grandma's Old-Fashioned Lemonade* on the front of it.

When her father finished hammering in the last nail of the lemonade stand he and Kayla stepped back to look at what they had built. A big smile crossed Kayla's face. "It's perfect!" she said and gave her father a big hug.

Kayla immediately made up her first batch of lemonade and soon had a bunch of curious people come over who had been watching what was going on. Every one of them bought a cup of lemonade!

Grandma's Old- Fashioned Lemonade was an immediate success!

Kayla thought she had great location being right outside
City Hall. As people went in and out doing their business with the
town they couldn't help but see *Grandma's Old-Fashioned
Lemonade* stand and most came over to see what was going on.
Many people came over and bought some lemonade from Kayla and
told her how proud they were of her to take a risk and start a
business like she did! It made the rent she was paying Mr. Henry
worth it. Even he came out and bought some lemonade from her!

After school Kayla would get to her stand as soon as she
could after finishing her homework. On the weekends she would
arrive late in the morning and work until it got dark. Friends would
try to get her to leave the stand to go to the local mall or hang out
in the park at the edge of town but she always said *no.* She really
loved being at her stand, selling lemonade and talking to her
customers. Kayla was also very grateful to be living in an area
where the weather was nice year-round. She didn't have to worry
about snow or freezing temperatures keeping people in their house
all winter and fall!

As time went by, Kayla's lemonade stand started to make a
big profit for her. All of her dreams of having a successful business
were coming true! She was able to buy a lot of the stuff she wanted
like new clothes and presents for her family. She also used some of
that profit to improve her business. First, she bought a few stools
for her customers to sit on. That helped the local furniture
business. She discovered the stools made her customers stay
longer and buy more lemonade! She also used some of her profits
to rent storage space from Mr. Henry to store her supplies. He had
an old barn on the property that wasn't used much anymore. One
section in the barn had an old freezer in it. Kayla rented the space

out from Mr. Henry and used the freezer to store her extra ice. She kept looking for ways to improve her business and wasn't afraid to spend some money to do so.

Another thing she did was to hire her old friend Hank again! He would work for Kayla on the weekends making lemonade, running to get supplies and helping customers. He even had a great idea to hang strands of Christmas lights around the stand. Not only did they look nice and attract attention, they enabled Kayla to keep her stand open into the evening when the sun went down! That too increased her revenue and profits! She gave Hank a bonus for the idea which made him very excited!

Kayla discovered she loved going to work. She loved seeing the long line of smiling people in their brightly colored clothes waiting patiently to buy her lemonade and she loved the fact that her profits, the money she had left over after her expenses, kept getting bigger and bigger. She was making a lot of money!

Her business continued to grow and grow. Not long after Christmas, when she finally got her driver's license, she was able to buy her first car without asking for any money from her parents. That made her feel great!

As the winter turned into spring and the weather got warmer she realized that her lemonade stand would be able to keep growing...if she wanted it to.

She did.

As the end of her senior year in High School approached Kayla made a big decision. She decided to put all her energy and time into growing her lemonade business full time.

At first her parents were skeptical. They wanted her to go to college because they felt that getting a college education was important. Their argument was that you had more of a chance to be successful in life with a college degree.[6]

Kayla argued that there were lots of successful people who never went to college, or who dropped out, and did very well for themselves.[7]

They compromised. Kayla agreed to go to college part time at night while she ran her business during the day. Her parents agreed on one condition...

"If your business fails, you will go back to school full time," her mom said.

Kayla said, "That's a deal." But deep down she knew she would do everything possible not to fail!

---

[6] "Unemployment rates and earnings by educational attainment, 2017." *United States Department of Labor Bureau of Labor Statistics.* https://www.bls.gov/emp/chart-unemployment-earnings-education.htm Posted March 27, 2018. (Retrieved June 26, 2018)
[7] Hess, Abigail. "10 ultra-successful millionaire and billionaire college dropouts." *CNBC.* https://www.cnbc.com/2017/05/10/10-ultra-successful-millionaire-and-billionaire-college-dropouts.html Posted may 10, 2017. (Retrieved June 26, 2018)

Minimal Government

(City Hall – The Freest Place on Earth)

Soon enough Kayla graduated high school. While all of her friends were busy hanging out and enjoying the freedom that graduation brought, Kayla was making plans for her business. She knew she had something good going and wanted to capitalize on the hot summer weather to make as much money as possible.

The more time Kayla spent at the lemonade stand running her business, the more she realized that some of her customers came from all the way across town to buy her lemonade. Many of them told Kayla they wished she had a stand closer to where they lived so it would be easier for them to buy her product. Kayla thought hard about this. After she paid her rent and paid for her supplies and other operating costs, she still had a lot of money left over. That was her profit. She thought to herself that maybe she should open another stand across town. After all, if she was making so much profit at one stand, imagine what another would do!

Kayla told her parents she was thinking about opening another lemonade stand and they thought it was a great idea too. Soon after Kayla and her dad went out and found another location for her second lemonade stand. She set it up the same way she did her first one. Realizing she could not be in both places at once, she knew she would have to hire someone to run it for her when she was not there. Kayla was thinking long term. She wanted to be able to have more time to concentrate on growing her business by looking for new locations and finding ways to keep improving profits. Kayla hired one of her friends at a wage they both thought was fair and the second lemonade stand was up and running quickly with the same long lines and positive feedback from customers as the first.

Soon Kayla opened a third stand. Then a 4th and a 5th... and she kept opening stands and hiring people until she had ten lemonade stands around town. She was so happy! Her business was growing, her customers were happy and Kayla felt a great sense of accomplishment and pride in her successful business. She was providing a product that people wanted, gave people jobs and was making money.

Many other people were happy as well!

Her employees who ran her lemonade stands were happy because they all had jobs and were able to feel good about making money and being able to support themselves. The other businesses around town were happy because now those people who worked for Kayla had money and were spending it in their stores on the things they sold. Things like clothes, cosmetics, and items for their homes.

The man who owned the store where Kayla bought her lemons and sugar from was *really* happy because the more lemonade she sold, the more lemons and sugar he sold to her. His profits were growing because of Kayla's business! He now had more money available to expand his business and hire more people and that made those people happy!

The guy who owned the spring water company where Kayla bought her spring water from was happy because he was selling a lot more water to Kayla because of her growing business. He was selling so much spring water to Kayla that he had to buy another truck and hire another driver to help him. That made the new driver happy because now he had a job that allowed him to buy the things he needed (or wanted!) and that made those people he bought those items from happy as well!

The sales representative who sold the spring water guy the 2nd truck was very happy because with that sale he made more money and could buy some more things for his family. This made the people who sold those items to the truck salesperson happy as well!

The man who sold Kayla her cups was happy because was selling more cups and was able to hire more people to help his business and that made the people who he hired happy!

...and on and on....[1]

The people of Jefferson Township as a whole were happy. The great economy of the township and its reputation of being a place where people were free to pursue their dreams with virtually no interference by the government encouraged a lot of people to come to Jefferson Township to pursue their dreams of being successful and earning a good living.

Jefferson Township developed a reputation as the place to be if you wanted to open a business. The town had a simple tax

[1] "Every dollar released from taxation that is spent or invested will help create a new job and a new salary. And these new jobs and new salaries can create other jobs and other salaries and more customers and more growth for an expanding American economy."
From: President John F. Kennedy, Radio and television report to the American People on the State of the National Economy, August 13, 1962,
http://www.presidency.ucsb.edu/ws/index.php?pid=8812&st=&st1=
(Retrieved April 26, 2017)

system that allowed people and businesses to keep the vast majority of the money they earned to do with as they pleased. The taxes and revenue needed to run the very small government in the Town did not amount to much at all.

The people of Jefferson Township were very, very cautious about taxes. The first rule they liked to live by regarding taxes was: *The less taxes the better.* They knew that throughout history governments had used taxes as a way to expand its power over those being governed. In some other societies, the expansion of government was fueled by increasing the amounts and types of taxes that people were forced to pay. This forcing of taxes on people inevitably resulted in the people becoming less free because of the resulting expansion of government that all of those taxes funded. An unpleasant fact that Kayla was aware of is that as government grows, it intrudes further and further into people's lives.

High taxes also cause people to be less free because people control less of what their own money can be used for. The people of Jefferson Township knew that the less taxes they paid meant they had more money in their pocket to spend on things they needed, and that will help grow the economy. They also knew another benefit of being able to keep more of their own money meant they were able to give more to charity to help those less fortunate.

The people of Jefferson Township were very cautious about the power their government was allowed to have. They believed that some form of government was necessary because an absence of government, though in theory might sound like a great idea, in all reality would result in anarchy[2]. A society based on anarchy would

[2] "Anarchy." "1. (Government, Politics & Diplomacy) general lawlessness and disorder, esp

result in the simple concept of "might makes right" becoming predominant. This would very quickly result in strong factions of heavily armed groups dictating their version of society to everyone else. That would not be freedom.

The people of Jefferson Township understood that it is a very fine balancing act to have a government that is strong enough to enforce the law, but not so strong that it can usurp the law. Part of this balance includes people having the natural right to possess firearms to defend themselves against many things, including a government that is attempting to take away their Freedom and Liberty. With this in mind the people of Jefferson Township created a minimal government with very, very specific powers.

This government of Jefferson Township solely consists of:

- A town legislature (council) that has very limited and specific powers defined in the Town Charter. Including the ability to propose and make laws within the confines of the parameters set by the Town Charter.
- A Mayor, also with limited and specific powers defined in the Town Charter, one of which is to approve or veto laws passed by the Legislature.
- A court system, again, with limited and specific powers, to adjudicate disputes in the town as well as issues of law.

---

when thought to result from an absence or failure of government 2. (Government, Politics & Diplomacy) the absence or lack of government 3. The absence of any guiding or uniting principle; disorder; chaos 4. (Government, Politics & Diplomacy) the theory or practice of political anarchism" https://search.yahoo.com/search?p=define+anarchy&fr=ymyy-t-999&fr2=p%3Amy%2Cm%3Asb

- Police with limited powers to enforce the law and to defend against outsiders who may try to come into Jefferson Township to take away the people's Life, Liberty, and Property.

The government of Jefferson Township is also restricted by law to not engage in any business, professional, commercial, financial, or industrial enterprise except as specified in the Town Charter[3].

This minimal government in Jefferson Township receives its funding through revenue that consists of voluntary taxes. Some of those taxes are:[4]

- A *sales tax* on all final use goods and services with the exceptions of the purchase of a home and the purchase of securities (stocks and bonds).[5]
- Non-protectionist *Tariffs* (or *duties)* on some business transactions that occur on goods and services that come into Jefferson Township.[6]
- *Usage Fees* such as parking meters and tolls.

---

[3] Adopted from the *Liberty Amendment* which was introduced by Congressman Ron Paul multiple times. Ron Paul introduced the Liberty Amendment in 1998, 1999, 2003, 2005, 2007 and 2009. See: https://www.ronpaul.com/taxes/ (Retrieved July 24, 2017).

[4] Farrell, Keith. "6 Ways to Fund Public Services in a Libertarian Republic." *The Libertarian Republic.* http://cc.bingj.com/cache.aspx?q=ways+to+fund+public+services&d=4841727010147201&mkt=en-US&setlang=en-US&w=L1fQGg94I-eZwyWqVcI-NTSsainjNZg8 Posted September 22, 2013. (Retrieved July 20, 2017)

[5] Moore, Stephen. "Replacing the Federal Income Tax." *CATO Institute.* https://www.cato.org/publications/congressional-testimony/replacing-federal-income-tax (Retrieved July 24, 2017)

[6] "Protectionist: The advocacy, system, or theory of protecting domestic producers by impeding or limiting, as by tariffs or quotas, the importation of foreign goods and services." (http://www.thefreedictionary.com/protectionist)

Citizens within Jefferson Township had complete freedom to trade amongst themselves and some had suggested that a tariff went against the principles of a free market, but most of the people of Jefferson Township did not believe so. They thought that in theory, if every society outside of Jefferson Township had a free market, the tariffs would not be necessary.[7] Unfortunately, that was not the case.

For one, many other societies were protectionist, meaning they heavily taxed items that they imported from Jefferson Township in order to favor their own internally produced goods. Some also gave money, known as subsidies, outright to businesses. This hurt Jefferson Township's businesses. The people of Jefferson Township believed the tariffs they placed on imported goods should equal those placed by other societies on goods they received from Jefferson Township. If other societies did not tax goods imported from Jefferson Township, no tariff would be placed on that society's goods being imported into Jefferson Township. Most everyone in town thought this was fair.

---

[7] This is why many so-called "free traders" in America have it wrong. We cannot truly ever have a "free trade" system unless the parties involved do not allow their governments to be involved in the economy. The minute a tax break, subsidy or "investment" in a business by one of the involved government's occur, it is no longer "free trade". True free trade based on a true free market does not have any involvement by the government. When the market picks winners and losers, not a politician or a bureaucrat, you will only then have the most efficient, and fair, economy. How can we ever have free trade with a country like Communist China, for example, when their government essentially owns all of the business in that country and pumps huge sums of money into those businesses and their economy as a whole? If a country wants to sell their goods in our country free of any tariffs, they need to reciprocate for American goods into their own country. We can't have one way free trade, meaning we allow all sorts of imports into our country free of any tariffs while our exports are heavily taxed upon entering a foreign market. That's not free trade, that's stupid trade.
Spiering, Charlie. "Donald Trump Calls for Total Tariff Removals at G7 Summit." *Breitbart*. http://www.breitbart.com/big-government/2018/06/09/donald-trump-calls-for-total-tariff-removals-at-g7/ Posted June 8, 2018. (Retrieved June 10, 2018)

Some other societies collected tax money through something called an Income Tax. [8] For every dollar of income a person earned, the government took a portion of it from that person. Some places took over 61% of a person's income![9] Kayla could not imagine living like that! She thought if she had to give 61 cents of every dollar to the government, it would not even be worth working. *Heck,* she thought, *it wouldn't even take that much to make me feel like working wasn't even worth it!*

Kayla knew there were societies out there that had such high tax rates. They used the money to fuel a Welfare State,[10] but Kayla didn't want welfare from the government. What she did want was the freedom to use as much of her money as possible to do the things that she wanted to do, like grow her business and provide jobs for people.

Jefferson Township's Charter did not allow taxes on people's incomes because the founders believed this would be as if the government was stealing the hard-earned property, in the form of money, of its citizens. People were coming to Jefferson Township because there was a system of government in place that was small,

---

[8] The second plank of the Communist Manifesto by Karl Marx calls for "A heavy progressive or graduated income tax"
https://www.marxists.org/archive/marx/works/1848/communist-manifesto/ch02.htm
(Retrieved July 24, 2017) . This Communist goal was achieved by the Progressives in the United States with the passage of the 16th amendment to the US Constitution in 1913. "The Congress shall have power to lay and collect taxes on incomes, from whatever source derived, without apportionment among the several states, and without regard to any census or enumeration."
(https://www.law.cornell.edu/constitution/amendmentxvi Retrieved July 24, 2017)
[9] "List of Countries by Personal Income Tax Rate." *Trading Economics.*
https://tradingeconomics.com/country-list/personal-income-tax-rate (Retrieved May 25, 2018)
[10] "Welfare State: 1 : a social system based on the assumption by a political state of primary responsibility for the individual and social welfare of its citizens. Merriam-Webster.
https://www.merriam-webster.com/dictionary/welfare%20state Updated May 13, 2018. (Retrieved May 25, 2018)

was very limited in its power and scope, and had the simplest of rules to follow. There was not much for the government to spend money on.

A law on the books restricted Jefferson Township from going into debt[11]. Another law stated that if at the end of the year there was money left over in the town treasury, the surplus was to be refunded to every citizen in town at an even rate.

The town left most of the decisions to the people, unlike other governments, which were big, expensive entities that were involved in many aspects of ordinary people's lives.

There also was a growing, entrepreneurial populace in Jefferson Township that had the freedom to be as successful as they could. All of these things helped contribute to the booming economy that made Jefferson Township the envy of all the other towns.

Kayla's lemonade business was booming as well. It was not long before someone else in town decided that he too could make money by producing and selling lemonade, so he opened his own lemonade stand. When he first opened it, Kayla saw that less people were coming to her stands. She did a little investigating and found out that her competitor was selling his lemonade for a little less than for what she sold hers. She was still making money and still had many loyal customers but she definitely noticed that some people, who probably were very price conscious, had stopped coming in.

---

[11] Singman, Brooke and Chad Pergram. "House fails to pass constitutional balanced budget amendment." *Fox News.* http://www.foxnews.com/politics/2018/04/12/house-to-vote-on-balanced-budget-amendment.html Posted April 12, 2018. (Retrieved May 25, 2018)

Instinctively she knew she could only charge a price that people were willing to pay. That price was largely determined by supply and demand. The new lemonade competition Kayla now had was causing her to lower her prices because demand for her more expensive lemonade decreased.[12]

Kayla acted right away. She lowered her price to be close to what her competitor was charging and then advertised the reduction with the hope of generating demand for her product thereby getting those customers back. This was good for her customers because now their favorite drink cost less. Kayla was making a little less in profits but she did not mind. The competition inspired her to want to make her business even better. Not to mention she started buying advertising from the local advertising agency so their business benefitted as well!

Kayla enjoyed the competition for another reason...she liked to win! She got together with her father and asked him what he thought she should do. He told her that her business was growing, which was obviously a good thing, "...but you need to keep it fresh and relevant."

He said, "As you become more successful it's only to be expected that others would try to capture some of that success by developing their own version of your popular product." He told her she needed to distinguish herself from any competitors that may come along in order to keep her business unique and interesting. Kayla agreed and after much thought she made the decision to turn

[12] Hazlitt, Henry. "How Should Prices Be Determined?" *Mises Institute.*
https://mises.org/library/how-should-prices-be-determined Posted May 18, 2012.
(Retrieved May 25, 2018)

her lemonade stands into full-fledged *Grandma's Old-Fashioned Lemonade* stores!

Kayla hired a real estate agent whose job was to help find Kayla locations throughout town where she put her stores. In the days and weeks ahead, she spent a lot of time driving around town with the agent, looking for the perfect places to put her stores. It wasn't easy because there wasn't much retail space available. The town's economy was doing so well there weren't many empty storefronts available. Slowly but surely her agent found her several locations to rent. The agent was so happy because the commissions he made on finding the stores for Kayla helped him to buy things he needed for his family.

The owners of the shopping centers and the strip malls where Kayla put her lemonade stores very happy because they now had a tenant who was renting previously empty storefronts. The money from the rent would help them to afford the things they needed for their families and also gave them money to reinvest back into their businesses. All of this economic activity, the buying, the selling, the renting, all of it, helped the people of Jefferson Township become prosperous. They were free to grow and be profitable because the town's government largely left them alone. Kayla loved the fact that as long as she respected people's Life, Liberty and Property, she was free to run her business as she saw fit without government interference.

As Kayla secured the locations for her new stores she knew she wanted them to have bright attractive colors, sleek interiors and a big window where people could watch the lemonade being made. To help her accomplish this she hired an interior designer who came up with ideas for the stores which Kayla thought would be very appealing to her customers. The interiors were a bright, yet subtle yellow and every store had clean, comfortable rest rooms for the customers. The designer helped Kayla create an environment in each store that encouraged customers to spend lots of time there and to enjoy things like free Wi-Fi and complimentary snacks.

The interior designer appreciated the extra money that Kayla paid her and was able to budget more of her increased earnings to grow her design business by hiring another designer to help her.

This transformation of Kayla's lemonade stands into actual stores wound up drawing in a lot more customers and helped Kayla gain back all of the customers and profit she lost to her competition... and then some. She began to see completely new customers who said they were attracted by the fresh new look her stores had.

Her competition responded by trying to make his lemonade business even better much to the delight of everyone in town. The competition between the lemonade businesses was great for the town because each lemonade business owner constantly worked to make their business the best of its kind. The lemonade customers appreciated this because the level of service and quality they received from either of the lemonade businesses kept getting better.

One night, Kayla's father came to see Kayla as she was closing up one of her stores. They walked out together and Kayla locked the door. It was a warm night with a full moon in the sky. It was right after the grand opening of the last of her new stores and she was exhausted but elated. It had been a great day! The Mayor had come out to help with the ribbon cutting ceremony and then said a few kind words about how great it was to see yet another business opening up in town. The local news station was there filming everything which they were going to run on the evening news. Kayla loved all the publicity!

As they walked home Kayla's father said, "I am very proud of you dear. Through hard work and determination, you created a successful business that has changed many people's lives. Think about that for a minute. Think of all the people who are better off because of your business and the money it generates. You have become wealthy because of your business and you should never be ashamed of that. You earned your money, you built your business. It was your idea and your hard work, with the help of the hard work of your employees that made your business the success that it is today. No one can tell you that you did not build this business. No one handed you anything for free, and no one can take credit for what you have done. Sure, there are others involved, like your employees who make the lemonade and the people you pay rent to for example, but none of them would be doing what it is they are doing if it weren't for you. Always treat them right, appreciate and respect them for what they do, but never be ashamed or feel guilty of the success you now have because your success has become many other people's success as well."[13]

Kayla grabbed her father's arm and made him stop walking. She turned him around and hugged him tightly. She thanked him

---

[13] Shontell, Allison. "25 Self-Made Teenage Millionaires Have These 7 Things In Common." *Business Insider.* http://www.businessinsider.com/25-kid-millionaires-all-share-these-7-atrributes-2010-11 Posted November 4, 2010. (Retrieved July 6, 2018)

for believing in her and lending her the money to get her business started, which she had paid off in full by the way!

Kayla was wealthy and she was able to buy a whole bunch of things with her money. She bought her parents a new car, and that made the car dealer happy. She had contractors come and fix up her parents' home. They put in a pool; they hired a landscaper, all of these things made the owners and employees of those businesses happy because if not for *Grandma's Old-Fashioned Lemonade*, none of this economic activity would have existed.

One day while working at one of her stores Kayla heard that the local solar panel factory had gone out of business and the workers had lost their jobs. Someone in town had though that people would like to buy solar panels to provide energy to their homes and built a factory to make the panels. Unfortunately for the people who worked there the product never caught on. This made Kayla feel bad. For one; she knew some of them; and two, some of them were customers and she knew they would not be able to buy her lemonade anymore if they were not working.

Her parents also had taught her that it was her job as a Christian to try to help those less fortunate than she was.

There wasn't any kind of welfare or government assistance in Jefferson Township because the town charter did not list that as one of the functions of the general government, so Kayla knew it was up to the community to help those who had lost their jobs until they could get back on their feet again. Kayla went to all the businesses she dealt with, all of the ones who were doing so well because of her lemonade stand, and got most of them to agree to set up a charity and relief center for those who fell on hard times[14]. They pooled a portion of their incomes together and agreed to keep the center running with donations from their businesses as well as from the community at large. Kayla's mom agreed to run the center as a volunteer and soon many more donations were coming in from other businesses and people who wanted to help.

The laid off solar panel factory workers were able to keep on paying their bills and feeding their families because the center provided them with temporary financial help. Most weren't unemployed for long because the economy of Jefferson Township was doing so well that they were able to find jobs again. The man who sold lemons and sugar hired some; the spring water guy hired another. Others found jobs around the town with businesses that were doing well in Jefferson Township's growing economy.

The free and unfettered economy of Jefferson Township created an environment where being unemployed was a very temporary situation. Almost everyone who wanted a job was able to find one. All without the interference or "help" of the government.

The people of Jefferson Township had a great sense of pride and commitment to community. They felt blessed to live in Jefferson Township with its environment of freedom and entrepreneurship. This sense of pride and community inspired

---

[14] "As the economic recovery has begun to lift jobs and wages for the masses, so too has it stirred the philanthropic spirits of the wealthy, new research shows. An overwhelming majority of Americans (91%) with a net worth of at least $1 million, excluding their home, or at least $200,000 in annual income, gave something to charity last year, according to a survey from U.S. Trust and the Indiana University Lilly Family School of Philanthropy. Most (83%) intend to give as much or more the next three years."
Kadlec, Dan. "Wealthy People Are Giving Away More of Their Money." *Money*. http://time.com/money/4543503/wealthy-giving-money-philanthropy/ Posted October 25, 2016. (Retrieved June 21, 2018)

many in town to want to share their success with others and to help those who needed a helping hand. Not just by helping others who were facing hard times. People also wanted to share the things in their life that inspired and motivated them.

Kayla was a person who loved to read. She always wanted to get others to discover books and love them the way she did. Because of this she opened a library with some of the profits from her business[15]. She bought a building, books, furniture, and computers and hired a few people to run it. She set it up as non-profit, which simply meant it was there not to make a profit, but to exist as a service to the community. Its income came from the money collected from the services it provided such as renting out rooms for meetings and fines paid on overdue items, as well as by donations from the community.

The *Kayla Alexander Library* opened with great fanfare on a bright and sunny day. The community was very excited to have its own library and was very grateful to Kayla for opening it. During her dedication speech she thanked the community for their support of her lemonade because, she explained to them, if people did not like her product and buy it, she never would have been able to open this library for the community to use. She also thanked God to have been fortunate enough to live in a community that valued freedom, liberty, and opportunity. She expressed how she felt blessed to live in a community with a government that was limited

[15] "Philanthropic freedom is essential to a free society-A vibrant private sector generates the wealth that makes philanthropy possible-Voluntary private action offers solutions for many of society's most pressing challenges-Excellence in philanthropy is measured by results, not good intentions-A respect for donor intent is essential for philanthropic integrity." https://www.philanthropyroundtable.org/home/about/who-we-are (Retrieved June 21, 2018)

in its scope and not harmful to the opportunity that existed for everyone to be as successful as they could.

Kayla reminded everyone that it had not always been like this. She spoke of how at one time the town was ruled by Mayor King and a government that did as it pleased and stifled the people's opportunity to succeed by suffocating them with rules, regulations, and taxes. She spoke about the previous system which trampled on the Natural Rights of people and existed for the benefit of the few, powerful elites and their friends. She reminded everyone never to forget how, at great personal risk, Mayor Vernon and the other founders fought against Mayor King's oppressive rule and helped to secure the freedom and success that they now enjoyed today.

By no means was Kayla's library the only good deed that was done in Jefferson Township. Other successful people also began to voluntarily give back to the Township.

The spring water guy loved art, so he opened an *Art Museum and Exhibit Hall*. The grocer guy loved science so he made a big donation to the local college to build a new science lab. People throughout the town were making a good living and with their extra money they began to donate to the charities and causes they liked.

The business owners even set up a "Jefferson Township Charitable Business Fund" which had as its mission to help collect donations to the *Kayla Alexander Library* and the water guy's *Art Museum and Exhibit Hall*, or for things such as new benches near the bus stops and a new tennis court in the town park. The business owners were appreciative of the wealth they were able to create because of the freedoms enjoyed by them in Jefferson Township and they were eager to give back to the community. They also knew it was important for the people of Jefferson Township to have good quality of lives since they were the ones who bought their products and worked in their businesses. As long as their quality of life remained high, they would continue to live and work in Jefferson County and that was good for everyone.

Kayla's workers were happy as well. She paid them well and they were able to buy the things they needed and wanted. One day one of her workers came to her with an idea. You see, up to this point, *Grandma's Old-Fashioned Lemonade* workers had been cutting and squeezing the lemons by hand. The worker thought this was very inefficient so he designed and built a machine that could do the work of cutting and squeezing lemons much faster than doing it by hand. He knew that they now could make more lemonade to sell in less time by using his machine. He showed the machine he had built to Kayla and she loved it!

Soon every one of Kayla's lemonade stores had one of the machines that her employee invented and they were turning out more lemonade in less time than ever before! This allowed Kayla to sell even more lemonade and to make even bigger profits.

Kayla was now making so much more lemonade with the new machine that her inventory started to pile up. She started to have more frequent promotions of her product at a lower cost. She would advertise these promotions on the local TV station and in the local newspaper and that made the advertising sales people of those businesses happy because now they were making more money. Her customers were happy with the lemonade promotions because the promotional price of the lemonade meant they would have more money in their pockets to spend or save as they saw fit. When her customers spent the money they saved from the promotional price of the lemonade this made other businesses happy and increased their profits. This enabled them to spend, save or invest more money as well!

Kayla had a problem though. The machine worked almost too well. She was making so much extra lemonade now that she had to think of something else to do with the excess product before it started to pile up in inventory. The promotions she was running only took care of part of the problem. She didn't want to keep dropping the price because she would then be losing more of her profit. People liked the lower price of the lemonade but the fact was they were willing to pay more for it because they thought of it as a premium product that was worth the extra money. If Kayla kept the price lower than what people were willing to pay for it she would only be losing money. Money she could use to grow her business and help the community. She also did not want to stop making extra lemonade because she thought of that as lost potential. Lost potential to grow her business even more and hire even more people.

She asked her father about this dilemma. "Well dear," he said, "right now people can only buy your product at your stores. Why don't you see if maybe you can start to bottle your lemonade and ship it outside of town so people outside of Jefferson Township, you know, people who live too far away to make the trip to one of your stores, can buy it in their local store?"

Kayla thought this sounded like a good idea. *Why not expand the market for my product?* She asked herself.

Kayla spent the next few weeks researching what it would take to expand her product into other markets. She knew she would need a factory to make the lemonade and trucks to ship the product. She also knew she would have to hire a lot more people to make, sell, and transport, the bottled version of her lemonade!

On the outskirts of town, near the rail yard, Kayla found a big piece of land for sale. She liked that it was near a rail yard because she knew that if she could ship her product by rail as well as trucks, her distribution and product expansion prospects were even greater. Kayla tracked down the owner of the land and made an offer that was accepted right away.

The land had once been part of a big farm and the owner of it wasn't planning on farming anymore so he was happy to sell it to Kayla.

Because Jefferson Township was a place where there weren't many governmental regulations on business Kayla very quickly had an environmentally responsible, sleek, efficient, safe lemonade factory built.[16] The construction of the factory created a

---

[16] "Physical construction projects, like the building of new factories, pipelines, broadband cables, energy plants, etc., are important drivers of American economic growth. These projects shore up infrastructure, enhance productivity, and are an important source of jobs. But excessive government red tape means it is harder and takes longer than ever to build in America today.

As a witness at a 2012 congressional hearing noted, 'The Hoover Dam was built in 5 years. The Empire State Building took 1 year and 45 days. The New Jersey Turnpike needed only 4 years from inception to completion. Fast forward to the present day... Cape Wind has needed over a decade to find out if it can build an offshore wind farm. Shell Corporation is at 6 years and counting on its permits for oil and gas exploration in Beaufort Bay. And the Port of Savannah, Georgia has spent 13 years reviewing a potential dredging project, with no end to the review process in sight.'

lot of jobs for people in the construction industry which was good for them and the economy as a whole.

When Kayla had the factory built she was very careful to make sure that it complied with the principle of no harm coming to someone else's Life, Liberty or Property. That was why she was careful to make sure it generated minimal pollution and was a very safe working environment for her employees.

Speaking of employees, Kayla's next move was to go on a hiring spree to staff her new lemonade bottling business. It was not easy at first because the economy of Jefferson County was so strong that not many people were without a job. Kayla had to offer above average pay and benefits to attract people to work for her. She hired hundreds of factory workers, drivers, and salespeople. Many of them were local people, young people fresh out of school, some were enticed to leave their current job by the higher pay Kayla was offering. She also had many applicants from outside of Jefferson Township, people who were motivated to move to Jefferson Township by its booming economy and substantial Freedom and Liberty.

No wonder a recent global survey placed the U.S. behind 40 other countries when it came to ease of obtaining the necessary permits to construct a warehouse. While much of this red tape comes from state and local governments, the federal government contributes more than its fair share.

For example, deploying physical broadband services can require up to eight separate reviews/permits from five different federal agencies. Building a pipeline means up to 13 different reviews / permits from seven separate agencies. The federal government's own "permitting dashboard" warns that complex reviews can take '4+ years' – the extent of an entire presidential term – to process. But even 4+ years is just an estimate; most permit processes lack hard deadlines, and the process can drag on as long as the agency wants or until the applicant gives up."

"Cutting Red Tape To Help Build American Infrastructure." *Conservative Reform Network.*" http://conservativereform.com/cutting-red-tape-to-help-build-american-infrastructure/ (Retrieved June 26, 2018)

Next, she bought a bunch of brand new trucks from the local truck salesperson, which was great for their business. The trucks were all painted bright yellow with big *Grandma's Old-Fashioned Lemonade* logos on them. They really attracted people's attention!

Building the factory turned out to be a great move for Kayla. The line of bottled lemonade helped Kayla's business profits to grow even more. Soon full trucks of bottled *Grandma's Old-Fashioned Lemonade* were making their way out of Kayla's factory to locations way beyond the borders of Jefferson Township. Not only did her own wealth increase, others associated with her business did as well.

The more the money rolled in, the more Kayla was also able to reinvest in her business. For example, she thought it would be much better for her business if she did not have to buy all her lemons from someone else. She had long toyed with the idea of growing lemons to use in her lemonade herself. But it was never a "need to have" for her business. It was always a "nice to have". But now that she had the money, she decided it was time to do it!

There was another big open field right next to Kayla's new bottling plant. It was owned by the same man who sold Kayla the land she built her factory on. She negotiated a good deal and bought it from him.

But the problem was, Kayla didn't know the first thing about growing lemons! So, she had the local employment agency start to look for people she could hire who knew how to grow lemons. The employment agency found a person named Rafael whose family grew lemons and other fruit back in his home country when he was a kid. Kayla interviewed Rafael and although he hadn't been growing lemons since arriving in Jefferson Township many years ago, and although he was just a kid when his family had the fruit business, she liked him. He seemed like a hard-working man and even though he didn't know everything about growing lemons, he knew more than Kayla! So, she hired him.

Kayla and Rafael got to work right away building the lemon orchard. Rafael knew of a place where they could buy mature lemon trees so Kayla bought enough to fill her orchard so it would be ready to go quickly next season. She also hired a lot of new employees to help her run the orchard.

Kayla had built a genuine business empire in her beloved Jefferson Township. She had multiple retail locations throughout the town where she sold fresh squeezed lemonade. With her most recent purchase of land she soon would have a fully functioning lemon tree orchard which would supply a large portion of the lemons she needed to make her product. She also had a factory where a bottled version of her lemonade was produced and then shipped throughout the region from her distribution center utilizing her fleet of delivery trucks. Kayla employed hundreds of people and the economic activity from just her business alone was a critical component of the overall economy of Jefferson Township. All of this occurred because Kayla had a dream about building a successful business and then was fortunate enough to live in a society built on the foundation of the protection of Life, Liberty and Property and which was free enough for her to pursue that dream.

It got to the point that the economy of Jefferson Township was booming so much and the businesses there had so many jobs to fill that there were not enough people in town to fill them all.[17] Since workers were in short supply it made those who were holding jobs in Jefferson Township even more valuable to their employers. Kayla had first discovered this when she was trying to hire people for her new bottling plant. She had a hard time finding people to fill all of her open roles.

Many businesses started to compete for workers and this caused salaries, benefits and other perks to go up as businesses fought to keep the employees they had by offering them more money and perks. It also helped to grow the population of Jefferson Township because people from all over were coming to town to take advantage of the booming economy by creating businesses.

In fact, so many people wanted to immigrate to Jefferson Township that the Town Council had to establish rules about who could move there to ensure that the town was able to handle the growth. They made it a rule that anyone who moved to the town had to apply for the right to move to the town and they had to have a skill, a job lined up and a place to live. They also had to agree to obey the laws of the town. This ensured that only the best of the best would be able to move into the community and that those who did immigrate to the town would already have a place to live and a job. They would not be a burden to the rest of the community.

Kayla was now one of the richest people in town. She was making a lot of money and that made her feel good because she

---

[17] The Associated Press. "U.S. employers post 6.6 million open jobs." *Arkansas Online.* http://www.arkansasonline.com/news/2018/may/08/us-employers-post-66-million-open-jobs/ Posted May 8, 2018. (Retrieved June 7, 2018)

was able to do good things with her money such as give to charities, help her family and grow her businesses which gave people jobs.

While everything with Kayla's business was going as good as she could ever have dreamed, something happened which caused her to worry that her business was in danger.

One of her lemonade stores had sold some lemonade that made someone sick. Over the next few days after the incident went public her sales started to drop off. Many people started to believe that all of her lemonade might be bad so they stopped buying it. This was a potential disaster for Kayla and her business. She knew that if she did not act fast, many people's lives might be negatively affected. Customers may keep getting sick if she didn't take steps to make sure there wasn't any more bad lemonade being sold, and her employees would get hurt because the drop off in business could potentially cause people to lay people off or to cut pay and benefits. She knew she had to act quickly to restore people's faith in the quality of her product.

The first thing she did was to close all of her stores until she could determine what had happened. She did not want to take the chance on selling anymore bad lemonade. While the stores were closed she had every inch of every store cleaned and sterilized. Then she took a whole day to retrain all of her employees on the proper procedures to follow in the making of the lemonade as well as a reinforcement of the proper sanitary practices they all needed to follow. Finally, when she was satisfied with her progress in those areas, she reopened the stores and advertised the exact steps she had taken in her stores to help ease her customer's minds regarding the quality of her product.

At the same time, she was doing all of that she launched an investigation into exactly what happened and how one of her stores was able to sell bad lemonade. What she discovered was the manager at the lemonade store where the bad lemonade had been sold did not obey the strict quality assurance rules Kayla had set up in order to ensure only high-quality products were produced. The manager was making lemonade with dirty equipment because he was not following her strict cleaning guidelines. This was bad enough. She also found out he wasn't using lemons from her approved lemon vendor.

Kayla only would buy her ingredients, like lemons, from certain suppliers. This way she knew each of her stores was producing a consistent product. Kayla was especially strict about where her lemons came from. They were the main ingredient in her product and she wanted to make sure her lemonade only contained juice from the best lemons. It was more expensive for her to do it this way but she felt it was what justified her having a "premium" product.

Kayla trusted her managers and other employees to run her stores as if they owned them themselves. She paid them well and even incentivized them to keep making the stores better. The more profit the stores made, the more profits she shared with her employees.

Her managers handled all of the inventory and bookkeeping at the store they were in charge of. The manager who was making the bad lemonade wasn't buying lemons from an approved vendor. Instead, he bought lesser quality lemons from somewhere else. These lemons cost less but weren't as good as the approved ones. To make matters even worse, he falsified his inventory records to reflect as if he was buying the more expensive lemons but he continued to make Kayla pay for the more expensive ingredients. He then pocketed the difference. So not only was the employee making a product that made people sick, he was lying to Kayla and stealing from her as well.

Kayla still wanted to hear the manager's side of the story. Even though the evidence was incontrovertible that he had been stealing, she wanted to know why. She thought maybe he needed the money because someone in his family was sick and needed expensive medicine, or maybe he had a gambling problem. Whatever the reason, being a good person, she just wanted to see if she could help him if he was in some kind of financial trouble.

She had a meeting with him at one of her stores. When she asked him why he did it, he broke down and started crying. He offered no excuse other than he wanted more money, and that it was easy to do.

"Don't I pay you enough?" she asked him.

"Yes," he said. "You do. I don't know why I did it. But once I started I couldn't stop."

Satisfied there wasn't any extenuating circumstances to the manager's behavior she fired him.

Kayla paid the Doctors bills of the person who had gotten sick and started an ad campaign to get the lost business and customers back. Right away, she instituted stricter oversight of her stores and publicly admitted to what happened. She told her customers she was sorry for having broken their trust in her product. She gave a lot of her product away for free to encourage people to start drinking it again. This all cost Kayla's business a lot of money, but she knew she had to do it. One of the principles Jefferson Township was founded upon was to do no intentional harm to another person. That to do so was a violation of that person's Life, Liberty, and Property.

Kayla's employee violated this principle and suffered the consequences of his actions. Kayla had him arrested for stealing from her business and sued him for the damages he caused. The employee was forced by the court to pay restitution to Kayla for the damage he inflicted on her business. His reputation ruined by his selfish and criminal behavior, the guilty employee could no longer find work in Jefferson Township and eventually had to move away. Save for the involvement of the Police and Courts when the employee was arrested, none of this episode involved the government at all.

In Jefferson Township's free market-based economy a person's reputation is a key component to how they are able to interact in the overall economy. A bad reputation limits someone's ability to participate in the economy and be successful. A good reputation is vital for a person to build trust and gain the confidence of the consumers. Cultivating and fostering a good reputation is vital to every person participating in the economy of a free market.[18]

Soon enough Kayla's efforts paid off as people began to trust her products again and her business recovered. People liked that she was honest with them, did not make excuses or try to hide anything and that she made good with the person who had gotten sick. They also liked that she fired the responsible employee right away.

Things in Jefferson County were going great. The economy was booming, people were happy and enjoying the fruits of living in a free society!

Soon enough Election Day was right around the corner once again.

While at work one day, Kayla heard some of her customers and workers talking about this man named Mr. Woodrow who was telling everyone who would listen about how great things were over in Europa Township.

Kayla did not think much of it, but she began to hear more and more talk of this sort from people around town.

One late afternoon Kayla saw her old classmate Hank outside one of her stores. She always felt good when she saw Hank because he was her first employee. He was talking to someone and she overheard him say how great Europa Township was. She asked him exactly it was about Europa Township that made it so great.

---

[18] Mauzy, Stephen. "Why Free Markets. " Americanthinker.com. Posted August 26, 2012. http://www.americanthinker.com/articles/2012/08/why_free_markets.html (Retrieved October 26, 2017)

"Oh!" he said. A big smile came across his face. He started to gush, "Over there the people really have a say in what is going on in their town. Everyone is equal and there isn't anyone who is better than anyone else. Everyone gets exactly what they need to live and everyone contributes to society according to what they can. It's all made fair by the government because they have the smartest people running things. Everyone in government has gone to college! They all have more college degrees than they have fingers! The government over there is great! No one gets a special advantage over anyone else and everyone has a guaranteed job, gets guaranteed medical care and a guaranteed education! They even get guaranteed time to rest and relax! It's wonderful!"[19] Hank seemed almost breathless as he spoke about it.

Kayla asked Hank, "So the Town government over there does all that? Where do they get the money to pay for all of those things? Who gave the government the power to do those things?"

Hank said, "They have a stash of cash[20]! Everyone gets a piece and it doesn't cost a thing! It says it right in their town charter!"

Kayla thought about that.

Hank went on, "Mr. Woodrow says if we vote for him we can start to be just like Europa Township! Isn't that great?"

---

[19] The Constitution of the USSR: Chapter 7 Article 40 Citizens of the USSR have the right to work...Chapter 7 Article 42 Citizens of the USSR have the right to health protection...Chapter 7 Article 45 Citizens of the USSR have the right to education...Chapter 7 Article 41 Citizens of the USSR have the right to rest and leisure. (See: http://www.constitution.org/cons/ussr77.txt) (Retrieved August 1, 2017)
[20] http://www.urbandictionary.com/define.php?term=Obama%20Stash and https://youtu.be/_Ojd13kZlCA Retrieved August 1, 2017

Kayla did not know if it was. Things seemed to be going pretty well here in Jefferson Township. But what about all of those "free" things? That might be nice too.

In the days leading up to the election Kayla heard a lot of talk about what was going on in Europa Township. People seemed excited by it.

She also noticed something else. People began to take notice of how much money she was making. The comments were little ones at first such as, "Oh...you can afford it," or, "How *much* money do you need to make?"

Then she started to read about some of the things that Mr. Woodrow was saying. Things like:

"The government needs to do more. "

"The government needs to keep people safe."

"The government should do more to help."

"The government needs to guarantee things."

"How big should the government *allow* a business to be?"

"Should the government really *allow* someone to make *so much* money when others make less? Shouldn't the government control that in the spirit of *fairness*?"

"Aren't rich business people just greedy because all they want to do is make more money?"

"Shouldn't things just be a little bit *fairer*?"

Kayla started to feel a little uncomfortable. She was proud of all the good things her *Grandma's Old-Fashioned Lemonade* business had done. The talk of making things "fairer" didn't make sense to her simply because she thought things were pretty fair already in Jefferson Township. You were free to be as successful as you could. What was fairer than that?

One night she asked her father about the good things she heard people saying about what was going on in Europa Township. Her father told her, "Sometimes people just do not realize how good they have it. They become comfortable and they let their guard down. Many begin to think that the grass *is* greener on the other side. Even though they have more than enough to live comfortable lives by way of material things and plenty of opportunity always to better themselves, as they have here in Jefferson Township, they begin to covet what others have."

"Sometimes," he said, "people are simply jealous. They see what others have and they want it for themselves, but without the sweat and hard work it takes to get there. Many times, people conclude that the easiest way to get what they want is through government. If what you hear is going on in Europa Township is true, I would guess the people there are getting a little too lazy and a little too comfortable with giving more power to their government. That can't be good."

He told Kayla that unscrupulous politicians would sometimes exploit the jealous and covetousness part of human nature to gain power for themselves. They promise things to groups of people, special interests her dad called them, which they can only get by taking it by force from someone else. This helps those politicians gain and then hold onto power.

"Problem is," he said ", once it starts, the taking that is, it's hard to stop. That's why it's so important for the people to always guard against it. But that's hard work. It is very hard for people to choose what they know is the hardest road, even if it is the right thing to do. It takes a lot of work to stay free. When people lose the desire to work for their freedom, it allows people to take control who are more than happy to take their freedom away. Sometimes people just like to have power over others. Sometimes people feel good by making others feel bad."

That is terrible, Kayla thought.

Kayla wanted to learn more about why people seemed so fascinated by what was going on in Europa Township so she invited Hank over to her house to talk about it. One Friday evening he arrived carrying a box of donuts, "I thought we could have these while we sat and talked!" he said. "I can't wait to tell you about why Mr. Woodrow would be a great Mayor!" Kayla noticed Hank had a "Woodrow for Mayor" campaign button attached to his shirt.

Kayla let Hank in and they went into Kayla's kitchen.

"Sit Hank," she said, pointing to a chair next to the table, "I'll make some coffee." After the coffee brewed she poured Hank a cup of coffee and sat some sugar and milk down on the table in front of him. She asked him how his sister Jennie was doing.

"She's great!" Hank said. "Doing really well in school. She is a big admirer of yours!"

"Is that so?" Kayla asked with a chuckle. "Why is that?"

Hank grabbed one of the donuts he brought over and started to eat it. In between bites he said, "Because you built this great business and she loves the lemonade! She tells everyone how she was one of the first people to work for you! She says it with such pride! As if she hadn't been there when you started your business would never have succeeded!"

"Awww! That's great!" Kayla said. "I will always have a soft spot for Jennie!" Kayla thought fondly of Jennie. And Hank too. They were both there at the beginning when Kayla set up her first lemonade stand several years before. Hank and Jennie certainly helped Kayla get her business going that first day and Kayla was very appreciative of it. It taught her a very important lesson early on that no business like Kayla's could ever succeed without good employees, and a good boss recognizes that and treats them fairly. Kayla did just that with Hank and Jennie. Although Jennie was too young at the time to realize what was going on...she just liked talking to people and pouring the lemonade!

That first day Kayla paid Hank a wage he was happy with for his work and she did the same for every employee she hired since. All without the government ever getting involved! As a business owner Kayla knew it was very important to always treat employees with fairness and respect. Doing so created an environment of trust, cooperation and good will between Kayla and her management team and her employees. It also created an environment where everyone felt an obligation to help make the business succeed and grow. And if one of Kayla's employees didn't believe in the culture or business Kayla created, they were free to leave, just as Kayla was free to let them go if she didn't feel they belonged working for her. There was freedom based on respect for Life, Liberty and Property!

That thought brought Kayla back to why she wanted to talk to Hank and had invited him over.

"I heard you talking the other day about how great things are over in Europa Township and why Mr. Woodrow would be a great Mayor."

"Oh yes!" Hank said, a big smile appearing on his face.

"I want to learn more," Kayla said. "Tell me about it."

"Absolutely! Mr. Woodrow firmly believes that Jefferson Township is the greatest society ever created," Hank said in a professorial tone.

"I agree," Kayla replied.

Hank continued, "But he is worried that the economy here is now built in such a way that there are only a very few powerful people who are controlling everything to do with the prosperity the town now enjoys. He is afraid that the people at the bottom only get the crumbs[21] that the super-rich allow to trickle down[22]. He

---

[21] Cawthorne, Cameron. "Pelosi Defends 'Crumbs' Comment About Workers' Bonuses." *The Washington Free Beacon.* http://freebeacon.com/politics/pelosi-defends-crumbs-comment-about-workers-bonuses/ Posted: January 29, 2018 (Retrieved May 29, 2018)
[22] "Trickle-down: Of or relating to the economic theory that financial benefits accorded to big businesses and wealthy investors will pass down to profit smaller businesses and consumers." *The Free Dictionary.* https://www.thefreedictionary.com/trickle-down

believes wealth should be created for the benefit of all and in order for society to really be great…and fair, the Government needs to assume more responsibility to make that happen. He thinks the Government must partner with business in keeping our economy running at full speed and he also believes it is the Government's responsibility to see that every American has a chance to obtain their fair share. I agree with him that we cannot maintain our prosperity unless we have a fair distribution of opportunity in our town."[23]

Hank sat back in his chair when he finished speaking and seemed very pleased with himself. He was sure that what he said made complete sense to Kayla. To Hank, it was just common sense that the government needed to do more! He truly believed that private enterprise and the government needed to work together for the benefit of all.

Kayla however was dumbfounded by what Hank said. Because if you didn't know any better it would all make complete sense. After all, who doesn't want prosperity for all? Who doesn't want a society that is fair? But Jefferson Township had all of that already without the government getting involved! There seemed to be something else going on with what Mr. Woodrow was saying and that Hank was buying wholeheartedly into. Kayla had her suspicions of what that something else was, and she felt a new sense of urgency to talk to Hank about it. She was a little nervous

(Retrieved May 29, 2018)

[23] "The Government must work with industry, labor, and the farmers in keeping our economy running at full speed. The Government must see that every American has a chance to obtain his fair share of our increasing abundance. These responsibilities go hand in hand. We cannot maintain prosperity unless we have a fair distribution of opportunity …"
Truman, Harry S. "Annual Message to the Congress on the State of the Union January 5, 1949." *The American Presidency Project*. http://www.presidency.ucsb.edu/ws/?pid=13293 (Retrieved May 29, 2018)

that this whole "government needs to do more" thought was starting to get into people like Hank's head.

"Hank," Kayla said, "there's a lot wrong with what you said."

Hank's smile faded and now he looked offended, "How so?" he asked.

"Because your premise doesn't make sense," she answered. When she said that Hank sat up straight in his chair and folded his arms, a scowl on his face now.

Kayla continued, "Our town has operated successfully for a very long time on the belief that a minimal government is the best kind. The government was given very specific powers in the Charter, and those powers centered on making sure that people's Life, Liberty and Property remained sacred and protected. That's it! Short of those very specific powers the government has no reason to be involved in anything else, especially the economy! Our economy does so well because the government has minimal involvement in it, not in spite of it! People pursuing their dreams to be prosperous and to have a better life for them and their family is what makes the economy great. People can pursue that dream much better when the government doesn't get involved by burdening people with taxes and regulations! Certainly, some are more prosperous than others, but that's what happens in a truly free society! Hank, you know better! You know if everyone maintains respect for each other's Life, Liberty and Property, everyone benefits! We don't need the government interfering to protect against imagined wrongs such as things aren't 'fair' enough!"

"But it's not fair that there are only a few people making more money than they ever could spend!" Hank said. Now he was leaning forward in his chair and clearly getting upset.

"Why?" Kayla asked. "Again, as long as they did it with respect to people's Life, Liberty and Property, why isn't it 'fair' to have more money than someone else?"

"Because it's just not," Hank answered.

"So, the government should have the power to 'fix' that?" Kayla asked him.

"Yes," Hank said. "It should."

"How? Why?" Kayla asked.

"Why? Because the Government is impartial and not focused on making a profit. The Government is only interested in everyone's own good, not like a corporation that is only after profits. Like I said earlier," Hank said. "Like Mr. Woodrow says. We need a fairer distribution of opportunity."

"You're wrong Hank," Kayla said. "Government is not impartial."

"Why not?" Hank asked, clearly annoyed.

"Because government is partial to itself. You talk as if government is some faceless entity but it's not. It is composed of people who have their own thoughts, ideas and even biases. And those thoughts, ideas and biases of the people who work in government get reflected in the policies it makes. The bigger the government, the more people working for it, the more they will want government to reflect their own thoughts. So, don't say government is impartial!"

"But what about the courts?" Hank said in a 'gotcha!' tone. "They are part of Government and they are impartial!"

"Yes," Kayla said, "courts are a part of government and should be impartial. In our minimalist government it is one of the very specific powers granted to government. But Mr. Woodrow isn't part of the courts, he's just a politician looking to further his own interests!"

At that moment Kayla realized what the "something else" was. Power and arrogance. Mr. Woodrow was trying to convince people to give him the *power* to change things because in his *arrogance* he believed he knew what was best for everyone (because he was smarter than them!). Things were going very well in Jefferson Township. It was by no means a perfect place without any problems. However, when problems did arise the people worked together to find solutions based in respect for each other's Life, Liberty and Property. Government, in the form of the courts, only became involved when there was an impasse between the parties who were having an issue with each other. People were free to live their lives or run their business or spend their money (or not spend it) as they saw fit as long as they didn't violate someone else's Life, Liberty or Property. It all worked. People were free. Apparently, Mr. Woodrow and his followers didn't like all of that freedom and they were looking to cut back on some of it. And they were going to use the government to do it.

Hank looked offended that Kayla wasn't just agreeing with him and going along with Mr. Woodrow's philosophy.

"Hank," Kayla said. "You also said something about 'fair distribution of opportunity'. What does that even mean?"

Hank was feeling exhausted at this point.

"Everyone should have an equal opportunity to be successful," he said.

Kayla thought about that word "equal". She realized that she and Hank probably had different ideas about what it meant. To Kayla "equal" meant everyone has the same opportunity to be free and to live their lives as they see fit. She believed being "equal" meant there weren't special rules for you that didn't apply to me, or vice versa. Being "equal" meant that respect for Life, Liberty and Property applied to *everyone*. It didn't mean that everyone should start off equally with the same money in the bank, or the same amount of knowledge, for example. That would be impossible.

But that was exactly what she thought Hank believed "equal" meant. Because someone had more money than someone else, for example, they weren't "equal" and, according to Hank, that wasn't fair. Hank's line of thought seemed to be that the government then needed to step in and correct that "unfairness". Mr. Woodrow seemed to think he should have the say as far as what was "unfair" or not and we should give him the power to correct it. Kayla was somewhat frightened by the fact that people like Hank were willing to let someone like Mr. Woodrow obtain that kind of power.

"They don't have equality of opportunity now?" Kayla asked.

"No," Hank said. "And that's what needs to be fixed."

"And how do you do that?" Kayla asked.

"Like college," Hank said. "It's not fair that some people have the opportunity to go to college because they can afford it but some can't because they don't have the money."

"So, what should happen?" asked Kayla.

Hank said, "The government should tax rich people to pay for college for poor people. That's one of the items in Mr. Woodrow's platform."[24]

Kayla said, "So the government should force me to pay for your college education? The government should steal my money and give it to you?"[25] Kayla was now talking to Hank as if she were asking questions of a child.

"That's not what I'm saying," Hank said derisively.

"It's exactly what you're saying!" Kayla exclaimed.

---

[24] Millionaire Socialist Bernie Sanders (http://www.newsweek.com/bernie-sanders-makes-one-million-dollars-second-straight-year-book-deals-992845) wants to steal your money to pay for 'free' college tuition:
"It's Time to Make College Tuition Free and Debt Free." *Berniesanders.com*
https://berniesanders.com/issues/its-time-to-make-college-tuition-free-and-debt-free/
(Retrieved June 26, 2018)
[25] Luebke, Bob. "Why Free College Tuition is a Bad Idea." *Civitas Institute.*
https://www.nccivitas.org/2016/16909/# Posted February 4, 2016. (Retrieved June 26, 2018)

"Well then what would you do?" Hank asked rather excitedly. He was leaning forward now and practically out of his chair.

"Well," Kayla said, "If I needed engineers to design my next factory and none were around I would offer to pay for someone's college education to learn it on the condition they come work for me for a little while after completing their education.[26] Or if I was in high school and wanted to go to college after I graduated and I knew my parents didn't have the money for it I would study hard to get a scholarship, or take advantage of a company's internship program, or I would go get a good job and save money or go to college part time taking classes I could afford to take. I would figure it out while being very, very, grateful to have been blessed to live in a society that would allow me the freedom to do just that...to figure it out. I certainly wouldn't want the government forcing someone else to pay for it for me!"

"You always think the market place is the solution Kayla. You always believe Government is a problem[27]," Hank said. "Free college would be a great thing for everyone. Everyone would benefit from having more college educated people around. Don't you agree?"

"I think more educated people is a great thing," Kayla said,

[26] Carrns, Ann. "To draw workers, employers offer to help with student loans." *The New York Times / MSN.* http://www.msn.com/en-us/money/careersandeducation/to-draw-workers-employers-offer-to-help-with-student-loans/ar-AAzbnwW?ocid=ientp Posted June 26, 2018 (Retrieved June 26, 2018)
[27] Yates, Al and Anne Bartley. Progressive Thinking: A Synthesis Of American Progressive Values, Beliefs and Positions. Denver: American Values Project. 2012. Page 7.

"If it's such a great thing and we agree on that, why shouldn't the government be able to tax everyone to provide that for society?" Hank asked. "It would benefit everyone!"

"Because you can't give me something I didn't ask for and then demand payment for it in the form of taxes!" Kayla said. "Whatever the purpose, government can't act to give out benefits and then seize payment from people for it without prior agreement. It's the same as if you gave me something for 'free', let's say a book, then demand I pay you for it! I appreciate the book if it's 'free', but if you 'give' it to me and then demand payment from me for it, I don't want the book! I'd rather keep my money because the book isn't really 'free'. You are forcing me to do something with my money that I don't want to! You are violating my Liberty and my Property![28]

Kayla continued, "Now if people donated a bunch of money, donated meaning they didn't have it taken from them by force through taxes or whatever, and then that donated money was used for 'free' college for people, no strings attached, that may be OK."

"What do you mean 'may be OK'," Hank asked.

"Meaning the government shouldn't be involved in it at all," Kayla said. "And that's exactly what is happening now in town! Businesses like mine which have been successful have set up various charities, scholarships and financial aid for people using donated money! Government is not, and should not, get involved!"

Hank fell back in his chair and looked exhausted.

---

[28] Nozick, Robert. Anarchy, State, and Utopia. New York: Basic Books. 2013. Page 95.

Kayla didn't want to let Hank off the hook just yet. She wanted to know more because she knew, based on Hank's whole attitude and thought process, that she was witnessing the start of a big problem in her community. This developing seed of thought that government needs to "do more" and "*take* more responsibility". A thought process that ran counter to everything the town was founded on and everything Kayla believed about the role of government. Kayla wanted to know more because she wanted to be prepared to fight against it.

"So, what else does Mr. Woodrow believe?" Kayla asked.

Hank sat back in his chair. "Do you really want to know?" He sounded exasperated.

"Yes," Kayla said, "I do."

For the next hour Hank spoke to Kayla about all of the things he knew Mr. Woodrow believed and the things he wanted to accomplish as Mayor. Kayla listened intently and tried not to interrupt.

Hank told her Mr. Woodrow was going to work on things like, "Creating more jobs and fixing the town's infrastructure. He is going to look after worker's rights and fight climate change. He is also going to look into demanding a minimum wage for workers and make sure everyone has access to 'free' healthcare and paid sick leave from their jobs, to name just a few!"[29]

---

[29] "Working Family Issues." *Working Families Party.* http://workingfamilies.org/issues/ (Retrieved May 30, 2018).
The *Working Families Party,* or WFP, is an ultra-radical left wing group with close ties to the *Communist Party USA (CPUSA).* One of the goals listed on the CPUSA's web site is to: "strengthen relationships with unions, left/progressive electoral forms like Our Revolution

"All done by the government and funded by taxes on the "rich" people and corporations," he said.

Hank spoke a lot about how the government needed to "invest" in creating all of these great services and programs for the community. Kayla asked him where the government would get all of this money to "invest".

"By people paying their fair share," Hank said.

"So, you mean by taxes?" Kayla asked. "So, the government should tax people more in order to get the money they need to invest? Is that what you are saying? The government should force me to give it my money so someone like Mr. Woodrow can decide where to spend it? Why shouldn't I think he will use that tax money to further his own ambitions? By giving it to people who support him for example?"

"Because the Government is impartial and represents the people and does what's best for people," Hank answered.

"Hah!" Kayla laughed, "Hank, you're so naïve! The more money the government takes from us for people like Mr. Woodrow to do with what they please, the less freedom we have! The difference between you and I Hank is you believe that government's job is to preserve people's freedom[30]. I believe the people can preserve their own freedom without government getting involved. I

(OR) and Working Famlies Party (WFP), etc;"

[30] Yates, Al and Anne Bartley. Progressive Thinking: A Synthesis Of American Progressive Values, Beliefs and Positions. Denver: American Values Project. 2012. Pages 30 and 67, for example. "The unique mission and purpose of government is to promote the public interest…" and, "…(Progressives) defend an accountable, efficient and well-run government as essential to the preservation of individual liberties, justice and quality of life."

also believe a government powerful enough to supposedly preserve my freedom is powerful enough to take it away."

Hank of course didn't agree. He continued to reiterate the lines that government needs to help things be more "fair", that it should "invest" in things to make our lives better, and that its job is to "protect" people from harm. The more Hank spoke and the more Kayla tried to reason with him, the more she realized that he wasn't interested in hearing her side. The more points that Kayla made based in fact and reason, the more emotional and hysterical Hank's attitude became. It was a trait that Kayla would come to see in most people who believed as Mayor Woodrow and Hank did.

After several hours Hank finally prepared to go home.

As he opened the front door to leave he turned to Kayla and said, "Thank you Kayla for listening." He smiled and gave her a hug. "I know we don't agree on a lot of these things but I will always be your friend."

"Of course," Kayla said. "I feel the same way. Goodnight Hank."

"Goodnight Kayla."

And with that Hank walked out onto the porch and Kayla shut the door behind him.

A nagging thought entered her mind...

We're in trouble...

Kayla didn't know it, but unfortunately that nagging thought was there to stay.

Progressivism

(Community Hall-The Fairest Place on Earth)

Mayor Woodrow

A few days after Hank left Kayla's house it was Election Day in Jefferson Township again. The sky was not as blue as it was on election days in the past, nor did it seem quite as warm. Nevertheless, City Hall was again decked out in all its red, white, and blue bunting. The Flag still fluttered proudly from atop its flagpole in front of the old, big building.

Mayor Ronald ran a good campaign, but after the votes were tallied it seemed Mr. Woodrow was able to convince enough people that his vision for Jefferson Township was a good thing. He was elected Mayor by a slim margin much to the delight of those who supported him, like Kayla's old friend Hank. The town also elected a bunch of Mr. Woodrow's supporters to the Town Council as well.

Mr. Woodrow told everyone to get ready to *progress* forward. He said that everyone who agreed with him was a *Progressive*. He said those who did not support him would remain stuck in the past or they were simply not smart enough to realize all of the great things they can accomplish as *Progressives*. Well, he did not say that last part *exactly*, but that was what he believed.

Mr. Woodrow was an unassuming looking man. He was short in stature and had thinning hair. He wore thin wire framed eyeglasses and looked very much like the Professor he once was. He always wore three-piece suits that seemed just a little bit too tight on him.

Kayla didn't like what she knew about Mayor Woodrow's policies so far, but many in town seemed to be fine with what he was proposing. She was feeling a little uncomfortable though because one of the first things he did was to change the town's motto on the sign outside of City Hall from *The Freest Place on Earth* to *The Fairest Place on Earth*. He also changed the name "City Hall" to "Community Hall". "After all," he said, "the good of the community is the most important thing. We all need to be ready to contribute for the sake of the community and the Government needs to make sure everything is fair."

The day after the election Kayla heard Mayor Woodrow on the TV talking about all of the wonderful things he wanted to accomplish. He wanted to have clean air and clean water. He wanted to make sure that "big business" was not hurting anyone. He wanted to make sure that people weren't doing anything that might cause harm to themselves...or someone else. All of these things sounded good on the surface to Kayla. After all, who in their right mind would want people to get hurt? But it was how he wanted to do these things that made Kayla nervous.

He said, "People who like to drink sugary beverages are a problem! This selfish lifestyle choice might lead to diabetes or other health issues which may cause those people to go to the Doctor. Now this bad choice by one person affects everyone else because the Doctor now has to take time and use resources to help that person instead of someone else. That's not fair!"

The Mayor proposed the town should pass a special tax[1] on sugary beverages to discourage people from drinking them. What

---

[1] Many cities have made efforts to impose taxes on sugary beverages under the guise of

was he going to do with the tax money collected form the sugary beverages? He said it will go to "help people". But he never explained what that really meant.

Not only that, he also said that he wanted to limit the size of sugary beverages people could buy. He did not think anyone should be allowed to buy a sugary drink bigger than 16 ounces... "For their own good" of course!

Kayla thought this was ridiculous[2]. What business is it of the government if someone wants to drink a sugary beverage? *Aren't we living in a free society and allowed to make our own choices?* She thought to herself.

Apparently not, she answered herself back.

Limit the size of drinks to 16 oz.? She thought. *How stupid is that? Couldn't a person who wants 32 oz. just buy two 16 oz. drinks? What good is banning drinks over 16oz.?* But Kayla was beginning to get the sense that it wasn't really about the sugar.

---

helping to prevent numerous health issues as well as to recoup costs associated with the treatment of diseases such as diabetes and obesity. New York City, under Mayor Michael Bloomberg, attempted to limit the size of sugary beverages allowed to be sold in 2012 by passing a law, but the law was declared unconstitutional in 2013. Berkeley, CA was the first city in the US to pass a tax on sugary drinks in 2014. Philadelphia, PA became the first major city to do so in 2016.
See: http://www.foodsafetynews.com/2012/05/nyc-poised-to-limit-size-of-sugary-drinks/#.WP4P_tKGPRY
http://www.reuters.com/article/us-sodaban-lawsuit-idUSBRE96T0UT20130730
https://www.usatoday.com/story/news/nation-now/2014/11/05/berkeley-passes-soda-tax/18521923/ and http://www.npr.org/sections/thesalt/2016/06/09/481390378/taxing-sugar-5-things-to-know-about-phillys-proposed-soda-tax (Retrieved April, 24, 2017)
[2] "Kids poke fun of Cook County sugary beverage tax at lemonade stand." *ABC 7 Chicago.* http://abc7chicago.com/food/kids-poke-fun-of-cook-county-sugary-beverage-tax-at-lemonade-stand/2280324/ Posted August 6, 2017. (Retrieved August 19, 2017)

She asked her father about this. "Well Kayla," he said ", my guess is it's more about collecting all that tax money. With all that money, the Mayor can use it to do all sorts of things for the people who support him. I bet he hopes that will get them to keep voting for him. In the end, I think that's the real reason for him wanting to do it. It will bring him money that will bring him power. It could be possible that in his heart he really believes this will help people, as misguided as that is. However, that's not how *I* see the role of government. I believe in a free society where people can make decisions, good or bad, for themselves, and as long as they don't hurt others it's none of the government's business."

"But he's saying that sugar does hurt people", Kayla said.

"Then why doesn't he just try to make sugar illegal?" Her father asked. "If it's truly as harmful as he seems to be saying it is, isn't it immoral of him to let it continue to be a legal item for people to purchase?"

Kayla thought for a few seconds and then said, "Even if it's illegal people could probably still get it on the black market. Right?"

"That's right," her father said, "at one point in its history the town made alcohol illegal. Once again it was done for 'people's own good' by the politicians of the day. But what happened?"

Kayla remembered her history, "People started bootlegging it and selling it anyway. It created an underground industry and spurred the growth of organized crime. Many people died and got hurt during that period because of it."

"That's right," her father said. "If people truly want something like alcohol or sugar, they will get it. I am against is the government taxing things simply to control people's behavior. They have no right to decide what I think is right or wrong for myself. However, it's up to our elected Representatives to make sure they are taxing the right things. And the people should have a say in it too. I would have more respect for the man if he simply came out and said he is taxing sugary beverages because the town needs the money. But the minute he says he is doing it 'for my own good', I become very skeptical."

Many people agreed with Mayor Woodrow but it did not make any sense to Kayla.

Now she understood completely what her father was talking about when he warned that there were unscrupulous politicians who had a desire to control other people's lives to gain power for themselves. This new Mayor was more about telling people what to do than actually wanting to help. The fact that he said, "force people" proved it to her. Kayla's dad always told her a government only gets its way through force. Sometimes it is a "soft" force, sometimes it is a "hard" one. But either way it is force[3].

Mayor Woodrow also said he wanted to make sure everyone was being treated fairly and it was government's job to make sure it was happening. "But..." he said, "...I need people in Government to make sure it is all getting done correctly and fairly. Because Government people are all very smart and are all very unbiased and have only the best interests of *everyone* in mind." Mayor Woodrow

[3] Richman, Sheldon. "Government Is Force." *Foundation for Economic Education.* https://fee.org/articles/government-is-force/ Posted September 16, 2011. (Retrieved May 30, 2018)

said, "Only the Government would be able to make sure that everything was fair because you can't trust a business or an individual person to do it. After all, they are only interested in profits and their own self-interests." He said you needed government to decide for people what is right or wrong, because regular people do not have the time to figure it out themselves.

"What we need are 'experts' in the Government to handle things." He said.

"The great thing is," Mayor Woodrow said, "I just so happen to know who those very 'experts' are!" He said they are the smartest of the smart with all sorts of degrees from big name universities and they knew just what to do so don't worry about it! They can be trusted to do what is right for everyone equally.

"But", Mayor Woodrow said, "all that takes money, and the Government needs more money to hire all of the special Government 'Experts' who will make sure everything runs smoothly and that no one is doing anything to hurt themselves or each other."

Mayor Woodrow announced that in order to fund this expansion of government he would seek to institute an *income tax.* He said, "The money from the income tax will be used to hire the Experts who will work for the Government making sure everything is fair!" He also said they needed to *invest* in new government agencies and departments whose job will be to "look after" other things that are important to people such as the environment, education and even labor. All of which needed more "Experts" to staff them. "For your own good of course!" he said.

It wasn't missed by Kayla that Mayor Woodrow said these "experts" will work *for the government*. Traditionally in Jefferson Township government workers were considered to work *for the people*.

Mayor Woodrow said some of the income tax money would also be used by the government to pay for things that he called *investments*. He said the town needed to *invest* in things like widening the roads, building a new post office and installing new streetlights and street signs.

Kayla didn't think the town really needed any of those so called "investments" because the roads and street lights seemed just fine the way they were, their post office seemed to be big enough and she really did not need or want the government "experts" deciding exactly what "fair" and "safe" was. Kayla also thought about the town Charter and knew that it specifically said the government could not collect an income tax from the people. She remembered that she learned a long time ago that an income tax was taught to be a bad thing because it took (stole) money (property) from people and denied them the opportunity to spend that money as they saw fit for their own best interests.

The income tax seemed like a punishment to Kayla, or a fine. Just because she earned an income, *was that a bad thing*, she thought to herself? At the very least Mayor Woodrow seemed to think people didn't *deserve* to keep all of the income they earned.

Apparently, Mayor Woodrow suspected some people might have negative feelings about his Income Tax because he said, "This Income Tax will not be for everybody! In fact, it will only apply to the very wealthy! It is only *fair* that the wealthiest among us, those who can afford to pay more, do their patriotic duty, and pay their *fair* share! For the good of the community! And what is their fair share? Why it is a very small 1% for the rich and up to 7% for the super-rich! And the super-rich are getting a great deal because the first $400,000 of their income will be exempt from the tax! Not being taxed on that first $400,000 is the government's gift to them! Anyone making more than $400,000 can certainly afford a small tax to pay for the great things the Government needs to do!"[4]

Kayla thought it was funny how the Mayor thought that allowing someone to keep something that was already theirs a "gift".

As for the "Experts" Mayor Woodrow wanted to hire (he now called them "Agents") he said that their job was to protect the people[5]. He also said that those who had to pay the "very small and fair" income tax should be happy they are being given an opportunity to work together as a community for the good of all. He said it was their "patriotic duty" to "give" this money to the government and just to make sure everyone was being "patriotic" and "giving" their money to the government, he was going to take it right from their boss's bank accounts. He was also going to hire more "Agents" whose jobs would be to make sure that no one "cheated" by not giving their taxes to him, ehhhh...., to the government.

---

[4] See the original Income Tax Rates https://www.irs.gov/uac/brief-history-of-irs (Retrieved April, 24, 2017)

[5] "He has erected a multitude of New Offices, and sent hither swarms of Officers to harass our people and eat out their substance." From the US Declaration of Independence

During a press conference when Mayor Woodrow was talking about his plan for the income tax someone said to him, "But you cannot do that! The power is not given to the government by our Township's Charter!" He was an older man with faded blue jeans, work boots, and a flannel shirt on. He looked as if he spent a lot of time outdoors.

Mayor Woodrow answered, "But the Charter is a 'Living Document' whose meaning can change as we need it to. We can make it mean anything we want it to. That is what makes it so great! Remember the charter was written a long time ago under different circumstances. It can only be relevant if it *evolves* to reflect our much more modern world!"

A man in the audience said, "The Charter isn't a 'living document' meant to change with the times. It's principles of freedom and liberties are timeless. Calling it, a 'living document', which says that it can have different meanings to different people, is like saying it should not exist at all. What's the sense of having rules and laws if we say can be interpreted differently based on the current circumstances? A law against theft is a law against theft, for example. According to the law, theft is bad. You can't interpret it any other way. If you want to change a law, or change the charter, there are processes you have to go through. You can't just say 'I think it means this...' and that makes it so!"

Some in the crowd seemed to agree with the man who spoke up. But many others were murmuring their approval of what the Mayor was doing. A few of the younger people up front were looking at the man in the audience and snickering. It was obvious they saw him as some sort of relic who was stuck in the past.

Not too long after Mayor Woodrow announced his plan for his Income Tax, Kayla woke up one morning and went to her computer to check the news as she did most mornings.

The first headline she saw was, "The Income Tax Is Here!" As she read the story, she found out the Town Council, in a special nighttime session, amended the Town Charter to allow the tax on income!

Kayla did not feel good about that at all. It used to be the people who made up the town's government worked part time and could be counted on to further freedom and liberty because when they went back to their regular jobs all that freedom helped them as well. However, one of the other things Mayor Woodrow did was to make all of the town government jobs full time. "We need people working full time for the citizens," he said, "Because there's a lot of work to be done!"

The government workers also got official government cars to drive and the town paid for their medical and dental benefits as well. All out of the taxpayer's money of course. No wonder they liked what Mayor Woodrow was doing.

Kayla thought about that man at the press conference who had challenged the Mayor when he called the Charter a "living document". The Mayor seemed to have followed the proper process and was able to change the Charter after all. *But what did that mean? Kayla thought. Just because a Progressive Mayor could change the Charter did it mean the change made to it was right?* Kayla knew that earlier leaders of the town did not think an income tax was a good thing. They believed it should only to be used during extreme emergencies, and only for a limited, defined period, but Mayor Woodrow was able to get people to agree it was such a good thing that it should become permanent.

Kayla thought about something else. In the past, the people of the town would never have agreed with Mayor Woodrow. People enjoyed their freedom and enjoyed their limited government. They never would have wanted the government to be so involved in everything because they learned from the past that government could become very oppressive. They did not trust government, so they controlled it with laws that laid out specifically what it could do.

Many people, like her friend Hank, also didn't seem to care that Mayor Woodrow was slowly starting to get involved in areas he never was allowed to before, and technically still wasn't allowed to! This made her nervous! People like Hank were actually encouraging the Mayor to keep taking more unilateral actions. They believed it was ultimately for the good of everyone in spite of the fact that in many cases it was illegal!

"I will take action!" the Mayor would yell at rallies.[6]

Kayla watched Mayor Woodrow give a speech where he said, "With the passage of this Income Tax, this patriotic tax, we have instituted fairness in our society! The very wealthy, those making over $400,000 a year who will not even notice this money is missing, will now be doing their patriotic duty by paying this tax.

---

[6] Slattery, Elizabeth and Andrew Kloster. "Obama Administration's Unilateral Actions." *The Heritage Foundation.* https://www.heritage.org/the-constitution/report/executive-unbound-the-obama-administrations-unilateral-actions Posted February 12, 2014. (Retrieved May 30, 2018)

Thanks to this tax we will now be able to hire the 'Experts' we need to ensure our community remains a fair place to live for all. Those 'Experts' will become Agents of the Government. To make sure all those wealthy people pay the Income Tax some of those Agents will be checking up on them. Now I am sure they will find that every wealthy person who must pay the tax is doing the right, patriotic thing by paying it. No one would want to risk going to jail by not paying it I would suppose. After all, how unpatriotic would that be?"

Kayla did not understand how paying a tax made someone a patriot, especially when they did not have a choice in the matter and would go to jail if they refused to pay it.

It was not long before Kayla started to see other things start to change. In the past, Kayla never really saw any Town Officials come around on official business or send official letters unless something bad or unusual happened like when her employee sold the bad lemonade. In fact, there were not many Town Officials at all.

Now Kayla started to see more and more Town Officials driving around in their taxpayer funded government cars. She started to get official letters in the mail quite frequently as well. The Town began to tell her things like she could only use paper cups, not plastic, because paper was better for the environment. Kayla thought that did not make any sense because paper came from trees that needed to be cut down to make the paper. Aren't trees part of the environment? The paper cups also cost more money to buy but the Town government did not seem to care.

The government told Kayla she needed to install the more expensive "energy efficient" light bulbs in each of her stores because incandescent bulbs used "too much" energy. The government also said each store had to be built to certain dimensions and could only be made using certain materials. The government then told Kayla she could only allow her employees to work a certain number of hours each day. When the workers complained because some of them wanted to be able to work a lot to make more money, the Town did not care. They said it was for the good of everyone because some people were working very hard and long hours and they might get tired and hurt themselves. They also said it was not fair that some people worked so much that they were making a lot more money than those who were not.

Kayla thought all of this was ridiculous.

Mayor Woodrow had some other ideas he said were "transformational" for Jefferson Township. One involved its currency.

Jefferson Township always had its currency tied to gold. If you have a dollar, theoretically you could go to the bank and get a dollar's worth of gold. By keeping the currency linked to something tangible, like gold, helps people to trust it. Because of this the currency is stable, so the economy also tends to be. Having the currency linked to something like gold also makes the currency worth something. In this case, it's worth the gold that backs it up. Since there could only be as much of Jefferson Township's currency in circulation as there was gold backing it, people came to think of Jefferson Township's currency as the "Gold Standard" throughout society. They trusted its value.

This also served another purpose, it helped to keep spending and prices under control. If you wanted to spend money on something, you needed to actually have the money to do so. If you didn't have the money, you couldn't spend it. This keeps prices stable and helps the money that is in circulation maintain its value because there is only a limited amount of it. Again, remember, the more of something there is, the less its worth. Even currency. Because the supply of money was limited by how much gold was backing it, you couldn't create money out of thin air. The only way to increase the supply of money in circulation is by actually getting more physical gold, typically by mining for it and digging it out of the earth. That's a very expensive and time-consuming process.

Mayor Woodrow and his fellow Progressives did not like this. "Why should we restrict ourselves to having our currency tied to gold?" he asked during another one of his speeches. He also did not like the fact that people had been turning in their dollars for actual gold a lot more since he became Mayor. Kayla knew some people were a little nervous about all the changes that Mayor Woodrow was bringing to their town. They were worried things might get a little turbulent, so, as often happened when there was some uncertainty, especially in the economy, people would stock up on gold because it tended to always hold its value. And, many thought having an ounce of actual gold in hand was much better than having just the paper currency.

But Mayor Woodrow said that if the town removed its currency from the gold standard they would be able to have a lot more "flexibility" with the economy.

"We would then be able to have all of the smartest money experts set our money policy for us!" the Mayor said. "By putting more paper money into circulation or by taking it out of circulation, these experts can make sure that our economy is always strong![7] With the currency tied to gold, these very smart experts will not be able to manipulate the money supply so easily, which would hurt the people of the town! Don't you all want the experts to take care of us?"

A news reporter asked the Mayor, "If the currency isn't tied to gold anymore, how could the people be confident a dollar was worth anything anymore?"

The Mayor said, "Why... your trust in the Government makes it worth something!"

"But what if I don't trust the government?" someone else asked the Mayor.

A look of disgust crossed the Mayor's face. With as much incredulousness as he could muster the Mayor said, "Why wouldn't you trust the Government? The Government has everyone's best interests at heart and hires only the smartest people to make sure we are all taken care of. These monetary experts will create a stronger economy for us all. You'll see!"

"But everything has been great the way it is." An older lady in the crowd chimed in. "Why should we change it?"

---

[7] Kadlec, Charles. "Nixon's Colossal Monetary Error: The Verdict 40 Years Later." *Forbes*. https://www.forbes.com/sites/charleskadlec/2011/08/15/nixons-colossal-monetary-error-the-verdict-40-years-later/#5a744f3c69f7 Posted August 15, 2011. (Retrieved August 7, 2017)

"Because it will be even better, and fairer!" the Mayor said.

Kayla didn't like this idea of taking the town off the gold standard at all. To her it was simple. The more of something there is, the less it is worth. If the government no longer needs to have a dollar tied to actual gold, and they can print[8] as much money as they want, to pay for things like expanding the size of government, Kayla believed the value of a dollar would go down because more of them would be in circulation.

She talked to her father about this to see if she was right.

He said, "You are right. If a government keeps dumping more of its currency into circulation, prices start to rise and inflation begins to creep in. History shows this as fact. It has happened before with big, rich countries. Germany in the early 1900's for example. During a period of economic hardship Germany's government kept printing more and more money in a misguided attempt to control their economy. At one point the German currency became so worthless a wheel barrow full of paper money couldn't even buy a loaf of bread! Eventually we can get to a point called hyper-inflation where your currency is worthless. And that is scary!" [9]

[8] Schoen, John W. "How does Fed 'inject' money into the system?" NBCNews,com Answer Desk. Updated August 12, 2007. http://www.nbcnews.com/id/20218020/ns/business-answer_desk/t/how-does-fed-inject-money-system/#.WhRJ-tLrtQI (Retrieved November 21, 2017)

[9] See: Boesler, Matthew. "WEIMAR: The Truth About History's Most Infamous Hyperinflation Horror Story." *Business Insider.* http://www.businessinsider.com/weimar-germany-hyperinflation-explained-2013-9?op=1/#e-inflations-roots-were-in-world-war-one-which-germany-financed-with-outsized-budget-deficits-1 Posted September 20, 2013. (Retrieved August 15, 2017)
Gillespie, Patrick. "Venezuela: the land of 500% inflation ." *CNN Money.* http://money.cnn.com/2016/04/12/news/economy/venezuela-imf-economy/index.html Posted April 12, 2016. (Retrieved August 15, 2017)

"Could that happen here?" Kayla asked.

"Of course, it could." Her father said. "Anytime government gets involved in manipulating the supply of a currency, anytime it gets involved in disrupting the natural flow of supply and demand, a country is in danger of its economy having real problems, right up to the point of collapsing. That's what makes removing the currency from the gold standard so dangerous. It removes a check on government power. If a government can arbitrarily start to 'print' money, it can use that money to expand its scope, size and power at its own whim. If the Mayor wants to hire 100 more agents to harass people, a gold-based economy would limit his ability to do so because the supply of money he has available to do so would be limited by the amount of gold available to back it. He couldn't do it unless he somehow increased the amount of gold available. However, if he didn't have to worry about the money having gold to back it, he could just 'print' whatever money he needed to pay for the new agents. Not only does this make the money in circulation less valuable, the government's power becomes almost limitless."

"I see." Kayla said. "If money is no object, there is almost no limit to what you can do. Good or bad. Removing gold from backing our currency means we are giving almost limitless power to a government which may not always have our best interests at heart."

"Exactly!" Her father said. "In the end, allowing politicians or other government bureaucrats[10] to have complete control over

---

[10] "Bureaucrat: 1. an official of a bureaucracy. 2. an official who works by fixed routine without exercising intelligent judgment." *dictionary.com* http://www.dictionary.com/browse/bureaucrat (Retrieved May 18, 2018)

the supply of money is dangerous. Dangerous to the economy and dangerous to people's freedom."

He then said to Kayla, "Now let me ask you...what happens to prices when more money is in circulation?"

Kayla thought about this logically. *If people have more money to spend on something they want, they would probably be willing to pay more for whatever it is. If people are willing to pay more for something, its price will rise.*

She answered her father. "Prices go up."

"That's right!" he said. "The price of something is determined by what people are willing to pay for it. If I have more money in my pocket because the government printed more of it, I may be willing to pay more for things I want, which makes prices rise. That's called inflation.[11] If the government keeps dumping money into circulation, because they are not restrained by the money having to be backed by gold..."

"Then prices keep going higher and higher..." Kayla finished the sentence for her father.

"Now think about one other thing," her father said. "What if the government starts to print all of that money but only gives it to people they like. What happens then?"

---

[11] "Inflation: a persistent, substantial rise in the general level of prices related to an increase in the volume of money and resulting in the loss of value of currency (opposed to deflation)." *dictionary.com. http://www.dictionary.com/browse/inflation?s=t* (Retrieved May 18, 2018)

Kayla thought about this for a second and said, "If prices keep going up and I don't get any of the extra money the government hands out I am in real financial trouble."

"That's right." Her father said. "And the government can make it that if you want the extra money you have to do certain things or give up certain rights. People who are seeing their savings constantly decline in value because of inflation, people who start to worry about how they will pay for the things their family needs may be willing to do what the government wants to get that extra money. Giving the government unlimited control over the supply of money is a dangerous thing."

Soon after, as expected, Mayor Woodrow ended Jefferson Township's practice of linking its currency to gold. Because of this, Mayor Woodrow now had the government's mint start to print more paper currency. He used this newly printed money to hire more government workers, build more government buildings, and ultimately grow the size of the town's government, just as Kayla's father had said they would.

Many people in town agreed with Kayla and her father that taking the currency off the gold standard was a bad thing. People inherently trusted the value of actual gold more than the town's unbacked paper and electronic currency. The Mayor said their new currency would be a *fiat*[12] currency and was the best thing for the long-term success of their township.

---

[12] "Fiat Money: money (such as paper currency) not convertible into coin or specie of equivalent value." *Merriam-Webster.* https://www.merriam-webster.com/dictionary/fiat%20money Updated June 20, 2018. (Retrieved June 25, 2018)

But the people didn't believe in the fiat currency's promise of value provided by the government so they started to acquire actual physical gold and to save it. Many had started to do this in anticipation of the Mayor's expected action to rid the town of its gold standard. The town's gold supply started to dwindle and this made Mayor Woodrow nervous.

"We can't have people hoarding gold!" he yelled during one of his many speeches. "It's unpatriotic and unfair! Going forward, the private possession of gold, except in personal jewelry you already own, is illegal! You must all exchange your stockpiles of gold for Jefferson Township currency! Failure to do so will have you in violation of the law and make you subject to punishment!"[13]

Kayla thought that this latest action by the Mayor, confiscating gold and making the possession of it illegal, was absurd. She realized this was something a Dictator would do.

With all this extra paper money floating around things started to go up in price. Just as Kayla's dad said it would. For example, when the government bid out a job on a new government

---

[13] "By virtue of the authority vested in me by Section 5 (b) of the Act of October 6, 1917, as amended by Section 2 of the Act of March 9, 1933, entitled "An Act to provide relief in the existing national emergency in banking, and for other purposes," in which amendatory Act Congress declared that a serious emergency exists, I, Franklin D. Roosevelt, President of the United States of America, do declare that said national emergency still continues to exist and pursuant to said section do hereby prohibit the hoarding of gold coin, gold bullion, and gold certificates within the continental United States by individuals, partnerships, associations and corporations...The term "person" means any individual, partnership, association or corporation".
"34 - Executive Order 6102 – Requiring Gold Coin, Gold Bullion and Gold Certificates to Be Delivered to the Government. April 5, 1933." *The American Presidency Project.* http://www.presidency.ucsb.edu/ws/?pid=14611 (Retrieved May 5, 2017)
See also:
Salsman, Richard M. "The Bank Runs of the Early 1930s and FDR's Ban on Gold." *Forbes.* https://www.forbes.com/sites/richardsalsman/2011/04/06/the-bank-runs-of-the-early-1930s-and-fdrs-ban-on-gold/#457b0bd73ee5 Posted April 6, 2011. (Retrieved May 5, 2017)

office building, the contractors knew the government now had all this extra cash lying around so they increased the amount they wanted the government to pay to get the job done. The lumber company knew the contractor got more of the government's cash so they increased the price of the lumber they sold to the contractor...and so on.... The government didn't care about the inflated prices and were willing to pay them because now they just printed more money to cover it!

Kayla started to pay much closer attention to the bills she received from her suppliers. She noticed that everything was going up in price. Inflation was happening everywhere. And it turned out it wasn't just because of all the excess cash being printed now.

She asked the grocery store owner why he was now charging more for his lemons. "Well Kayla," he said, "I now have to charge more for lemons because the government told me I must wash every single lemon I sell because I can't sell dirty fruit. They said it may be harmful to people. Because of this new regulation, I had to hire more people to wash the lemons."

Kayla tried to find another place to buy her lemons from but all of the lemon sellers told the same story. Government intervention in their business by way of regulation was causing them to have to try to raise prices. She could have refused to pay the increased prices but then what? She wouldn't be able to buy lemons to make her lemonade. She begrudgingly paid the higher price for the lemons.

She also didn't think the lemon washing regulation made any sense. She peeled all the lemons before squeezing them, so how dirty they were on the outside did not really matter. She had no choice though, she needed them to make her product. However, because her supply of money was not endless, she had to cut back elsewhere to make up for the added expense of the more expensive lemons.

Kayla had been using part of her profits to pay for very generous fringe benefits for her employees. One of this was a tuition reimbursement plan. If one of her employees went to college and got straight A's, *Grandma's Old-Fashioned Lemonade* would pay for the course. As much as it broke Kayla's heart she had to end that benefit for her employees.

When she did that something unexpected happened. Some of her employees got mad. "Why don't you just cut back on your profits or your pay?" some asked her angrily. "Why cut back on *our* benefits?"

This took Kayla by surprise. She was always very generous with her employees and they always were very appreciative. She has never heard talk like this from them before. This new attitude from some of her employees made her mad.

"Not that it's any of your business," she answered angrily, "I *have* cut back on my pay. As much as I hated to do it because I use a lot of my own pay for charitable giving. So now I can't give as much to charity as I would like. I also need to maintain some kind of profit margin to stay in business and provide jobs for people. As the owner of the business I need to make hard decisions sometimes about what is best for the business and everyone that works here. But remember one thing, it's not my fault. All of this is occurring because the government has been getting more and more involved in our lives and our business. Their constantly increasing regulations and taxes have been hurting all of us."

Kayla knew this sense of *entitlement*[14] exhibited by some of her employees could be attributed to the Mayor's constant talk that people are owed something by the government. That the government should be the one providing things for them to make everything "fair". That and his constant disparagement of profit and business was creating a frame of thought in some people that those were things which should be controlled by the government.

One afternoon an Agent came into Kayla's lemonade factory to "inspect the lemons". He had on khaki pants and a green golf shirt with an embroidered patch on the chest that read, "Jefferson Township Health Department". This was one of the new Departments the Mayor created. Around his neck was a black lanyard that had a clear plastic pouch on the end of it that contained an I.D. card that had the Agents name and photo on it. The lanyard and I.D. hung down to the Agents belt buckle. He asked the secretary for the manager and when the manager appeared the Agent casually flashed his I.D. at him and said, "Health Department". The manager of the factory, who was an agreeable sort of person, let the Agent in. The agent asked to "see the lemons" so the manager took the agent into the storage room and showed him the crates of lemons which they used for making the lemonade.

---

[14] "Entitlement: belief that one is deserving of or entitled to certain privileges." Merriam-webster.com. https://www.merriam-webster.com/dictionary/entitlement Updated June 13, 2018. (Retrieved June 25, 2018)

The Agent asked, "Why are there two separate sections for storing the lemons? And why are those lemons ", he said pointing to one group of lemon crates ", in different crates than those lemons?" he asked while then pointing at the other group of lemon crates.

"Well," the manager said, "those are the washed lemons we get from our lemon supplier and those are the lemons we get from our own lemon farm. We keep the washed ones separate from the others so they don't get dirty again."

"Hmmmm," the agent said. "So, you don't wash the lemons you get from your farm?"

The manager thought this was an odd question, why would they have to wash their own lemons? "No sir, we don't. We don't grow enough of our own lemons to make all of our lemonade so we have to buy some from the grocer. The grocer we buy the lemons from washes them before he sells them to us as the regulation says. But we don't wash the lemons we grow ourselves, well...because we grow them ourselves!"

The manager was genuinely perplexed as to why the agent thought they would wash their own homegrown lemons.

"Hmmmm," the Agent said again. "Thanks for your time. Tell your boss she will get my report and findings in the mail." With that, he turned and left.

The manager scratched his head and watched the Agent get into his government vehicle and drive away. He went back to work.

The next day Kayla was at the lemonade factory. The manager told her what had happened with the government agent.

"He asked if we washed the lemons we grow ourselves?" she asked the manager.

"Yes," he answered. "Then he just basically ran away!"

Kayla thought the whole interaction was strange but she didn't think much of it. She didn't like the fact that a government agent just appeared at her factory and started to demand to see things, but she figured it was just part of the Mayor's plan to make sure all of his "experts" looked busy to justify their existence.

That is until she got an official letter in the mail from the government that very same day. When she opened it she almost couldn't believe her eyes:

From: The Jefferson Township Health Department

To: Kayla Alexander

Subject: Health Violations Observed in the Grandma's Old-Fashioned Lemonade Factory

- *After an inspection by an Agent of the Jefferson Township Health Department Grandma's Old-Fashioned Lemonade Factory is found to be in violation of the town ordinance against the sale of unwashed fruit.*
- *Said Agent observed, and was told by the facilities manager, that lemons obtained from a farm owned by*

the Grandma's Old-Fashioned Lemonade Corporation are being used in the production of lemonade without being first washed.

- *Grandma's Old-Fashioned Lemonade Corporation is to immediately discard all lemons currently on these premises.*

- *Grandma's Old-Fashioned Lemonade Corporation is also to immediately discard all lemonade that has already been produced and is currently on the premises.*

- *In the spirit of fairness, the Health Department will not, at this time, require a total recall of all Grandma's Old-Fashioned Lemonade which is currently for sale in the marketplace.*

- *Going forward Grandma's Old-Fashioned Lemonade Corporation is required to wash all lemons obtained from any source before being used in production. This is required to be performed in a sterile "fruit washing room" located in a structure separate from the factory where the product is produced. Any wastewater created because of the wash process must be filtered before being disposed of. All lemons transported from the "fruit washing room" to the factory must be done so by way of cleaned and sanitized vehicles.*

- *Grandma's Old-Fashioned Lemonade Corporation has six weeks to comply or face the stoppage of all production of Grandma's Old-Fashioned Lemonade at this facility.*

- *Grandma's Old-Fashioned Lemonade Corporation must have its "fruit washing room" and*

accompanying improvements inspected before being
certified as compliant by the Health Department.

- *As a food producer and because of Grandma's Old-*
  Fashioned Lemonade Corporation status as an
  offender all facilities will also be subject to periodic
  inspections by the Health Department for a period of
  three years and no less than once a year after.

Thank you for your cooperation,

The Jefferson Township Health Department

Kayla almost fainted. This would cost her thousands of dollars. She called the Health Department and asked why this was happening to her company? She explained that her lemons did not fall under the fruit washing regulation because she wasn't selling them to anyone; she was using them in her own factory.

"Well Ms. Alexander," the annoyed voice on the other end said, "*technically* you are selling them to someone, albeit to yourself. You pay wages and such to have those lemons grown in order to use them in your factory. What is 'selling' and 'buying' other than receiving or giving money for something? Those lemons cost money to grow, the money used to grow those lemons creates the situation where you are *technically* buying those lemons. Since there cannot be 'buying' and 'selling' exclusive of each other you are in effect selling and buying the lemons from your farm, therefore they fall under the fruit washing regulation. Understand?"

Kayla thought her head was going to explode. "That doesn't make any sense," she said to the voice on the other end while trying to remain calm. "How am I selling and buying to myself?"

"I'm sorry this isn't clear to you," the voice said. I will send you a pamphlet which explains the fruit washing regulation in great detail. It has pictures!"

Kayla hung up.

By the time Kayla got her factory up to "compliance" with the regulation, it had cost her thousands of dollars. She had no choice but to cut back on the reinvesting in her company. Sure, building the washing room and other regulation related expenditures created work for others but that work was short lived. Kayla had wanted to create long term work for people by expanding her business, but she had to cut back on that now because of the added expense of getting her company into compliance with the regulation and then maintaining it. Besides, none of that work was created because of the free market. It came about because of the taxes taken from people as well as government creating a problem where none existed. There wasn't one instance of someone getting sick from "dirty fruit" on record. But since the government said it *could* happen, they said they had to act to prevent it. All of this seemed decidedly *un-free* to Kayla. Kayla's company was lucky though because it could afford to make the changes. It had become quite a big operation that generated a lot of income. She was still profitable, though less so, and paying for the regulations, in the end, affected her workers the most, because she could not invest as much in them anymore.

For example, she had been working on a plan to give the kids of her employee's free dental care, including expensive braces for their teeth if they needed them. But now the cost of complying with the fruit washing regulations had forced her to eliminate that idea. Everyone suffered...except the government.

Who was unlucky though were a lot of the smaller businesses who could not afford to keep up with the costs associated with complying with all the new government regulations that were being imposed on business. Many of those businesses closed and the employees found themselves unemployed.

The thing that irked Kayla the most was the fact that these extra expenditures, expenditures that took away from her growing her business, helping her employees, and yes...even further enriching herself, were coming about because a few people in government said they should. It had nothing to do with business or competition. It had nothing to do with Kayla making a wrong or right decision out of her own free will. Instead, it was occurring because of the *whims* of a few power-hungry people.

Kayla's customers suffered as well. They loved her lemonade and were willing to pay more for it, but doing so left them with less money to spend elsewhere. This of course negatively affected other businesses. Kayla's customers spent more for her lemonade but cut back on their purchases elsewhere. Those other businesses suffered financially from the drop in their business. This caused them to also do things like cut benefits and lay off workers. And this went on and on for months. A new regulation or tax of some kind seemed to come down from the government every day.[15]

One afternoon Kayla was outside one of her stores sweeping the sidewalk. She liked to do that from time to time just to show her employees that no job was beneath even the owner. Kayla did that a lot. Sometimes she would clean the bathrooms, sometimes she would go around wiping down tables. Being it was a pretty nice day outside she figured she would get some fresh air.

She looked down the block and saw a heavy set, balding man rapidly approaching her. He seemed to be in a hurry. His white apron was flapping wildly in front of him and he was pumping his arms vigorously. He looked as if he would burst into a run at any moment. She noticed a piece of paper clutched tightly in his hand. As he got closer Kayla could see it was the local grocer. She stopped sweeping and looked up at him as he pounded to a stop in front of her. He didn't look happy. His normally pale, smiling face was bright red. Beads of sweat were dripping off his forehead.

"CAN YOU BELIEVE THIS? CAN YOU BELIEVE THIS?" he yelled waving the paper in his hand in the air in front of Kayla.

For a second she thought he was yelling at her. But then realized he was just yelling in general. It took Kayla by surprise because he was normally so happy. In fact, he was normally one of the nicest people Kayla knew. He was well known around town for not charging families who were struggling financially for their groceries. He always seemed willing to help someone and always had a smile on his face. But not now. It was the first time she ever saw him so upset.

---

[15] Gattuso, James and Diane Katz. "20,642 New Regulations Added in the Obama Presidency". *The Daily Signal*. https://www.dailysignal.com/2016/05/23/20642-new-regulations-added-in-the-obama-presidency/ Posted May 23, 2016. (Retrieved May 21, 2018)

"Ed, Ed," she said, taking a step back. "What's going on? What's the Matter?"

Ed then proceeded to explain to Kayla he just got another letter from the Town Government (that was the paper he was waving around) that now he would have to pay a special tax on the sugar he sold.

Excitedly he ranted, "The government said that in their efforts to 'fight obesity' sugar has been identified as something that contributes to that disease.[16] The government also said that in addition to possibly contributing to obesity, sugar can cause cavities in your teeth and the government wanted to protect people from that as well! So, Mayor Woodrow got the Town Council to pass this tax on sugar!"

She remembered that a sugar tax was one of the proposals Mayor Woodrow made when he was first elected. Now Kayla suddenly felt some of the same anger Ed was feeling. After all, her drinks were made with sugar! She believed it wasn't any of the government's business if people wanted to consume sugar. Shouldn't they be able to do so if they wanted?

"That's ridiculous!" Kayla said.

The grocer agreed.

---

16 "The evidence for taxing soft drinks (or any other source of calories) as a means of reducing obesity is weak
and largely theoretical. In practice, people in prosperous countries are not easy to manipulate with blunt tax
instruments given the diverse food environment."
Snowden, Christopher. "Sugar taxes: A Briefing." *Institute of Economic Affairs.*
https://iea.org.uk/wp-content/uploads/2016/07/IEA%20Sugar%20Taxes%20Briefing%20Jan%202016.pdf Posted January 11, 2016. (Retrieved May 21, 2018)

"What are you going to do?" Kayla asked him.

"Now I have to lay off some workers," he said. "It hurts me to do so because many have been with me for years, BUT I DON'T HAVE A CHOICE IF I WANT TO STAY IN BUSINESS!"

"Ed, I am so sorry," Kayla said.

Ed just grunted and stomped away, muttering to himself. Kayla watched him disappear around the corner. It looked like he was heading towards Community Hall.

Kayla thought back to the conversation she had with her father when the sugary beverage tax was introduced. She had wondered why the government didn't just ban sugar if it was so bad. Not that she wanted that to happen, she just thought it showed how disingenuous the government was being. Kayla's had father told her the sugar tax was probably more about the government taking more money from people rather than out of concern for people.[17] It seemed to Kayla that he was exactly right, the government was more interested in taking more money from people.

Kayla was about to turn around and head back into her store when she looked across the street towards *Tony's Barber Shop*. The barber shop had been a Main Street staple for close to forty years. Kayla's dad, for example, had been getting his hair cut at *Tony's* since he was a kid. She saw her old friend Hank come out of the barber shop followed closely by Tony.

---

[17] Basham, Patrick. "Sugar Taxes Are Unfair and Unhealthy." *Usnews.com.* https://www.usnews.com/debate-club/should-sugar-be-regulated/sugar-taxes-are-unfair-and-unhealthy Posted March 30, 2012. (Retrieved May 21, 2018)

Hank apparently had gotten a job with the town because he had on the same khaki pants and golf shirt they all wore. He also was holding a clipboard in one hand. Clipboards seemed to be the something every government agent carried around nowadays. Hank looked as if he was trying to explain something to Tony because he kept pointing to his clipboard as he spoke. Tony had his arms crossed across his chest and was looking down towards the ground. As Hank was speaking Tony was shaking his head. Kayla set her broom against the wall and went across the street to see what was going on.

As she approached them Hank stopped speaking to Tony and said, "Oh, hi Kayla."

Kayla noticed there was a patch on the front of Hank's shirt that read *Jefferson Township Department of Licenses and Permits.* "Hi Hank," she said politely. Turning to Tony she said, "Is everything OK Tony?"

Tony looked up at Kayla and said, "No, Kayla. It's not. After almost forty years in business, forty years of cutting hair in this town...including this kid's," he said pointing his thumb at Hank without looking at him, "the government says I am not qualified to cut hair unless they say I am."

Hank shuffled uncomfortably but didn't say anything.

"What's he talking about?" Kayla asked Hank.

Rather sheepishly Hank said, "The Government has decided that for the good of the people, Barbers, and some other occupations, will now have to follow certain guidelines in order to get a license to operate."

"What guidelines? What are you talking about Hank?" Kayla asked.

Hank went on, "Well, the Government wants to make sure that certain businesses, like Barbers, are running clean and sanitary operations, for the good of the health of the people of course."[18] Hank sounded a little more confident when he spoke about the government.

Kayla heard that similar line, *good for the people,* quite a bit since Mayor Woodrow was elected. "So that's your job now Hank? Looking out for the good of the people? 'Protecting' them from people like Tony who have been in business for forty years without ever having a problem?"

Hank didn't answer.

"Let me see those guidelines," Kayla said. She grabbed the clipboard from Hank. He said, "Hey!" but didn't resist.

Kayla read down the list of guidelines the town now thinks Tony the barber, a man who had been cutting hair for decades, has to now abide by "For the good of the people".

---

[18] Carpenter II, Dick M. Ph.D. and Lisa Knepper, Kyle Sweetland, Jennifer McDonald. "License to Work: A National Study of Burdens from Occupational Licensing. 2nd Edition." Institute for Justice. http://ij.org/wp-content/themes/ijorg/images/ltw2/License_to_Work_2nd_Edition.pdf November 2017. (Retrieved May 20, 2018)

It read:

What are the requirements for a barber's license?

• *Successful completion of a course of study*

• *Submit an application*

Note: A license to practice barbering does not allow the operation of a business. A separate Barber Shop license is needed to operate a business.

What qualifications do I need for licensure?

• *Successful completion of a course of study*

• *Completed a one-time course of study regarding "the transmission of contagious diseases and the proper methods of sanitation and sterilization"*

• *Successfully completed the town's practical examination within 2 years*

• *Jefferson Township Education – completed barber course in a town approved school*

• *Experience – Certification from state board proving 3 years of experience and 2 Experience Statements*

How many hours of training is required for barber?

Hours are determined by the approved Jefferson Township barber schools.

All applicants must complete a one-time course of study regarding "the transmission of contagious diseases and the proper methods of sanitation and sterilization to be employed in barber shops." The course curricula must be approved by the Education Department and proof of course completion must be submitted with your application

Do I need a physical to be licensed?

Yes. You need to be examined by a physician, physician's assistant or nurse practitioner to apply for a license in Barbering. Your physician, physician's assistant or nurse practitioner must complete and date the Health Certification section of the application. You must submit your application within 30 days after it is signed.

Who must apply for a Barber shop owner license?

*You must obtain a Barber Shop Owner's license to own, control or operate a barber shop, whether as a sole proprietor, partner, shareholder or officer. See chart on page 4. **Note: A shop owner's license does not permit you to practice barbering. Each person performing such service must be licensed as a barber operator by the Department of State.***

Are there any barbering prohibitions?

Yes. A business license will not permit the practice of barbering at your business location if you have not first obtained a barber shop license pursuant to Article 28 of the General Business Law. [19]

---

[19] Adapted from: New York Department of State. Division of Licensing Services. https://www.dos.ny.gov/licensing/barber/barbering_faq.html#1 (Retrieved May 20, 2018)

Kayla handed the clipboard back to Hank. "This is ridiculous," she said.

"In what way?" Hank asked. He seemed genuinely offended by Kayla's attitude.

"Tony has been cutting hair for forty years. Could he have done that if he gave bad haircuts or ran a dirty shop? Of course not! The free market would have taken care of that. If he didn't provide a good service people wouldn't go to him and he would have gone out of business. This whole thing is nothing more than an attempt by the government to take more money from the people, to control business and gather more power," she said.

She went on, "All this is going to do is make it harder for the little guy to start a business. It's stupid. How much does it cost to comply with all of these regulations?"

"The permits and stuff cost a couple of hundred dollars, the school can cost thousands,"[20] Hank answered.

"Wow!" Kayla said. "Just...wow!

Tony, who had been standing there silently, listening to Kayla express the very thoughts he was feeling, spoke up. "So, Hank, what happens if I don't get the Barber License?"

---

[20] "The total cost of the program, including a non-refundable $100.00 registration fee, is $4,600." From: *American Barber Institute.* http://abi.edu/courses/500-hours-barber-operator-program (Retrieved May 21, 2018)

"Well," Hank said in a tone that he wished this whole conversation would just end already, "you will face fines and potential seizure of your business and accounts by the town."

"Hmmph," Tony said.

Kayla started to speak up again. She was completely agitated at this point, but Tony held up his hand to her.

"Don't worry honey. It's OK," he said in a calm voice to Kayla. "I've been cutting hair and have had a successful business for many, many years. I am fortunate to be in a position that I can retire. Because God knows I won't comply with any of these stupid rules. What the government is doing is robbery. Even worse, it's bordering on dictatorial. And you're right, the government doesn't really care about doing this 'for the people' as this moron says," he pointed at Hank with his thumb. Hank went to say something but then thought better of it and kept his mouth shut.

"It's all about money, and power," Tony said. "So, don't you get upset," he told Kayla. "I will be OK." He smiled at Kayla and then turned to Hank. "Congratulations Hank. You and your idiot government did something the free market never did, you put me out of business. I lasted all these years operating without any of your dumb government licenses and regulations, now all of that is gone because of you and your government buddies. Tell me I need to take a course on how to cut hair? Absurd. Tell me I need the government to say it's OK for me to make a living by cutting hair? Ridiculous. Tell me I am not qualified to be a barber unless you say I am? It's a joke. Who are you to make that decision?"

Hank started to say something about how all the rules were for the good of everyone but one harsh look from Kayla made him pause. Instead, he turned around and walked to his government car, got in and drove away.

Kayla and Tony hugged each other. She had tears in her eyes. She told him to take care and the turned and walked back across the street to her store. Tears streaming down her face. She couldn't believe what was happening to her town she loved.

The rules and regulations didn't stop at Tony's barber shop. Kayla soon stared to feel the pinch of an intrusive government even more and more as well.

Yet another letter from the government came to Kayla in the mail. She received a fine from the government because she had too many thermometers in her walk-in refrigerator and her cutting boards had cut marks on them![21] This was all uncovered during yet another government inspection.

Kayla really couldn't pass her continually increasing cost to do business on to her customers. They too were already cutting back on their spending because of the new fines and taxes taking more money out of their own pockets. She wound up having to lay some workers off. Some thought they could go get jobs washing the lemons for Kayla and the grocer, for less money by the way, but those jobs were few and far between now, and besides, soon the grocer had to lay off even more workers because his business was slowing.

[21] Briquelet, Kate. "City fattens coffers with 'frivolous' slaps at local businesses." *New York Post*. http://nypost.com/2012/09/30/city-fattens-coffers-with-frivolous-slaps-at-local-businesses/ Posted Sept 30, 2012. (Retrieved May 19, 2017)

It used to be there weren't enough workers for jobs in Jefferson Township. Because of that employers offered things such as higher wages and more perks and benefits to keep the employees they had, or to even lure workers away from other businesses. Now, largely because of the declining economy brought on by all of the government intervention, just the opposite was occurring. Businesses were cutting back on jobs and benefits to cover their increased costs and declining revenues and profits. Workers were finding it harder and harder to get a job because there simply wasn't a demand for their services by the hurting businesses. When a worker did find a job, it was usually at a lower rate of pay with reduced benefits than it had in the past.

Of course, Mayor Woodrow blamed businesses for the shrinking job market and economic pain most were feeling. He said, "Don't be fooled when business tells you they can't hire more people because they can't afford it! That's not right and that's not fair! They are still making plenty of money and have plenty of profits! They are just greedy!"

What Mayor Woodrow said made Kayla very mad! Yes, she was still making a profit, less than she used to but still making one. But that's what her business is supposed to do! That is, make a profit which benefitted many people besides just the business owners. Mayor Woodrow sounded as if he would be happy if businesses made no profit at all! As if that would be the most "fair" thing to happen. Mayor Woodrow didn't know, or didn't care, about how a business operates. All he seemed to care about is demonizing other people to further his own agenda.

Kayla received a bill from her spring water guy who sold Kayla the water she used in her lemonade. She noticed right away that his prices went up too. She believed she already knew the answer but she asked him why anyway.

He said, "My prices went up because one of the government 'expert' scientists said that the plastic water bottles I use are unhealthy for people and the government needed to protect us from the harm plastic bottles can cause. When I asked him for proof he said I needed to 'look it up'. So, I did. There isn't any definitive proof the plastic is bad for people but since the 'expert' scientist said it was so, then it was."

Based on this sketchy science the town government passed a regulation directing the spring water guy to start using only glass bottles for his water. However, if wanted to keep using the plastic bottles he could pay a "plastic bottle tax". Which again led Kayla to believe it was more about the money. Because if the plastic was proven to be harmful to people's lives a "plastic bottle tax" would mean the government was OK with people being harmed by it as long as a tax was paid. So much for the government "protecting" people from the harm they claim plastic bottles cause.

The spring water guy knew glass bottles broke a lot more often than plastic ones, so he would have to replace them more frequently which would add a significant amount of additional expenses to his business. They also cost more than plastic bottles as well. Yet another expense. He would have to cut back on investing in his people and his business to cover the additional expenses caused by yet another government regulation.

Normally the spring water guy would sell his broken plastic water bottles to a scrap guy. The scrap guy would then use the plastic to make other things like household items, jewelry and even park benches, but as the water guy slowly switched over to glass bottles, because he didn't want to pay the plastic bottle tax, he sold less and less scrap plastic to the scrap guy. Eventually the scrap guy went out of business and found himself and all his workers unemployed. Sure, the glass bottle manufacturer saw a slight increase in revenue from her higher prices, but she was getting hit with so many government regulations of her own that she wasn't seeing any significant increase in her businesses profits because the government was taking most of it in the form of fines and regulations as well.

Again, Kayla thought to herself it wasn't so much that the government thought the plastic was bad for people, they just wanted the money from the tax on the plastic bottles. On the other hand, maybe they did think the plastic was bad for people, but they didn't care about that because all they really care about is getting the tax money. Because if the plastic was really that bad for people, why wasn't it just banned outright?

The spring water guy told Kayla that the government also told him his delivery truck was not acceptable because it "polluted the air". So now, the water guy had to pay a tax on his truck to keep using it. They said he could buy one of the government approved electric trucks to avoid the tax, but the water guy said they couldn't carry as much water as the diesel truck and cost twice as much money to buy one, so the electric truck wasn't a good option for him. Kayla also found out that a lot of pollution is created when the batteries for electric vehicles are manufactured.

138

She also knew that the electricity used when electric vehicles are plugged in to charge comes overwhelmingly from power plants which create their own kind of pollution.[22] *So are electric vehicles really all that environmentally friendly,* she asked herself? Apparently not. Once again, it seemed the real reason behind what the government was doing was to get more money from people and to increase its own control over how people live and work.

The price of fuel also went up for the water guy because the government decided to start heavily taxing the fuel used in "dirty trucks". They told the fuel guy he could keep selling his fuel if he paid a "fuel pollution" tax though.[23] Of course, the fuel guy had no choice but to pay the tax. This cut into what was already a very thin profit margin. This hurt his business.

The next day the same government agent who visited her friend Ed the grocer to tell him about the sugar tax he would have to start paying came to Kayla's lemonade store. He told her that she too would have to start paying a tax on every serving of lemonade she sold because she is selling something that is made with sugar, and it is therefore an "unhealthy" product.[24]

The agent told Kayla the same story about sugar she had heard before. He said the tax was to help pay for the medical care of people who had "sugar related" diseases like diabetes. He said,

[22] Conca, James. "Are Electric Cars Really That Polluting?" *Forbes.* https://www.forbes.com/sites/jamesconca/2013/07/21/are-electric-cars-really-that-polluting/#4f86c80b325a Posted July 21, 2013. (Retrieved May 19, 2017)
[23] Karplus, Valerie J. "The Case for a Higher Gasoline Tax." *The New York Times.* http://www.nytimes.com/2013/02/22/opinion/the-case-for-a-higher-gasoline-tax.html?mcubz=0 Posted February 21, 2013. (Retrieved August 19, 2017)
[24] Jordan, Karen. "Backlash grows over Cook County's sugary drink tax." *ABC 7 Chicago.* http://abc7chicago.com/politics/backlash-grows-over-cook-countys-sugary-drink-tax/2289457/ Posted August 9, 2017. (Retrieved August 19, 2017)

"Because some people consume so much sugar, and they may develop diabetes, people who sell them the sugar need to be held responsible."

He said it wasn't "fair" that Kayla made a profit on something that made other people "sick" and she owed it to them to help pay for the expenses related to the medical conditions that she caused by making an "unhealthy" product. Kayla asked the agent why the people didn't just stop buying the lemonade if it made them sick. After all, she wasn't forcing them to buy it. The agent said that if she didn't sell it, they couldn't buy it.

"But what about all the people who drink responsible amounts of lemonade?" Kayla asked the agent. "They know too much of it is bad for them so they limit the amount they drink. Isn't it more about people who have no self-control or accountability for their individual choices? Why should everyone else be held responsible and have to pay for the bad decisions of a few?"

The agent said, "Those who don't drink so much lemonade to make themselves sick have some responsibility in this as well. If they didn't buy it and help make it popular and something that people want, then you wouldn't make any money from it and wouldn't sell it. Since they do buy it, they have to pay for the right to drink it."

"So, it would be better if I went out of business and didn't sell the lemonade?" Kayla asked.

"Woah woah woah!" the agent said. "No one said anything like that! The Government just wants you to take responsibility for your product by paying for what it does to people."

"So, I have to take responsibility for it, but those who abuse it don't?" Kayla asked. "That doesn't make any sense! I have done so many nice things for people by selling this legal product. I have made jobs and donated money. People's lives have been made better because of my product. If people abuse just about anything it could be bad for them. Heck, if you drink too much water you could die! Are you going to tax water?[25] You can burn yourself with matches. Are you going to have a special tax on that?" Kayla was getting really upset now because she knew that she wasn't doing anything wrong. She did not like the idea that now the government is making decisions as to what is good or bad for an individual. Isn't that up to the individual?

The agent looked at Kayla with a surprised look. He yelled, "YOUR PRODUCT IS EVIL AND IT'S YOUR FAULT PEOPLE ARE GETTING SICK!", and simply turned around and walked away. Kayla noticed that many of these "progressives", who seem to think they are so smart and know what is the best for everyone, like to yell and run away when faced with the truth or when you don't agree with them.

The Mayor called the new tax the "Unhealthy Product Tax". Because of it Kayla wouldn't be able to expand her business or hire as many new people as she wanted. She really had no choice but to pay the tax. She couldn't raise her prices to cover the entire tax because people would stop buying her lemonade as it would be too

---

[25] California has proposed just that! "Currently being proposed by the Brown administration through a budget trailer bill, this tax would be a first, but it probably wouldn't be the last." See: Pommering, Bill. "Why a tax on drinking water is wrong." *The San Diego Union-Tribune.* http://www.sandiegouniontribune.com/opinion/commentary/sd-utbg-california-water-tax-20180406-story.html Posted April 6, 2018. (Retrieved May 21, 2018)

expensive. So, she had to absorb the loss herself. It was either that or go out of business entirely and she didn't want to do that.

Another day yet another government agent came to Kayla's lemonade store. He had on khaki colored pants and a green golf shirt. On the left breast of the shirt was embroidered *Jefferson Township Department of Charities*. That was something new to Kayla. He had a big, cheesy smile and said to Kayla, "Great news! The government has decided that to ensure charitable giving is distributed equitably among the different needy parts of our township, and to ensure that no one charity is better off than another, starting immediately the government will assume the responsibility of handling all charity in town![26] Instead of relying on the whims of individuals to donate money to charity, the government will now start to collect a charity tax from all citizens! That tax will be used to pay for things such as welfare for those out of work, food for those who don't have enough and other worthy items! Being that I have a degree from a very prestigious university in the field of Charitable Management, I have been appointed the Director of the Department of Charities by the Mayor. I am just visiting various people around town to say thank you for paying the charity tax."

Kayla came out from behind the counter and stood in front of the man. She stood several inches taller than him and noticed that he was balding on the top of his head. She asked, "So is the tax voluntary? I already do a lot for charity and don't feel I need to pay a tax to support charity as well."[27]

[26] Dehaven, Tad. :" Charity and the Federal Government." *Cato Institute.*
https://www.cato.org/blog/charity-federal-government   Posted August 9, 2011.
(Retrieved June 1, 2018)
[27] Tanner, Michael D. "Government failure, private success." *Cato Institute.*

The agent took a step back and struggled to maintain his smile. "Voluntary? Oh no! That wouldn't be fair. Everyone has to pay in order to ensure everyone is doing the right thing!"

"So, who decides where the money goes?" Kayla asked.

"Why I do! "The agent said, his face brightening again. "Didn't you hear me when I said I have a degree in Charitable Management? I am very qualified for this job!"

Kayla took a step closer to him and said, "But who is watching you?"

The agent's smile went away. He turned around abruptly and stormed away. Kayla heard him muttering something like "troublemaker" under his breath as he left.

Over time the "Charity Tax" forced Kayla to close down the *Kayla Alexander Library*. The library relied on the good will and donations of others to operate. With the cost of living rising so much people didn't have as much money to donate to charities and cultural institutions anymore. The other not for profits started to close one by one as well.

People like Hank were happy though. "It's better off the government takes care of charity anyway," he said. "That way everything is fair."

https://www.cato.org/publications/commentary/government-failure-private-success
Article originally appeared in Christian Science Monitor on Sept. 20, 2005. (Retrieved August 19, 2017)

Less and less people were coming in to Kayla's lemonade store now, and the ones who did come spent less and less money. They were telling Kayla because of the new taxes and the cost of everything going up they had less money in their pockets to spend. Some started to question what the government was doing about it. Why wasn't the government helping more? Kayla did not quite understand that though, because she knew that she had less money in her pocket because the government kept taking more of it from her in one form or another. She noticed too that people weren't dressing as nicely any more. They also didn't smile as much anymore either.

Everyone looked burdened. Everyone that is except for the government workers. More and more of whom she started to see around in their khaki colored pants and variously colored golf shirts driving around in government cars.

Then Kayla heard about another law which had been passed.[28] This law said if a union was voted into a place of business by the workers everyone who worked there, except for the owners and managers, had to join the union, or at least pay dues to the union, whether they wanted to or not.[29] Apparently, this was a part of Mayor Woodrow's efforts to "protect worker's rights." Kayla wasn't worried about it. For one, everyone always had the right to join a union, and she was OK with that. Because people were free

[28] http://legal-dictionary.thefreedictionary.com/Wagner+Act (Retrieved August 19, 2017)
[29] "Federal law allows unions and employers to enter into "union-security" agreements which require all employees in a bargaining unit to become union members and begin paying union dues and fees within 30 days of being hired. Employees may choose not to become union members and pay dues, or opt to pay only that share of dues used directly for representation, such as collective bargaining and contract administration."
"Union Dues." *National Labor Relations Board.* https://www.nlrb.gov/rights-we-protect/whats-law/employees/i-am-represented-union/union-dues (Retrieved June 3, 2018).

to *not* to join one as well. She also wasn't worried because she always treated her employees fairly. What bothered her about the new law was it forced employees to join a union or pay dues to one even if they didn't want to. That was new. She knew unions were a special interest group and wondered what business was it of the governments to mandate workers had to support this special interest group, or any special interest group, for that matter. It just didn't seem fair.

It did not take long for Kayla to start to see union organizers hanging around her lemonade stores. She didn't mind it at first, because they were only handing out flyers and talking to people. But then they started to interfere with her business, her customers and her workers. They started to carry signs in front of her stores which said she wasn't paying her workers fairly and that her workers were losing their "rights". People whom she had never seen before, who had never worked for her, and who knew nothing about her started to call her "greedy" and a "robber baron"[30], whatever that is. With a lot of hatred in their voices they said she was a *Capitalist*, as if that were something evil. They told her workers that she was "stealing" from them and, "who does she think she is making all of that money and keeping it for herself?" Which wasn't true in the least.

One day, Kayla attempted to reason with them, the union organizers. She said to them she paid her workers well and all of her workers worked for a pay that they both, her as the owner and they as individual workers, thought was fair. But the organizers

---

[30] DiLorenzo, Thomas J. "The Truth About the 'Robber Barons'." *Mises Institute*. https://mises.org/library/truth-about-robber-barons Posted November 1, 2017. (Retrieved August 22, 2017)

just yelled at her and called her names. They said she could afford to pay her workers more because she was "rich". "I mean look at the house you live in and the car you drive," they said. "How much money do you really need? Don't you think you make too much money?"

Kayla said, "What business is it of yours how much I make, what I do with money or what I pay my employees? I worked hard. I took the risks. I pay my people well based on what we agree on together. Each worker individually gets a salary we both think is fair. They get raises based on how well they perform. They are happy."

"HAPPY?!?!" an organizer yelled in her face. The veins popping out of his neck, his voice shrill while grasping his picket sign like a weapon that he wanted to beat her with. "THEY CAN NEVER BE HAPPY AS LONG AS YOU KEEP STEALING FROM THEM! THEY BUILT YOUR BUSINESS, NOT YOU! IT WAS BUILT ON THE SWEAT OF THEIR BACKS, NOT YOURS! YOU GET TO SIT IN YOUR FANCY HOUSE BY YOUR FANCY POOL AND ROLL IN THE MONEY THEY MAKE FOR YOU AND YOU STEAL FROM THEM!"[31]

"But," Kayla said, "I built this business. I took the chance. Yes, people sold me their labor of their own free will and I pay them well for that labor. If they are so unhappy why don't they just quit?

---

[31] "People have been taught to hate and fear their employers, who are portrayed in Obama mythology as heartless predators, scarcely aware of the hapless Little People they gobble up in their quest for outrageous wealth. ('You didn't build that! Someone else made that happen!')"
Hayward, John. "Selling your labor." *Red State.*
https://www.redstate.com/jhayward13/2013/09/03/selling-your-labor/ Posted September 3, 2013. (Retrieved June 27, 2018)

I don't force them to stay. If they wanted more money we can talk about it together, one on one. They don't need you to speak for them. They have a voice. "

But the organizers were relentless. They went to her employee's homes. They followed her employees to work. They called her employees at night on the telephone. They said anything they wanted, whether it was true or not, to convince her employees that Kayla was treating them poorly and if they only let the union represent them, they would make more money and be much happier.

They could do all of those things, but according to the law, business owners and managers like Kayla weren't allowed to threaten, interrogate, promise anything or lie to her employees who were the subjects of the union's organizing attempts,[32] yet the union could do all of those things.[33] Kayla didn't think that was fair but Mayor Woodrow certainly did.

Soon there was a vote. Some of Kayla's workers did not vote because they did not think the union had a chance. They liked how Kayla dealt with them. They never thought in a million years that half plus one of Kayla's employees at a *Grandma's Old-Fashioned Lemonade* would ever vote in a union.

But after the election they were shocked to find out that the union won! They found out too late that the law did not require a

[32] Purdie, Celeste and Jim Rhollans. "Union Communication Guidance: TIPS and FOE." *Society for Human Resource Management.* https://www.shrm.org/resourcesandtools/hr-topics/labor-relations/pages/tips-foe.aspx Posted April 26, 2016. (Retrieved June 3, 2018)
[33] "Can a Union Lie to Workers?" *Truthaboutunions.org.* http://truthaboutunions.org/2017/07/11/can-a-union-lie-to-workers/ 2017. (Retrieved June 3, 2018)

majority of Kayla's employees to vote for the union, as one would expect, but only a majority of those who voted![34] The union organizers never told anyone this. So now, because only a few of Kayla's total employees voted, and a majority of them voted for unionization, *Grandma's Old-Fashioned Lemonade* stores were a unionized shop. Going forward all of the workers in Kayla's stores were forced to join the union if they wanted to keep working for Kayla. The employees also had to start paying union dues out of every paycheck they earned. And the dues were a lot of money![35]

Those employees who did not want the union, but did not show up to vote, were out of luck. Now they were forced into paying dues to the union as well.

The union hurt Kayla's business.[36] The union demanded much higher wages than what Kayla and her individual employees had agreed to. Kayla had a payroll budget she needed to stick to for her business to be successful so the new, artificially higher union wages caused Kayla to hire less workers. This hurt those people who otherwise would have had a job but the union didn't care about "those people", it only cared about union people.

Kayla now also had to pay everyone who did a certain job the same. The workers who did a great job got the same pay as

---

[34] Hunter, Robert P. "The Union Representation Election Process." *Mackinac Center for Public Policy.* https://www.mackinac.org/2319 Posted August 24, 1999. (Retrieved June 3, 2018)
[35] Sherk, James. *The Heritage Foundation.* "Unions Charge Higher Dues and Pay Their Officers Larger Salaries in Non–Right-to-Work States." https://www.heritage.org/jobs-and-labor/report/unions-charge-higher-dues-and-pay-their-officers-larger-salaries-non-right Posted January 26, 2015. (Retrieved June 3, 2018)
[36] "Research indicates that the cost of running a unionized operation is 25% to 35% greater than for a non-unionized one, and this figure does not reflect any negotiated changes in unionized employee wages or benefits."
"What is the Cost of Unions?" *Adams, Nash, Haskell and Sheridan.* http://anh.com/the-cost-of-unions/ (Retrieved June 3, 2018)

those who did a mediocre job. At this point, there weren't many of Kayla's employees who did a very poor job left because she had fired them all, but even that changed with the union now in her place of business. The union told Kayla that in the future she wouldn't be able to simply fire someone who did a bad job. They said she would have to get the approval of the union first. So now, the union was telling Kayla how to treat her employees!

Kayla soon discovered this new, more expensive union-wage payroll was much higher than she could afford. She had to cancel her plans to open more lemonade stores which would have meant more jobs for the township. She also couldn't hire as many people as she wanted because she couldn't afford it with her hirer new payroll coats. What the union didn't seem to understand was that Kayla did not have an endless supply of money. Union or not she had a budget to follow as any good businessperson would. As the owner of the business she was compensated well, but she felt she deserved it. She took all of the risks with the business, she paid her people well, and she created jobs.

After a while Kayla noticed that some of her best workers began to slack off and not perform any better than her worst. She asked one of them what was going on and he said, "Listen Kayla, I used to have an incentive to do the best job possible because I knew that you would reward me for the good job that I did more than what any slacker got. But now my raise will always be the same as even the worst worker, so it doesn't matter how good of a job I do. Why would I work as hard as I used to? In fact, the slower I go, and the longer it takes me to finish my job, the more money I will make with overtime. I know you cannot just fire me anymore so what's the point in working hard and being efficient?"

149

"Not only that," her worker said. "Do you see how expensive things are getting around here? The cost of living has gone up a lot! Say what you will about the union, now at least I can afford to live here."

Kayla thought about this for a second then said, "But the cost of living is only going up because the government keeps taxing everyone more and more and getting involved in things where it isn't supposed to, such as supporting unions. Didn't you live pretty nicely before Mayor Woodrow was elected?"

"Yes, I did, "he said.

"So back then you lived well and you still do," she said.

"Yes, because of the union," he said. "I couldn't afford living here if it wasn't for my union wage."

"But the union wage is one of the reasons why the cost of living has increased. The sad thing is because of the union wage, which is artificially high and not based on the free market, I cannot hire as many people as I want. I even had to lay people off. Unions aren't good for *all* workers, just union workers, isn't that right? Despite what they say about being for the working man."

"I guess you're right," he said. "But who cares? I still have my job. Besides, sounds to me like we need *everyone* in a union!"

Kayla said, "But if more people are forced to join a union, many more businesses wouldn't be able to afford their current workforce anymore. They probably would not be able to hire as many people either. This would mean we would have even greater unemployment."

"So what?" he said. "As long as I have my job. Besides, I think big businesses like yours can afford it. You people just want all of the money for yourself."

At that point Kayla gave up the conversation. She realized that unions weren't about helping all working people; they were for helping only *unionized* working people. They didn't seem to care much about non-union people who were unemployed.

Union bosses knew that as long as the union members were paid, those members were able to pay dues to the union. Union dues kept the union bosses driving around in nice cars and living in nice houses.[37] Most union bosses made more money than her managers and some made a bigger salary than even Kayla drew from her business! Kayla thought it was funny how union bosses accused her of being greedy and rich yet many of them lived in big houses, had fancy clothes, and drove expensive cars.[38] The only difference was the union bosses had those things because of the money that Kayla paid her workers who then paid the dues to the union. Without her business, there wouldn't even be a union. She

---

[37] For a detailed profile of unions, including union boss salaries, go to the "Find a National Union" section and click on "Leaders & Salaries": https://www.unionfacts.com/cuf/
[38] "But the AFL-CIO report neglected to include the average salary for all CEOs in the U.S. in 2016, which, according to the Bureau of Labor Statistics, was $194,350. These same union leaders who criticize the salaries of CEOs earned on average $252,370 in 2016 — nearly $60,000 more than their private-sector counterparts.
The Center for Union Facts, the union watchdog that unveiled the average presidential salary from nearly 200 unions, found that some union leaders are earning lucrative salaries north of $700,000"
Yack, Austin. "Union Leaders Earn More than Most CEOs." National Review. https://www.nationalreview.com/corner/union-leaders-ceo-salaries-union-leaders-earn-more/ Posted May 15, 2017 (Retrieved June 3, 2018)

could, and had, run her business without the union, but the union could not exist without her business and all of those union bosses and workers would be unemployed. None of them would ever admit it, but they needed her more than she needed them...IF the government didn't get involved. But that was the union's trump card. The government. As long as the government forced unionization on people, the unions would exist with an unfair advantage.

Kayla didn't think all union members were bad. She didn't even think private sector unions were bad in general. What she didn't like was the government getting involved and stacking the deck in favor of the unions. That wasn't fair!

But, hypocritically, Mayor Woodrow didn't care about fairness here. Oh no! Mayor Woodrow thought this was all great! He loved the unions! He loved them even more around election time because he knew all he had to do was promise them some more goodies and they would campaign and vote for him.

He especially loved the public-sector unions, the ones who the government employed! But as far as Kayla was concerned, public sector unions, those composed of people who earn a living by getting paid from taxes, should not be allowed to exist. She felt they were a conflict of interest. Because the members of public sector unions were paid by taxes, it was in their best interest to vote for people who would keep raising the taxes needed to pay them. And of course, because they were such a big voting bloc, they could demand that the politicians raise taxes on only certain people and things and never on them! How was that fair![39]

[39] "Public-sector unions thus distort the labor market, weaken public finances, and diminish

152

One day, one of Kayla's employees came into her office and told her he was quitting because he got a government job.

"Oh, that's too bad Jim," she said to him disappointedly. She liked Jim. He was one of her best workers. "No offense Jim, but I don't know how the town can afford to keep paying all these new government workers," she said to him.

A quizzical look crossed Jim's face. "What do you mean?" he asked.

"Government workers..." she said. Realizing by the blank look on his face Jim had no idea how government workers were paid. "They get paid from taxes the government collects from the people. If a government worker makes $50,000 a year, that 50 grand comes from the people's taxes they pay."

"But I will be paying taxes too," Jim said defensively.

"Not really,"[40] Kayla answered.

"How can you say that?" Jim asked with a touch of agitation in his voice. "Public sector workers pay just as much as private sector workers in taxes!"

the responsiveness of government and the quality of public services. Many of the concerns that initially led policymakers to oppose collective bargaining by government employees have, over the years, been vindicated."
DiSalvo, Daniel. "The Trouble with Public Sector Unions." *National Affairs.* https://www.nationalaffairs.com/publications/detail/the-trouble-with-public-sector-unions Posted Fall 2010. (Retrieved June 3, 2018)
[40] Bankert, Matthew. "Public Servants: Who is Serving Whom?" *Mises Institute.* https://mises.org/blog/public-servants-who-serving-whom Posted may 8, 2016. (Retrieved August 25, 2017)

"Let me explain something to you Jim," Kayla said. "As a government worker you don't pay any taxes because your entire paycheck comes from the taxes other people pay. If you make 50 grand a year as a government worker, paid from taxes, and you pay two thousand in taxes, that's just a rebate from you back into the treasury. In all reality your actual pay, in this example, is 48 grand a year. It's the same as the government just saying your pay is 48 grand a year and then not require you to 'pay' taxes. Either way you are not really paying taxes."

Jim still looked confused.

"Let me put it this way," Kayla said. "If there is no money in the treasury and we want to hire one government worker, where does the money come from to pay him?"

"Taxes," Jim said.

"Right!" Kayla exclaimed. "Or the government can borrow money to pay the worker, but for now we will say just taxes. Private sector taxes to be exact. The private sector pays taxes into the treasury and then we pay the government worker."

"I get that," Jim said.

"If the pay to the government worker keeps reducing the treasury, and no taxes are coming in to replenish it..." Kayla lets the last part of her statement hang in the air to see if Jim gets it.

Jim thought for a minute then says, "Eventually the treasury runs out of money again."

"Right!" Kayla said. "If we pay a government worker 50 grand which brings the treasury to zero, then that government workers pays two grand in taxes, that only puts two grand back into the treasury, right?"

Jim looked like he was getting it. "That's right," he said.

Thinking she could solidify his understanding Kayla said to Jim, "So what's the difference if we just paid him 48 grand and told him to pay no taxes? Either way there is two grand left in the treasury. All a government worker paying taxes is, is a bookkeeping trick to make people think that government workers are paying taxes.[41] We need ten private sector people making 50 grand a year and paying the same taxes to fill the treasury back up again. Get it?"

Jim nodded his head that he got it. "But that's OK Kayla," he said. "I love the Mayor! He gave me a job making a lot of money!"

"But that money comes from the pockets of your friends and neighbors, many whom are struggling financially right now," Kayla said. "Do you think it's right the government keeps hiring more government workers which puts more and more of a burden on everyone who doesn't work for the government?"

---

[41] "In short, government bureaucrats do not pay taxes; they consume the tax proceeds. If a private citizen earning $10,000 income pays $2,000 in taxes, the bureaucrat earning $10,000 does not really pay $2,000 in taxes also; that he supposedly does is simply a bookkeeping fiction. He is actually acquiring an income of $8,000 and paying no taxes at all." Rothbard, Murray N. Man, Economy and State with Power and Market 2nd ed. Ludwig Von Mises Institute: 2009. Page 908 https://mises.org/system/tdf/Man%2C%20Economy%2C%20and%20State%2C%20with%20Power%20and%20Market_2.pdf?file=1&type=document (Retrieved September 2, 2007)

Jim thought for a second then said, "I feel bad for them, I really do. But I have a family too that I need to support. This job will help me do that. Besides, government workers spend their money in the community and that helps businesses like yours, doesn't it?"

He asked that last question as if he was unsure.

"Jim, it's just a redistribution of wealth scheme," Kayla answered. "Sure, you'll spend money in my stores, for example. But part of what you spend was mine to begin with before the government confiscated it from me with taxes! If your job didn't exist, I and all the other taxpayers would have been able to keep that money and spend it or save it as we saw fit. The government took away my freedom to do that when it taxed me to pay your salary. What makes it worse is when the government jobs aren't even necessary! When politicians like the Mayor created patronage jobs just to reward their friends and keep a base of power it's even worse!"

"Patronage?" Jim asked.

Kayla couldn't believe just how clueless Jim was.

"Yes Jim, patronage,"[42] she said as if she was talking to a young child. "The Mayor created government jobs like yours just so he has people who owe him something, like their livelihood, or as a favor for supporting him. It's corrupt."

---

[42] "Patronage: the power to make appointments to government jobs especially for political advantage...the power to give jobs or provide other help to people as a reward for their support...the control by officials of giving out jobs, contracts, and favors" *Merriam-Webster Dictionary.* https://www.merriam-webster.com/dictionary/patronage (Retrieved June 27, 2018)

"Listen Kayla," Jim said, "I'm just happy to have a job that pays well."

Jim thanked Kayla for everything and left. Kayla hoped this little lesson taught him something. But in her heart, she didn't blame Jim. She knew he was just trying to take care of his family. But she was astounded by just how clueless he was about how taxes worked.

She was also angered by what she saw the Mayor doing. His policies were hurting the economy of Jefferson Township and the people who lived there. He was purposefully creating different crises and then offering up government as a solution! His policies were causing people to lose their jobs, and then he would say "I can fix that" with a government program of some kind, all while blaming business and the private sector for the problems he created! Those government programs and government plans all needed government people to run them. Government people who owed their livelihood to the Mayor. It was a truly unscrupulous plan with the single goal of helping the Mayor and his cronies accumulate power and wealth at the expense of the people. And an ever-growing number of people in Jefferson Township were either a beneficiary of the plan or blissfully unaware and uncaring of it either by choice, laziness or stupidity.

Kayla's business wasn't the only one suffering with trying to handle the higher cost of wages.

People were complaining to Mayor Woodrow about how everything seemed to be going up in price. Mayor Woodrow's answer was, "That's because your bosses aren't paying you enough!

They make all this money and keep it for themselves. What we need is a minimum wage! Everyone should be paid at least $15 an hour!"

A lot of people cheered this. If you didn't think about it, wanting people to make more money seemed like an easy thing to support. Taking the cue from the Mayor some people started to protest outside of one of Jefferson Township's local fast food restaurants. They picked that business because it employed a lot of workers, most of whom didn't make $15 an hour and it was a popular spot for people in town to grab something quick to eat. The protesters thought protesting there would generate a lot of attention from the local news. Many of the people who worked for the restaurant were in front of the building protesting, but there were also a lot of people protesting who didn't live in Jefferson Township at all.

That evening, Kayla and her father watched on TV as a local news reporter interviewed one of the protesters. She was a woman about the same age as Kayla and was carrying a sign that said, "Fight for 15! End Corporate Greed!" The sign wasn't hand written, it was professionally printed with bright colors and slick graphics. If Kayla were able to look even more closely, she would see a small logo in the corner of the local union.[43]

The reporter asked the protester, "Why are you out here protesting?"

The woman said, "Because I've been working here for five years and never got a raise and only make $7.50 an hour!"

---

[43] Campanile, Carl. "Union spends $19M on effort to raise minimum wage." *New York Post.* http://nypost.com/2017/04/03/union-spends-19m-on-effort-to-raise-minimum-wage/ Posted April 3, 2017. (Retrieved June 2, 2017)

"You work here?" the reporter asked.

"Yes!" she said, "and for five years my boss never gave me a raise and barely pays me enough to cover my bills! How am I supposed to live?"

"You think your boss is unfair?" the reporter asked.

"He is unfair!" she yelled. "He treats us like slaves and it isn't right!"

At that point, a group of other protesters gathered around the woman and started yelling and cursing at the reporter. Kayla shut off her TV.

Her father said, "What's funny about that woman is she started at an entry level job five years ago being paid a low, entry level, wage. For the past five years, she has been unable to find one other person on the planet to pay her even five cents more than she was making. Over the past five years, she apparently did absolutely nothing to make herself more valuable to her employer or to any other employer for that matter. And now she wants the government to step in to force her boss to pay her more for her labor services than it is worth. In fact, based on what she said, she should be thanking her boss for keeping her employed all these years because she is clearly not qualified to do anything else."

The town council didn't seem to think the same way as Kayla's father because they soon passed a law that every business had to pay every one of their employees at least $15 an hour, under the threat of paying heavy fines or even going to jail. Kayla thought wanting people to make more money is fine, but wanting the government to force businesses to pay a minimum wage wasn't. As a business owner, she knew if the government forced her to pay her workers more than the free market demanded, she would employ less people.[44]

The minimum wage would only force unemployment to increase because business simply couldn't just absorb that kind of expense and keep everything the same.

The local fast food restaurant where the protest occurred wound up firing all of the cashiers, including the woman who was interviewed on TV, and replaced them with self-serve electronic kiosks. [45] [46]

However, not every business had the backing of a big multi-national corporation like the fast food restaurant that was able to help defray some of the costs of installing the kiosks. In fact, most local businesses couldn't. Like the local diner where Kayla and her family had been going to for years. The owner of the diner simply

---

[44] "In essence, minimum wage increases make it more likely that firms won't hire new people than that they will fire current employees. For example, movie theaters have stopped employing ushers almost entirely... Indeed, even the Congressional Budget Office estimates that increasing the minimum wage to $10.10 per hour will cost 500,000 jobs." See: Syrios, Andrew. "Yes, Minimum Wages Still Increase Unemployment." *Mises Institute.* https://mises.org/library/yes-minimum-wages-still-increase-unemployment Posted February 9, 2015. (Retrieved May 21, 2018)

[45] Hudson, Jerome. "Business Insider: Fast Food Workers Are Being Replaced by Kiosks." *Breitbart.* http://www.breitbart.com/big-government/2016/05/17/business-insider-fast-food-workers-becoming-obsolete/ Posted May 17, 2016. (Retrieved June 2, 2017)

[46] "I remember my father telling me of an effect from the minimum wage increase from $1.00 to $1.15 effective September 1961. The same legislation scheduled a further increase to $1.25 in September 1963. Dad described how the DuPont Company at that point decided to automate elevators in its office building in Wilmington, Delaware. The old elevators worked fine, but required an operator. Within a short time, all the elevators were automated and the operators of the old ones had no jobs." See: Poole, William. "Minimum Wage and Unemployment." *Cato Institute.* https://www.cato.org/blog/minimum-wage-unemployment-0 Posted January 15, 2014. (Retrieved May 21, 2018)

couldn't afford to pay his workers the new higher minimum wage and went out of business after having been open for decades.[47]

Kayla's business started to suffer even more. With the higher taxes taking more money out of everyone's pockets, the higher costs of doing business and the additional expenses brought on by all the new government regulations she simply could not afford to keep all her lemonade stores open anymore. She wound up having to close some of them just to keep afloat. Now, also, many of her unionized workers were out of jobs.

The lemon guy and the water guy got hurt by Kayla closing stores too. The town was hurt as well because less business meant fewer taxes. Or did it? What the town wound up doing was raising taxes even higher to make up for the lost tax revenue. But did the government save this new tax revenue? Oh no, not at all.

Proof of this was next to Community Hall where a big new building was constructed. The sign outside of it read "Department of Welfare". When Mayor Woodrow was asked about it, he said the government needed the building to help all the people laid off by the greedy business owners. "But," Kayla thought, "things were fine *before* the government got involved." It didn't make any sense to her.

Things were starting to get very ugly in town. People were getting angry about the lack of jobs and steadily declining economy. With nothing else to do and the prospects of finding a job getting

[47]Bain, Jennifer and Natalie O'Neill. "$15 Minimum Wage Shutters Old-School Brooklyn Diner." *New York Post.*
http://nypost.com/2016/07/22/15-minimum-wage-shutters-old-school-brooklyn-diner/
Posted July 22, 2016. (Retrieved June 2, 2017)

less with each new tax and regulation, large groups of unemployed workers now roamed the town carrying hammers and smashing things. They attacked the market where Kayla bought some of her supplies. They called Ed the owner a greedy businessman because he had laid off some of his newly unionized workers. When he attempted to explain to the mob that he didn't have a choice, that he simply could not afford to pay all those higher, union wages anymore, they threw tomatoes at him and smashed his windows. They pushed him around and yelled at him.[48]

"You've got plenty of money!" they yelled. "You're just greedy!" they screamed.

He begged them to stop. He said, "This is my business! This is my store that I built from nothing with hard work and my own money!"

The mob grew even angrier after hearing that. They yelled at him, "You were only successful because of your workers! You were only successful because of the government! Your workers did your work for you! The government made the roads and provided the electricity for your store![49] Your store?!? Hah! This is the workers store! This is the people's store!" And they pushed him down and ransacked his store while yelling "THIS IS OURS! THIS IS OURS!"

---

[48]Urbanski, Dave. "Labor Union Violence in America: A Brief History." *The Blaze.* http://www.theblaze.com/news/2011/11/07/labor-union-violence-in-america-a-brief-history/ Posted November 7, 2011. (Retrieved November 6, 2017)
[49]"Obama to business owners: 'You didn't build that'." *Fox News.* http://www.foxnews.com/politics/2012/07/15/obama-dashes-american-dream-suggests-nobody-achieves-success-alone.html Posted July 16, 2012. (Retrieved May 25,2017)

Mayor Woodrow realized that things were getting a little out of hand and amidst cries of "Do Something!" and "Protect Us!" coming from many of the people in town he decided to act.

During a press conference he said, "We need more Police to protect you but that will cost money. Going forward the income tax will now also apply to businesses as well as individuals. Everyone and every business making more than $250,000 a year will pay the very fair income tax of 2%. This will ensure that we can hire the best Police there is!"

Mayor Woodrow said that he just so happened to know someone who could run the new and bigger police department for them! He was very smart as demonstrated by his degree in Police Technology from the local university.

With that, he introduced his friend Mr. Bernie. Kayla watched as Mr. Bernie clambered up onto the podium next to a beaming Mayor Woodrow.

"My neighbors...my friends...," Mr. Bernie said, "...I promise you that all of this lawlessness will stop. I just ask that you let me and my Police Force of expert lawmen do what is necessary to get things under control." The crowd cheered. "We will weed out the trouble makers and restore order once again!" The crowd cheered even louder.

Kayla couldn't believe how happy Mr. Bernie looked. His chest was thrust out, his arms were thrown back and he was strutting back and forth on the stage like a Lion. His Police Badge and buttons on his tunic sparkling in the light. He looked ready to conquer the world!

Soon enough Election Day was right around the corner again. But Mayor Woodrow had some competition. Only it wasn't the kind of competition Freedom and Liberty minded people like Kayla, were hoping for.

Running against Mayor Woodrow was Mr. Franklin. Many people loved him because he was a great speaker who could stir their emotions with what he said. He said that Mayor Woodrow was on the right track but he had not gone far enough! What they needed was a government that would, "...*guarantee* everyone would have an opportunity to show the best that was in them!"[50] He said, "The essence of any struggle for healthy liberty has always been, and must always be, for the government to be able to *take* from some the right to enjoy power, or wealth, or position which has not been earned by service to their fellows!"[51] Kayla didn't quite understand what he meant by that so she asked her father to explain.

"What he means is the government should have the power to take away from others their money, their job, their property, if the government feels that person has not done enough to help others while earning those things. He is saying if you do something just to make a profit, the government should be able to punish you and steal from you. Take your lemonade stores for example, if someone in government doesn't think your stores serve some kind of benefit to the community at large, or that the wealth you have

[50] Roosevelt, Theodore. "The New Nationalism-Osawatomie, Kansas August 31, 1910." *Theodore-Roosevelt.com.* http://www.theodore-roosevelt.com/images/research/speeches/trnationalismspeech.pdf (Retrieved September 4, 2017)
[51] Ibid

earned from it doesn't 'serve' others, then the government should have the ability to take it away from you."

"But that's not fair!" Kayla said. "My business does benefit others! I provide a product people want and enjoy; and now I am forced to pay a lot in taxes! I also hire people and pay them, and *they* pay taxes. I think a lot of people benefit from my lemonade stores! I 'serve' others by the jobs and economic activity my business generates."

"I know dear," her father said. "What he is talking about is a subtle form of what people call *totalitarianism*. That's when the government does whatever it wants to people and you have to obey or be put in jail...or worse. Mr. Franklin is proposing an increase in government power well beyond what Jefferson Township was founded upon or what powers the Charter grants to the government. Imagine he is Mayor and then decides that your business isn't doing enough to 'serve' others. He then wants to be able to 'take' your wealth from you! It's crazy!"

While watching him on TV Kayla heard Mr. Franklin say during a speech, "I have the greatest contempt for wealthy people,"[52] and many in the crowd cheered and yelled and raised their clenched fists into the air. This made Kayla nervous as she looked around at her nice house with its beautiful furniture and the expensive cars in her driveway. She knew her family was wealthy and here was a man who might be Mayor saying that he had "contempt" for her when he didn't even know who she was or what she did with her wealth.

---

[52] Ibid

Kayla was starting to get the feeling that Mr. Franklin really didn't like business people in general by what he was saying:

"The citizens of Jefferson Township must effectively control the mighty commercial forces which they have called into being,"[53] he said. Kayla was a "mighty commercial force" in town but the citizens of the town didn't "call" her business "into being". She created it herself, not the townspeople. Now he wants the citizens of the town to control her business?

"There can be no effective control of corporations while their political activity remains. To put an end to it will be neither a short nor an easy task, but it can be done,"[54] Mr. Franklin said. *So*, Kayla thought, *he wants to control my business because I may be involved with politicians or policies he doesn't like? Who is he to tell me my business cannot have a voice or influence in politics? And what is this "effective control of corporations" he mentioned all about? He wants the government to control corporations?*

Kayla had a nice business selling her lemonade in bottles to other parts of the country. It was a profitable and growing business for her that helped her hire more people and expand her business. That is why she got really nervous when she heard Mr. Franklin say, "It has become entirely clear that we must have government supervision of the capitalization, not only of public-service corporations, including, particularly, railways, but of all corporations doing an interstate business. It is my personal belief that the same kind and degree of control and supervision which should be exercised over public-service corporations should be

---

[53] Ibid
[54] Ibid

extended also to combinations which control necessaries of life, such as meat, oil, or coal, or which deal in them on an important scale."[55]

Interstate Business? Kayla thought to herself. *Why, anything could be considered interstate business. It is almost impossible to make anything that doesn't have something in it that comes from somewhere else.*

Take for instance her bottled lemonade. Kayla makes the lemonade and bottles it right in her own State but she buys the empty bottles that she uses to put her lemonade in from a dealer in another State. He ships them to her over State lines. Her bottle labels are made by a local printer but he gets the material for the labels from a supplier outside of their State. The plastic caps for the bottles come from another State as well. So according to Mr. Franklin Kayla's corporation in engaging in "interstate business" therefore it should be under "government supervision". This scared Kayla a lot. She knew that "supervision" is not much different than control. After all, you only supervise things that you can control. Otherwise, what's the point?

Oh but Mr. Franklin was a slick one. He talked a lot about pride in being a citizen Jefferson Township. Except the pride he was speaking of wasn't based in the things the township was founded on like Individual Freedom, Liberty and Justice. Oh no, his pride seemed to be based more on being proud of the government and the things it does. To Kayla that was a subtle, but big difference. Her pride in being a citizen of Jefferson Township was always based on those other things...like Individual Freedom and

---

[55] Ibid

Liberty. She was always taught, and believed, that the government is there to serve the people, not the other way around as Mr. Franklin seemed to think.

Kayla wanted to see what her old friend Hank thought about Mr. Franklin so she invited him over her house again to talk about it.

Once again, as he did when they talked before Mayor Woodrow's election, he showed up with a box of donuts and they again sat in Kayla's kitchen to talk.

"Hank," Kayla said, "I know you are a big supporter of Mayor Woodrow but what do you think about this Mr. Franklin?"

"Well," Hank said excitedly, "there are a lot of things I like about what Mr. Franklin is saying!"

"Like what?" Kayla asked.

"I like how he talks about how business and Government need to be partners in the economy. I agree with that," Hank said.

"You do?"

"Yes, I do." Hank said. "I think that people should be allowed to own businesses and industry, but I believe the Government needs to control the overall direction of the economy for the good of everyone."

"How so?" Kayla asked.

Hank rubbed his chin for a second then said, "Let's take healthcare. I don't think the Government should take over the healthcare system, but I think it should direct it to make sure it is fair for everyone."

"What do you mean by that Hank?" Kayla asked.

"The Government should make rules that make sure everyone can get health insurance. It should also give money to insurance companies to make sure they are able to cover everyone, for example," Hank said.

"The government shouldn't own the health care system but it should make rules about how it should be run and then should provide money to insurance companies?" Kayla asked.

"Yes," Hank said. "That sounds about right."

"And the rules the government makes, rules such as how much the insurance should cost, who should be covered, what kind of treatments should be covered and so on? To make it all 'fair' is OK?" Kayla asked.

"Yes," Hank said.

"So, if government gives a company money to do something, then sets all the rules about how that money is to be used, doesn't the government actually control the company?" Kayla asked. "Especially if that company relies on that government money to stay in business?"

"Well I guess so," Hank said. "But the company is still making money and now everything is fair…"

"…except for the business!" Kayla said, finishing Hank's sentence. "That is, unless the company is willingly taking the government's money. If the company is working in cahoots with the government then it's not fair to everyone else. Because then our taxes are being used by the government to prop up and control those businesses rather than the free market determining whether a business will survive or not. If that's the case, then the government is using our taxes to pick and choose who it wants to be successful. Because if the government is able to provide money to a business to support it and prop it up, it can just as easily not provide money to a business, thereby giving the business that received the government money an unfair advantage. This isn't 'fair'. In fact, it's the epitome of being unfair! Those are things the government should not be involved in! The Charter does not give the government any authority to do those things!"

"How is it not fair for the business?" Hank asked. "They're still making money. The owner still owns it."

"Maybe so Hank," Kayla said, "but the business is under the thumb of the government. In essence the business can't do anything the government doesn't want it to. The owner may 'own' the business on paper but everything the business does is under the direction or financing of the government; the government controls the business! That's not freedom!"

"So, Hank," Kayla continued, "where is the government going to get all of this money to 'give' to business to make sure everything is 'fair'."

"Mostly through taxes I suppose," Hank said. "The Government could also borrow money if it needed to."

"So, more taxes and going into debt? That's how the government will operate? Does that sound like a good economic plan Hank?" Kayla asked.

Hank was getting annoyed again. "Kayla you are always so against everything the Government does! You don't think it does anything right and you are always against it!"

"I'm not against government in general Hank," Kayla corrected him, "I think there is a need for a very limited government like we had before Mayor Woodrow came along. But I am against a government that keeps getting bigger and bigger and is intruding and controlling more and more of our lives. Mayor Woodrow is bad enough," Hank frowned, Kayla ignored him, "but now we have this Mr. Franklin who wants even more power for the government to run our lives. That's what I am against."

"Well I like him, Mr. Franklin," Hank said. "He's a strong man of action. And that's what we need to get things back on track around here! A strong man of action!"

"Are you going to vote for him?" Kayla asked.

Hank thought for a second then said, "Probably. Well...umm...yes! I am going to vote for him. Mayor Woodrow is good, but Mr. Franklin is right. He's not doing enough and things can be so much better!"

"Well Hank," Kayla said, "unfortunately they are the only two running who have a shot at winning. Our choices are 'bad' and 'worse'."

Hank frowned.

"What happened to you Hank?" Kayla asked softly. She was truly saddened by what was taking place with her friend Hank. He seemed so...brainwashed. Like many others in town, his answer to the problems they were having in Jefferson Township was always more government. *Why can't people like Hank see that it was because of "more government" they were in the mess they were in and it was only getting worse?* She thought to herself.

"What do you mean?" Hank responded with a quizzical look on his face.

"I mean what happened to you? You used to love Life, Liberty and Property as much as me. What happened?"

"Kayla, I still love those things as much as you," Hank's tone was as if Kayla's dog just died and he was consoling her. "It's why I want society to be fair for everyone. We need to protect those things."

"I agree," Kayla said, "Except when you say 'we' you mean the government. When I say 'we' I mean the people."

"When I say 'we' I mean everyone, including the Government," Hank said.

They stared at each other without saying anything for a few seconds. Kayla was studying Hank's face. Looking for any sign that he was open to hearing what she wanted to say, any sign that she could convince him he was on the wrong path. But there was nothing. He was looking at her as if he felt sorry for her. Sorry for her because she was so naïve about everything she still believed in like individual responsibility and the freedom to live your life as you see fit as long as it respected others Life, Liberty and Property. Sorry for her because she just didn't "get it". That she was stuck in the past. Sorry for her for having such outdated thoughts and ideas. But Kayla felt sorry for him. Sorry for him because she knew he was lost.

And to prove it he said, "Everyone should enjoy life, liberty and property. That's why the Government needs to ensure everyone has the ability to enjoy it. There's nothing wrong with the Government, which is the people's representatives, making rules to ensure everyone can enjoy those things in a fair society. If the Government has to tax you more so someone else can get a fair shot, what's wrong with that? If the Government needs to make rules to ensure everyone gets a fair shot, why is that bad? Why is it wrong for the Government to be able to force people to do the right thing?"

"I'll tell you what's wrong with it," Kayla said, "My money is *my* property, and you think the government should be able to steal it from me to give to someone else. What about *my* Liberty to spend my money how I want to? You're saying it's OK for the government, or more accurately some politician, to violate someone's Life, Liberty or Property just because they think it's right. And you want them to have the power to do it! That's just insane! You did get one thing right though, and that's about force. Government is force. Give the government too much power and they will have too much ability to force us to do things. That's not freedom either. That's why we need less government, not more! To protect our freedom from the likes of Mayor Woodrow or Mr. Franklin who are all too willing to use the force of government against us."

"Don't you love Jefferson Township?" Hank asked.

"Of course, I do!" Kayla said emphatically.

"So do I," Hank said.

"But my love for Jefferson Township stems from the fact that it once was a place where Life, Liberty and Property were the most important things to protect," Kayla said. "It had nothing to do with Jefferson Township per se. It especially doesn't mean I love its government! The people of the Township at one time agreed that to best way to secure our Life, Liberty and Property was with a limited government with very specific powers. We knew as a society, and history proves it, that too much government leads to too much government abuse of our freedom. So, let me correct myself, I don't love Jefferson Township the way it is now. What I love is what it was. As it is my home I want the Township to be the best, freest place on earth! And I want to fight to restore it to that! Right now, I don't recognize it and it has become a hard place to love. It's become a hard place to love for one, because of the government we have allowed to take hold, and two, because the people have changed. The people of the Township, people like you Hank, have become much too comfortable and much too reliant on government to solve our problems and to 'take care of things'. We have lost a lot of our spirit of freedom and individuality."

"Individuality? Hah!" Hank said.

Kayla was annoyed now, "What do you mean by that Hank?"

"Individuality is what got us into this mess! If people weren't so greedy and so busy looking out for themselves the government wouldn't have to step in," Hank said excitedly. "I agree things need to change around here. But what we need is more respect for the Township! People need to understand that everything we do needs to happen to ensure the survivability of the Town! And that's why we need a strong Government making rules to make sure that happens! The Town is us! It's the community all together! When we are all dead and gone the Town will live on and we need to make sure it survives!"[56]

There was an awkward silence. Hank looked at the clock and said he had to go, it was getting late.

On his way out the front door he suddenly stopped as if he remembered he had forgotten something. He turned around and

---

[56] "Anti-individualistic, the Fascist conception of life stresses the importance of the State and accepts the individual only in so far as his interests coincide with those of the State...The keystone of the Fascist doctrine is its conception of the State, of its essence, its functions, and its aims. For Fascism the State is absolute, individuals and groups relative... The State, as conceived and realized by Fascism, is a spiritual and ethical entity for securing the political, juridical, and economic organization of the nation... If liberalism spells individualism, Fascism spells government."
Mussolini, Benito. "The Doctrine of Fascism: The Absolute Primacy of the State". *World Future Fund*. http://www.worldfuturefund.org/wffmaster/Reading/Germany/mussolini.htm (Retrieved June 7, 2018)

asked Kayla, "By the way, who are you going to vote for?" Hank asked.

Kayla hadn't really thought about it until that second. After a few seconds of thought she said, "Probably no one. Neither of them deserves it."

"Hmmm," Hank said, "OK Kayla, thanks for having me over and listening. Good night."

"Good night Hank," Kayla said as he walked out the door and she closed it behind him.

Fascism

(Homeland Hall- The Safest Place on Earth)

Mayor Franklin

Soon after Kayla had met with Hank at her house to talk about Mr. Franklin it was Election Day again.

It was a gray day with big gray clouds in the sky. It seemed dreary. A steady light rain fell from the sky which slowly pooled up in big puddles that people had to either jump over or walk through to cross the street. There was a slight breeze in the air that did not even move the fading and torn Flag which hung limply from the pole in front of Community Hall. It was the same flag that had hung there during the last election. No one had bothered to replace it.

Mr. Franklin, who was a very good speaker, had been able to get whole crowds of people to cheer and yell and agree with him. He had blanketed the area with flags and signs with patriotic slogans and made many people believe that honoring the flag and loving one's town was the same as loving the town's government. Many didn't notice the difference, but Kayla did.

Turns out the subtle differences that Kayla saw were lost on a lot of her neighbors because Mr. Franklin won the election. There was elation in the streets! People cheered, waved flags and played patriotic music and sang patriotic songs.

Kayla didn't vote for him or Mayor Woodrow. Instead she just wrote in her Father's name. She figured he would get a kick out of it!

One of the first acts Mayor Franklin did was to have the sign outside of Community Hall changed. He said, "Yes, we are a community for sure! A strong and vibrant one. But where would the community be without our homes? Our Homeland is what we are all here for! What we are working to make better! It is our Homeland where our exceptionalism lies. Therefore, I have instructed that Community Hall be changed to Homeland Hall! And we will have the safest and strongest homeland in history!"

Patriotism seemed to be the theme of the times. Kayla always thought of herself as a patriot. She was very proud to be a citizen of Jefferson Township and genuinely thought that the freedom and opportunity which were a result of the founding made Jefferson Township the best place on earth to live. She felt fortunate and blessed to live here. But Mr. Franklin's concept of patriotism seemed a little different. Oh, he also spoke of how great it was to live in Jefferson Township and how it was the best place on earth to live, but he also spoke about how great the *government* of Jefferson Township is. He also spoke a lot about how the government and businesses needed to "work together" for the benefit of the town. That also made Kayla nervous. She didn't want to "work with" the government. In fact, she wanted the government to stay away from her business. [1]

---

1 "Up and down the economy, at all levels of government, bureaucrats and planners dictate details in nearly all areas of economic behavior, with the principle that some sectors should simply be free of government intrusion having been totally discarded. If we have large swaths of economic liberty in America, and we do, this is by accident, or merely due to the state's institutional limits in being able to run everything. The ideological thrust of US economic policy is that we may live our commercial lives freer than in many places, but all upon the good graces of the state, its cartels, licensing boards, and regulatory apparatuses. Even our homes are private property only insofar as it serves the interest of the state, which claims the right to seize anything we own if it bolsters the tax receipts garnered through the state-business nexus. The business environment adheres to a rapidly expanding litany of commercial codes, many of them designed not even by legislature but by executive or judicial fiat. Taken together, this is the essence of economic fascism."
Gregory, Anthony. "America's Unique Fascism." *Mises Institute.*

That was a big difference to Kayla. She loved her town...but its government?

Just look at what Mr. Woodrow did, she thought. All of his new rules and regulations hurt her business, and also hurt the people who lived in the town too. All of the new taxes, regulations and fees came right out of the townspeople's pockets. What scared Kayla a lot about Mr. Franklin was him saying how the government should "control" business, and should "supervise" where business spends its money. That sounded to Kayla like Mr. Franklin was more interested in dominating businesses, not just regulating them.

Soon after Mayor Franklin took office he held a big town hall meeting where he announced a large-scale spending spree by the government. The room was all decked out in patriotic signs and banners. Behind the stage was a tremendous picture of Mayor Franklin. In the picture he had his arms folded across his chest and he was smirking down his nose at everyone. Mayor Franklin walked out onto the stage and took his place behind the podium. He started to talk about all of his wonderful plans for the town. He promised that he was going to "improve the infrastructure" of the town and would "create good paying jobs" by "investing in growth".

Someone asked the Mayor how much all of these big plans he had for the town would cost.

An annoyed look crossed the Mayor's face that he quickly covered up with a big smile. "The cost of *not* doing these

https://www.mises.org/library/americas-unique-fascism Posted October 21, 2011.
(Retrieved November 17, 2017)

investments in our community would be much greater! Thankfully there are people out there, other governments and such, who see our town as a worthy investment. So, we are going to sell *Patriot Bonds!*[2] Others know betting on Jefferson Township is a solid bet and we are sure many will invest in our homeland by buying our *Patriot Bonds!*" he said, without really answering the question.

"When you say 'investment' you really mean debt? Right?" asked someone else.

"Debt?" Mayor Franklin said, "Debt is such a negative word! Again, I prefer to think of it as an investment! Or a much-needed expenditure to fix what is broken! It takes money to fix things, you know.

"If you had a leaky roof in your house but no money in the bank to fix it, wouldn't you put the repair bill on a credit card if you could?" Mayor Franklin asked. He wasn't really looking for an answer. "Of course, you would! Jefferson Township's roof is leaking and we need money to fix it. We are borrowing money now to make these important investments and will pay it back later!"

Kayla remembered a time when the town would run surpluses every year and then return the excess money back to the people. Now the Mayor was talking about accumulating debt. And for what? And why? Kayla knew it was so the government could spend more money to "fix" things that never needed fixing before it started to get its hands in everything. Kayla also understood very

---

[2] "Government Bond: What is a 'Government Bond' A government bond is a debt security issued by a government to support government spending. Federal government bonds in the United States include savings bonds, Treasury bonds and Treasury inflation-protected securities (TIPS)." *Investopedia.* https://www.investopedia.com/terms/g/government-bond.asp (Retrieved May 21, 2018)

well that the Mayor *had* to take the town into debt if he wanted to keep getting reelected. He would take the town into debt so he could spend the money on projects and other things that created "fake" jobs for people. Fake in the sense that the jobs weren't created because of someone's entrepreneurship to create a good or service to meet the needs of what people were demanding. No, these jobs were created by government debt and the only way they could be sustained was by having even more government debt. Kayla knew that what the Mayor was doing was setting the town up for economic disaster in the long run. Sooner or later you have to pay back what you owe or stop borrowing to pay for what you can't afford in the first place. Either way the town was going to be in trouble.

If you keep using your credit card, to use the Mayor's analogy, to pay for someone to keep fixing your roof, sooner or later you run out of credit. Then what? You still have a leaky roof, but now you have a mountain of debt you owe someone. Then what does your creditor do when you can't pay them back? They take your house.

Even worse, what if you fix things in your house that don't really need fixing? Let's say you put in a new bathroom you really didn't need and charge it to your credit card? Then you remodel your kitchen, which didn't need remodeling...and put it on your credit card. Then you buy a new TV, which you don't need, for every room even...and put it on your credit card. Sooner or later you have to pay that credit card, back right? Maybe not. Maybe you open another credit card when the first one has no more credit left on it and you start charging things again. Sooner or later your payments become more than you can afford. Then what? Then what do your creditors do? Again, they take your house.

Kayla knew the same thing applied to government. If it keeps spending money it doesn't have, sooner or later it all comes crashing down. And who will pay for it? The regular people of course.

That evening Kayla just happened to have the evening news on. She had the volume muted so she could concentrate on some paperwork she needed to finish up when she glanced up at her silent TV.

The screen showed the news anchor sitting behind his desk pretending to read off a stack of papers in his hand. In the upper left-hand corner of the screen was a picture of Mayor Franklin giving a speech, underneath the picture it said *New Economic Plan*. Kayla turned up the volume to listen.

The news anchor said, "...And today at Homeland Hall the Mayor announced how he was going to make good on his promise to get the economy moving again..."

With that the picture cut to a video of the Mayor giving a speech earlier in the day.

"...so, my fellow citizens my economic plan will amount to an unprecedented investment in our town to create jobs and get the economy moving again by creating high paying jobs. We have businesses with plenty of shovel ready projects ready to get started but have been unable to get them moving because of a lack of

funding. [3] [4] [5] Well…THEY WON'T HAVE TO WAIT ANY LONGER!!!"
The crowd went wild with applause and cheering.

"We are going to sell *Patriot Bonds* to investors and then use the money raised by those bonds to invest in business as well as the improving the town's infrastructure with great public works!"[6] The screen then cut back to the news anchor. Kayla shut the television off.[7]

Patriot Bonds? Kayla thought, *Sounds like a scheme by the Mayor to find another way to "print" more money by the government.* The government didn't have the resources to pay back the principle plus interest of the *Patriot Bonds*. It would either have to "print" even more money, or borrow even more money and go further into debt…or both, to do so.[8]

---

[3] "PRES.-ELECT OBAMA: Well, I think we can get a lot of work done fast. When I met with the governors, all of them have projects that are shovel ready, that are going to require us to get the money out the door, but they've already lined up the projects and they can make them work." Meet the Press Transcript for Dec. 7, 2008.
http://www.nbcnews.com/id/28097635/ns/meet_the_press/t/meet-press-transcript-dec/#.WhQ-xNLrtQI (Retrieved November 21, 2017)
[4] Thinkfy. "Obama: Shovel ready not as shovel ready as we expected."
https://www.youtube.com/watch?v=O55aRrvXtio (Retrieved November 21, 2017)
[5] Jackson, Brooks. "Obama's Economic Speech." Factcheck.org. Updated December 11, 2009. http://www.factcheck.org/2009/12/obamas-economic-speech/ (Retrieved November 21, 2017)
[6] Ibid. Pages 187-188.
[7] To see how government can manipulate an economy see how Hjalmar Schacht did it for Nazi Germany:
"Hjalmar Schacht, Mefo Bills and the Restoration of the German Economy 1933-1939." *Fixing the Economists.* https://fixingtheeconomists.wordpress.com/2013/12/11/hjalmar-schacht-mefo-bills-and-the-restoration-of-the-german-economy-1933-1939/ Posted December 1th, 2013. (Retrieved June 15, 2018)
[8] To see an example of Schact's plan in action in America:
"Rohatyn pulled a debt-recycling scheme from Schacht's bag of tricks: It took in the old debt, created new debt, and then backed it with income streams looted from New York City's operating budget; to pay for this, Rohatyn demanded the imposition of draconian levels of austerity and service cuts, and then sought a bankers' dictatorship—the now-infamous Municipal Assistance Corporation or "Big MAC," and its Emergency Financial Control Board (EFCB), the latter having veto power over all city contracts and budgets for more than two decades.
The most important city in the world had its sovereignty stolen by the bankers, in much the

But Mayor Franklin knew the money from the sale of the *Patriot Bonds* would go far to ensuring that he remained popular with the people...for now. The bonds were going to enable him to keep spending money. He thought people would like this because after all, if they didn't have a job to feed their family and the government gave them one by using debt to create it, they probably wouldn't care how the job got created. All they would care about is they had a job which helped them to take care of their family. And who could blame them for that? And if you were someone who landed one of those government jobs you would probably look upon the person who gave you the job, like Mayor Franklin, as some kind of hero. Meanwhile the truth is he's no hero. He's just a man looking to enrich and empower himself. On top of that, he is only putting off the inevitable collapse of the economy due to all of the debt that couldn't be paid back at the expense of some future unemployed worker who will never find a job when the ultimate collapse comes.

But the Mayor was able to issue his *Patriot Bonds*, without any protest from anyone else in government, and the government started spending the money on all sorts of projects. Especially the Police Department. The mayor spent a lot of money on hiring more cops and buying all sorts of new fancy equipment. New Police cars, new uniforms and even a new Police station. He said this was necessary because, "we live in dangerous times and need to protect ourselves!"

same way Schacht had demanded that German sovereignty be ceded to the bankers to solve its fiscal crisis."
Wolfe, L. "Felix 'The Fixer' Rohatyn Is The Modern-Day Hjalmar Schacht." *The Schiller Institute*. https://www.schillerinstitute.org/economy/nbw/2004/rohatyn.html (Retrieved June 15, 2018)

He was right about that. Even after the election riots continued to happen very frequently. People were very upset and angry, seemingly at everything. Angry at business and corporations, angry at capitalism and now angry at the new Mayor. Every day there seemed to be a protest in town somewhere, and the demonstrations usually weren't very peaceful.[9] Many times they erupted into violence with innocent passersby getting assaulted and attacked by masked people who only seemed interested in causing mayhem. Setting fires also seemed to be a favorite activity of the protesters. At first it was just garbage pails and dumpsters that were being lit on fire. But that degenerated into cars being torched and, ultimately, businesses. Especially any business that was connected with a big corporation.[10]

Most of the businesses that were being attacked simply gave up and never reopened. Why would they? Only to see their windows get smashed and interiors get burned again and again?

The Mayor said he was going to act against the violence and put an end to it. He said, "We will fight a War against Anarchy!"

There was another thing about the Mayor and his cronies. They always seemed to be "at war" with something. "War on poverty"; "War on drugs"; "War on greed" and on and on. One thing all those "wars" had in common was they all required more and

[9] Helsel, Phil. "Protests, Violence Prompt UC Berkeley to Cancel Milo Yiannopoulos Event." *NBC News.* https://www.nbcnews.com/news/us-news/protests-violence-prompts-uc-berkeley-cancel-milo-yiannopoulos-event-n715711 Posted February 2, 2017. (Retrieved May 21, 2018)

[10] Corcoran, Kieran. "'This has turned into a riot': Chaos in Seattle as anti-capitalist demonstrators smash windows, set fires and attack police after May Day protest turns violent." *Dailymail.com.* http://www.dailymail.co.uk/news/article-3065042/This-turned-riot-Chaos-Seattle-anti-capitalist-demonstrators-smash-windows-set-fires-attack-police-Day-protest-turns-violent.html#ixzz5G9ZiLuoN Posted and Updated May 2, 2015. (Retrieved May 21, 2018)

more government money to run them. They also seemed to be teaching people that it was the government that needed to find answers to all of society's ills, and not the people, like how they used to think in Jefferson Township. And the people used to rely on God. Not so much of that any more either. Things were definitely changing in Jefferson Township.

"We need to stop the violence!" The Mayor thundered in another speech. "I am proud to say that in order to protect the people the town council has issued a total ban on guns! With the increase in the size and scope of our fine police force there no longer is a need for people to own a gun! We will protect you!"

Kayla remembered what her father had told her throughout her life...a government that disarms its people is up to no good. That when a government takes away law abiding people's guns, leaving them defenseless, the potential for real tyranny has arrived.[11]

Overnight, law abiding gun owners were turned into criminals by a government intent on removing any threat to its monopoly on force. Kayla also knew the Mayor lied. It wasn't a "total ban on guns" as he said because the government was still allowed to keep theirs. So, the average, and now defenseless, citizen's ability to protect themselves with a firearm had been removed and given to a government that may or may not have the people's best interest at heart. *It's not right*, Kayla thought, *a cop or a politician gets to keep themselves and their families protected by*

[11] Halbrook, Stephen P. "How the Nazis Used Gun Control." *National Review.* https://www.nationalreview.com/2013/12/how-nazis-used-gun-control-stephen-p-halbrook/ Posted December 2, 2013. (Retrieved June 14, 2018).
And... Jews for the Preservation of Firearms Ownership http://jpfo.org/filegen-a-m/about.htm

owning a firearm but I can't? Are their lives more valuable than mine? She knew the answer to that question as far as she was concerned is "of course not". But the Mayor and his supporters didn't seem to think so. Not at all. The Mayor and his family would continue to be protected by people carrying firearms, but he took that right from the private citizenry in a blatant and uncaring act of selfishness. "For your own good," of course.

One afternoon Kayla walked past what used to be City Hall read the new sign. *Homeland Hall-The Safest Place on Earth.* It made her feel uncomfortable. She knew that when people wanted to "protect" you, it came at a cost. Kind of like when organized crime would "protect" a small local business and want to get paid for it. If you didn't pay for the "protection", well then, maybe you or your store would have an "accident".

Kayla kept walking until she arrived at one of her stores. As she usually did she went inside and started to talk to her employees and some of the customers buying lemonade.

While talking to one of her customers about how everything keeps going up in price she looked over his shoulder and saw someone walk into the store. Right away she saw it was her old employee Jim. He had on the same khaki pants and wore the same loafers all the government workers did. He was holding a clipboard like all the rest as well. Except this time, he was now wearing a black shirt, buttoned all the way up to the top button. It looked like it was choking him.

He walked right up to Kayla and the customer and cleared his throat. The customer stopped talking, looked at Jim in his black shirt, then turned and walked away without saying another thing.

"Hi Jim," Kayla said, as cheerily as possible. "What can I do for you?" she asked.

Jim had a serious look on his face. "Well," Jim said, "It's nice to see you too," he said without much sincerity. Clearing his throat as an indication that was enough of the pleasantries and it was time to get down to business he said, "I am here on official business from the *Department of Government Syndicates.*"

He stopped talking and looked at Kayla for some sign of acknowledgement of his obviously important status. Kayla looked blankly back at him.

"Anyway," Jim said, with annoyance in his voice because Kayla seemed to fail to understand his important position, *The Department of Government Syndicates*[12] has declared that from now on all large businesses must coordinate their activity with the Government of the Homeland. This is to ensure that all business activity is, first and foremost, beneficial to the Homeland. Going forward all major business activity and decisions must be coordinated through my Department of which I will be your representative. You can still make day to day decisions, but anything that affects the *Big Picture* must be coordinated through me and my Department. My Department will, from now on, set

[12] "Another keystone of Italian corporatism was the idea that the government's interventions in the economy should not be conducted on an ad hoc basis, but should be "coordinated" by some kind of central planning board."
DiLorenzo, Thomas J. "Economic Fascism Planned Capitalism Lives On." *Foundation for Economic Education.* https://fee.org/articles/economic-fascism/ Posted June 1, 1994. (Retrieved September 15, 2017)

prices, production levels, minimum wages, and maximum hours within each industry[13]. Do you understand?"

"So, let me get this straight," Kayla said, "the government is taking over 'big businesses'?"

"Oh no no no!" Jim said. "The Government will just be coordinating business activity. You still own your business; the Government just wants to partner with businesses to ensure that everything being done is for the good of the Homeland. We will work with business to eliminate unfair competition."

"I see," said Kayla.

"Do you?" Jim asked, seeming to be quite annoyed. "Everything exists because of, and for, the Homeland. Business exists solely for the betterment of the Homeland. Because of this irrefutable fact, the government, which is composed of representatives of the Homeland such as me, can make laws and decisions to foster the survival of the Homeland, and of course, its people."[14]

"I thought everything existed because of God?" Kayla asked.

---

[13] The National Recovery Administration, FDR's scheme to control the American economy ala Fascist style was eventually ruled unconstitutional by the US Supreme court. However, the spirit of it lived and lives on with the political establishment elite.
"The National Recovery Administration." *Digital History.*
http://www.digitalhistory.uh.edu/disp_textbook.cfm?smtid=2&psid=3442 (Retrieved November 16, 2017) For a good read on what the NRA really was about see:
Hazlitt, Henry. "The Fallacies of the NRA." *Mises Institute.*
https://mises.org/library/fallacies-nra Posted June 30, 2003. (Retrieved November 16, 2017)
[14] "Anti-individualistic, the Fascist conception of life stresses the importance of the State and accepts the individual only in so far as his interests coincide with those of the State, which stands for the conscience and the universal, will of man as a historic entity." – Benito Mussolini http://faculty.smu.edu/bkcarter/THE%20DOCTRINE%20OF%20FASCISM.doc (Retrieved September 15, 2017)

A look of contempt crossed Jim's face. "What are you, some kind of Jew or Christian? Some kind of religious nut?"

"I am a Christian," Kayla said, "and I exist to serve my God and my Christ, not your Homeland."

Jim got very angry. His face turned red. His upper lip was quivering. "You are an intolerant bigot," he said through his teeth, "and intolerant bigots like you need to understand that there is no place for your ignorant thinking anymore". He sneered at Kayla. "You will get more information in the mail and as your official representative, I will be back." He then turned and left.

Kayla soon found out that there wasn't much "partnering" in being a "partner" with the government. The big businesses in town were told what they could make and how much of it as part of an "economic plan". They were also told how much to charge and how much profit they could keep.

Kayla's friend, the soda guy soon ran into some trouble. He couldn't afford to pay his extremely burdensome taxes anymore so the Tax Department seized his business and property.[15]

Not too long after the soda guy closed his doors for good, Jim, from the *Department of Syndicates* was back in Kayla's store.

---

[15] "Treasury Auctions." *U.S. Department of Treasury.*
https://www.treasury.gov/services/Pages/auctions_index.aspx Posted January 22, 2018. (Retrieved June 18, 2018)
Sibilla, Nick. "IRS Seizes Over $100,000 From Innocent Small Business Owner, Despite Promise To End Raids." *Forbes.*
https://www.forbes.com/sites/instituteforjustice/2015/05/05/irs-seizes-over-100000-from-innocent-small-business-owner-despite-promise-to-end-raids/#67f5f4d122ab Posted May 5, 2015. (Retrieved September 15, 2017)

"Ms. Alexander!" he said cheerily, he seemed to have forgotten how mad he was last time he was in the store. "I have great news! The Government has reset the price[16] of your lemonade. You now will charge a lower price for it, so more people can afford it!" Jim said this with what seemed like genuine happiness.

"Reset the price?" Kayla asked. *What more will this government do to interfere* she asked herself. "So, the government now is going to limit the profits I can make? The government thinks it knows better than the natural flow of the market?" Her voice was shaking now with aggravation.

Jim shuffled his feet uneasily. Sweat started to appear over his upper lip. He always liked Kayla when she was his boss. She always treated him fairly and never seemed to get upset about anything. Seeing her like this made him uneasy. *But I am a representative of the Government and deserve respect!* So he thought. He cleared his throat.

"No No No! Kayla! You will still make a good profit!" He said with as much cheeriness as he could. "But we are in an economic crisis and price controls are needed so people can buy the things they need. Besides, the Mayor has very smart people in Government who came up with this plan!"

Kayla took a deep breath to calm herself. She was realizing more and more that really was no point in arguing with people like Jim. "OK Jim," she said, "I don't believe the government has any

[16] Morton, Fiona M. Scott. "The Problems of Price Controls." *Cato Institute.* https://www.cato.org/publications/commentary/problems-price-controls (Retrieved September 15, 2017)

business setting prices. I believe the free market of supply and demand does. But it doesn't look like there is much I can do about it. So, if you don't mind..." Her voice trailed off and she eyed the door.

Jim realized he was being dismissed so he said, "OK then" and turned and left.

Kayla needed to clear her head so she decided to go for a walk. She let the store manager know she would be back in a little while. As she left the store she could see Jim down the block so she went in the opposite direction. She had no desire to see him again at this point.

She found herself out walking on Main Street. The street was lined on both sides for blocks on end with stores that used to be fully occupied. She remembered that they had big, clean glass windows that showed off so many great things for sale. Now, most of the storefronts were empty, covered with rusted roll down steel shutters that had been spray painted with graffiti. Many storefronts had scorch marks on them from the fires rioters had set. There was a lot of graffiti too. Much of the graffiti was of various slogans like "end greed!" or "Resist!"[17]

---

[17] "The plight of the inner cities is clearly worse than ever: more welfare, more crime, more dysfunction,
more fatherless families, fewer kids being "educated" in any sense, more despair and degradation. And now, bigger riots than ever before. It should be clear, in the starkest terms, that throwing taxpayer money and privileges at the inner cities is starkly counterproductive. And yet: this is the only "solution" that liberals can ever come up with, and without any argument—as if this "solution" were self-evident. How long is this
nonsense supposed to go on? If that is the absurd liberal solution, conservatives are not much better. Even liberals are praising—always a bad sign— Jack Kemp for being a "good" conservative who cares, and who
is coming up with innovative solutions trumpeted by Kemp himself and his neoconservative fuglemen. These are supposed to be "non-welfare" solutions, but welfare is precisely what they are: "public housing "owned" by tenants, but only under massive subsidy and strict

She walked across the street and looked through the dirty window into what had once been *Tony's Barber Shop*. It had been some time since he had shuttered his business and moved away. Kayla could see there was nothing left inside. Through the window she could see her own reflection looking back at her from the big mirror which lined the opposite wall. She thought she looked much older than she actually was. She thought of all the people who had watched themselves in that very same mirror get their hair cut by Tony. Now it was all gone. She walked away before she started to cry.

The lampposts used to have ornate iron scroll work near the top from which the town would hang flower pots filled with vivid flowers during the spring, or beautiful twinkling Christmas lights right after Thanksgiving. Now they were rusted and unkempt. The only thing hanging from some of them were random pieces of garbage. Kayla leaned on one of the lampposts and let out a huge sigh as a piece of plastic wrap stuck on the pole brushed against her face.

It pained Kayla's heart to see this once bustling, thriving commercial hub of the town now nothing more than a shell of its past glory.

Kayla moved away from the pole and noticed some activity down the block. She couldn't quite see what was going on and

---

regulation—with no diminution of the public housing stock; "enterprise zones" which are not free enterprise zones at all, but simply zones for more welfare subsidy and privileges to the inner city."- Murray Rothbard

Rothbard, Murray N. *Making Economic Sense 2nd Ed.* Auburn, Alabama: Ludwig Von Mises Institite, 1995, 2006. PDF.

https://mises.org/system/tdf/Making%20Economic%20Sense_3.pdf?file=1&type=documen t (Retrieved September 17, 2017) became immediately nervous. She saw a group of people milling around in front of one of the shuttered businesses and recent experience had her think that any group of people gathering on the street in the middle of the day could only be up to no good.

She squinted her eyes and shielded her face from the sun to look harder at the scene down the block, ready to run the other way if she detected even the smallest threat. You couldn't be too cautious these days. What with the all the violent protests by frustrated people going on lately, it was better to be safe than sorry.

Kayla chuckled to herself because she thought about the new sign outside of Homeland Hall. *Safest Place on Earth* it read. *Not so safe if you come across one of those violent protests,* she thought to herself.

When she saw one of the people holding a broom, she felt better. There weren't too many mobs running around sweeping things up lately. Her curiosity was piqued so she started to walk towards them. As she approached she saw they were in fact sweeping things up.

The shuttered business they were in front of had a lot debris and garbage strewn about near it. One of the big flower pots that businesses had lined the street with had been turned over at some point and the dirt and a small dead tree in it had spilled onto the sidewalk. Two young men were struggling to get the heavy pot righted while a third stood ready with a shovel to shovel the dirt back in. An older lady with a broom, who Kayla had seen from down the block, stood by waiting to sweep up what was left. They all wore well-worn clothes.

Kayla said hello to them and they all said hello back. "What's going on?" Kayla asked.

The man with shovel smiled and said, "We're cleaning up." He motioned towards the street and Kayla noticed a shiny new pick-up truck parked a few parking spaces away. It seemed to be towing a big cage that was filled with all sorts of debris and trash. The lady with the broom walked over and picked up the small dead tree that had falling to the ground. She carried it over to the cage and threw it in.

"Oh! That's nice!" Kayla said. "Are you volunteers?" Not an unusual question. Back when things were good there used to be a lot of volunteer organizations in the town. In fact, the big flower pot that the young men were struggling with were donated by the local businesses and set up by volunteers to help make the street nicer.

"Volunteers?" the man with the shovel said, almost laughing. "Lady, I can't afford to volunteer for nothing!"

"Oh," Kayla said. "Who do you work for?"

"The Government!" the man said. "The Mayor gave us our jobs! Thank God for him!"

The men struggling with the pot finally got it righted and joined in with the shovel guy. "That's right!" One of them said. "The Mayor started hiring people to help clean up the town. He's a great man who is taking care of us! My brother even got a job working on that new *Department of Works Progress* building they just started to build!"

195

"Department of Works Progress?" Kayla asked, "What's that?"

"That's who hired us!" Shovel man said.

Just then the headlights on the pickup truck flashed on and off. Kayla hadn't noticed before but there was a man sitting in the driver's seat of the truck.

Just then the lady came back from throwing the tree out. "The boss says we have to get back to work."

Kayla said goodbye to the workers and walked down the block towards the pickup truck. She noticed a man sitting in it, obviously a government worker because he had on the same kind of polo shirt that most of them wore nowadays. He smiled at her and she smiled back and kept walking. She didn't have much desire to interact with government workers these days.

As Kayla walked she noticed for the first time all of the colorful posters of Mayor Franklin hanging on the walls of building, on the fronts of closed up stores and everywhere else she looked it seemed. Someone had taken the image of the Mayor that hung behind his podium, the one with him smiling down his nose at everyone with his arms folded across his chest, and had turned it into a stylized print of red, white and blue. They had given the area around his head a glowing aura, like a halo, and underneath the image was one single word: HOPE[18]. Kayla thought it was creepy.

---

[18] https://en.wikipedia.org/wiki/Barack_Obama_%22Hope%22_poster (Retrieved November 20, 2017)

Kayla continued to walk and eventually found herself at her parent's house. She didn't even realize she was walking there having been so lost in thought. She walked in through the front door and found her father sitting on the couch in living room watching TV. She loved coming to see her parents. The house was warm and comfortable. There was a fire going in the fireplace and it smelled like her mother had just baked something delicious. She always felt safe here.

When he saw her walk in Kayla's dad said, "Hiya sweetie!" and muted the TV. She sat down next to her father on the couch. "What's up? You look like something is bothering you?" he said.

She grabbed one of the throw pillows and pulled it onto her lap. "Have you seen all of those posters of the Mayor around town?" she asked.

"You mean the ones that look like they took a photo and colorized it? Yes, I've seen them. What do you think?" he asked.

"I don't know," Kayla answered. "they just seem kind of creepy. It's like this guy is being made out to be some kind of savior. What I always loved about where we live is that the people made it great. Each individual trying to better themselves and their family made for a great system. We never relied on one person to do it for us. Never mind the whole government. It's what we got away from when our forefathers got rid of Mayor King."

"Things certainly have changed," her father said.

"On my way over I saw a group of workers cleaning up Main Street," she said. "When I asked them if they were volunteers they

197

basically laughed in my face. Then they told me that the Mayor gave them their jobs. They love him. They gave him all the credit for having a job. They don't even seem to realize that it's because of people like Mayor Franklin or Mayor Woodrow that things are so bad. That their policies are the reason why our economy is so bad." Kayla was getting upset by this and the agitation could be heard in her voice.

"And then there is this whole cult of personality developing around the Mayor. Like he's some kind of savior. Just look at those posters. It's ridiculous!" she said excitedly.

"You're right about that," her father said. "One of the traits of a Fascist totalitarian system is the leadership principle, or in other words a strong leader emerges who centralizes a lot, if not all, power in his own hands."

"Like Mussolini or Hitler or Stalin?" Kayla said.

"Mussolini yes," her dad said. "He was dictator of a Fascist system. Not Stalin. Stalin was a dictator, but of a Communist or Socialist system. There is a difference."

"There is?" Kayla asked.

"Yes," her father said. "Communism and Socialism is based on the government, or the State, owning the means of production, meaning industry. Fascism was called 'the third way'[19], a system

---

[19] "While failing to outline a coherent program, fascism evolved into a new political and economic system that combined totalitarianism, nationalism, anti-communism and anti-liberalism in a state designed to bind all classes together under a corporatist system (The "Third Way")."
"Benito Mussolini." *New World Encyclopedia.*

where private businesses still exist, but everything they do is basically dictated by the government."

"And Hitler?"

" Arguments have been made that Hitler was not the ruler of a Fascist State, but of a Socialist one instead," he said.

"What do you mean?" Kayla asked.

Her father said, "First of all it was in the name: National Socialist German Workers Party. But some scholars have suggested that because the Nazi government-controlled business and industry so completely, even though it didn't 'own' it, it was a de facto Socialist system.[20] As for Fascism itself, some scholars claim it was

---

http://www.newworldencyclopedia.org/entry/Benito_Mussolini#cite_note-Candeloro-6 (Retrieved July 11, 2018).

"In economics, fascism was seen as a third way between laissez-faire capitalism and communism. Fascist thought acknowledged the roles of private property and the profit motive as legitimate incentives for productivity — provided that they did not conflict with the interests of the state."
Richman, Sheldon. "Fascism-1st Edition." *Library of Economics and Liberty.*
http://www.econlib.org/library/Enc1/Fascism.html (Retrieved July 11, 2018)
[20] "Nevertheless, apart from Mises and his readers, practically no one thinks of Nazi Germany as a socialist state. It is far more common to believe that it represented a form of capitalism, which is what the Communists and all other Marxists have claimed.
The basis of the claim that Nazi Germany was capitalist was the fact that most industries in Nazi Germany appeared to be left in private hands.
What Mises identified was that private ownership of the means of production existed in name only under the Nazis and that the actual substance of ownership of the means of production resided in the German government. For it was the German government and not the nominal private owners that exercised all of the substantive powers of ownership: it, not the nominal private owners, decided what was to be produced, in what quantity, by what methods, and to whom it was to be distributed, as well as what prices would be charged and what wages would be paid, and what dividends or other income the nominal private owners would be permitted to receive. The position of the alleged private owners, Mises showed, was reduced essentially to that of government pensioners.
De facto government ownership of the means of production, as Mises termed it, was logically implied by such fundamental collectivist principles embraced by the Nazis as that the common good comes before the private good and the individual exists as a means to the ends of the State. If the individual is a means to the ends of the State, so too, of course, is his property. Just as he is owned by the State, his property is also owned by the State.

a form of heavily controlled Capitalism,[21] while others say the opposite,[22] and some say it is a mixture of both!"[23]

"So, are you saying we now live in a Fascist system?" Kayla asked.

Her father got up and went to his bookshelf and pulled a book off of it. He walked over and handed it to Kayla. She looked at the cover and read it out loud, *"As We Go Marching* by John T. Flynn."

But what specifically established de facto socialism in Nazi Germany was the introduction of price and wage controls in 1936."

Reisman, George. "Why Nazism Was Socialism and Why Socialism Is Totalitarian." *Mises Institute.* https://mises.org/library/why-nazism-was-socialism-and-why-socialism-totalitarian Posted November 11, 2015. (Retrieved July 11, 2018)

[21] "At this point we can say that fascism is (1) a capitalist type of economic organization, (2) in which the government accepts responsibility to make the economic system work at full energy, (3) using the device of state-created purchasing power effected by means of government borrowing and spending, and (4) which organizes the economic life of the people into industrial and professional groups to subject the system to control under the supervision of the state.

Flynn, John T. "What Is Fascism? Excerpted from As We Go Marching, part 1, chapter 10" *Mises Institute.* https://mises.org/library/what-fascism Posted April 26, 2008. (Retrieved July 11, 2018)

[22] "Socialists tried to pretend that fascism was simply the most developed, if also decrepit, stage of capitalism. But the fascists made their opposition to capitalism perfectly clear. For the dueling systems of capitalism and communism they proposed to substitute a "third way." The means of production would remain nominally in private hands, but the state would play a substantial role in production and allocation decisions. The classical liberal devotion to individual rights would of course be spurned in favor of collectivism, but in place of the communists' appeal to the worldwide proletarian struggle, the fascists' collectivism would be directed toward the nation."

Rockwell, Llewellyn H. Jr. *Fascism vs. Capitalism.* Auburn: Mises Institute, 2013. Page X.

[23] "As an economic system, fascism is socialism with a capitalist veneer...socialism sought totalitarian control of a society's economic processes through direct state operation of the means of production, fascism sought that control indirectly, through domination of nominally private owners. Where socialism nationalized property explicitly, fascism did so implicitly, by requiring owners to use their property in the "national interest" — that is, as the autocratic authority conceived it. (Nevertheless, a few industries were operated by the state.) Where socialism abolished all market relations outright, fascism left the appearance of market relations while planning all economic activities. Where socialism abolished money and prices, fascism controlled the monetary system and set all prices and wages politically. In doing all this, fascism denatured the marketplace. Entrepreneurship was abolished. State ministries, rather than consumers, determined what was produced and under what conditions."

Richman, Sheldon. "Fascism-2nd Edition." *The Library of Economics and Liberty.* http://www.econlib.org/library/Enc/Fascism.html (Retrieved July 11, 2018).

He sat back down on the couch. "It was written during the second world war. Flynn, a journalist, actually started as a leftist but had become disillusioned with the President and what he saw as the creeping Fascism of his policies[24]. It is a great history of Fascism and how that system came to be."

"What did he write?" Kayla asked. "How do you know if your country is becoming a Fascist State or already is one?"

"Flynn laid out a list of some key things that he believed signaled whether or not a system was a Fascist one.

- A government with unrestrained powers;
- A strong leader or dictator not responsible to the people but to his own establishment elite;
- An economy where production and distribution are owned privately but can only act within plans made by the government or under the government's supervision;
- A regulatory apparatus that overburdens society with regulations and directives;
- A financial system that is regulated by the government and not free enterprise, where the government controls the flow of money and is effectively the chief banker of society;
- Deficit spending and the accumulation of massive government debt and a society that is very militaristic in nature.[25]

[24] "Profiles: John T. Flynn." *Mises Institute.* https://mises.org/profile/john-t-flynn (Retrieved November 21, 2017)

[25] Flynn, John T. *As We Go Marching.* New York: Free Life Editions, Inc.,1973.November 21, 2017. Pages 161-162.

"I would also add that Fascists will not be afraid to use violence to shut down those who disagree with them. It could be organized violence committed by the State, or mob violence committed by those who have no desire to let an opposing viewpoint see the light of day, with the State a lot of times turning a blind eye towards it. Now think about where we live and see just how many of them apply. Fascism is also about one party rule. Especially when that one party uses the power and force of government to expand and solidify its rule at the expense of any true opposition. Knowing that I can say we are very close to a Fascist system here."

"But I thought Fascism was about racism and genocide?" Kayla asked, "Like Hitler hating Jews."

"Not necessarily," her father said. "But it can be, if the society it is taking root in allows it to be, like with Hitler, but fascism is more about power, control and economics. The mass murder Hitler committed had nothing to do with Fascism per se, it had to do with evil. Stalin murdered more people than Hitler. Mao even more. More people have been murdered under Socialism than any other system. Socialism is not Fascism. But it is evil. Millions and millions of deaths under Socialism make that a fact. Evil is evil and can be present in any system.

He went on, "We may never have a true dictator in the form of a single person where we live, even though Mayor Franklin is doing a pretty good job at trying to be one, but we could have a dictator of office so to speak."

"What do you mean by that?" Kayla asked.

"What I mean is lately we keep letting each successive Mayor take more power for himself, or, more correctly, his office of the Mayor. We, in essence, are allowing whomever we elect to that office to act like a dictator for his term. We don't force the Mayor to abide by the limitations set forth in our laws, we allow him to ignore them, thereby creating the situation where the office itself has dictatorial powers.[26]"

"I get it." Kayla said. "Fascism may look differently in the places it takes root in but the basics of it, excessive government deficit spending, heavy regulations, and so forth, will always be there."

"That's right," her father said.

Kayla always felt better after leaving her parents' house. She loved seeing and talking to her them. When she got home that night she did something she hadn't been doing much of lately and she turned on the news.

She saw the news anchor reporting how the Mayor gave yet another speech where he issued yet another directive. On the TV screen Kayla watched the Mayor once again standing at the podium in front of the big picture of himself.

He said, "It seems like some businesses in town are not doing their patriotic duty by purchasing *Patriot Bonds*. Going forward the Department of Syndicates will be coordinating a recurring purchase of *Patriot Bonds* by their member industries.

[26] Beatty, Warren. "Is it okay for Obama to Ignore the Constitution?" *American Thinker*. https://www.americanthinker.com/articles/2015/03/is_it_okay_for_obama_to_ignore_the_constitution.html Posted March 3, 2015. (Retrieved June 7, 2018)

Each business will be required to contribute a percentage of their profits to the purchase of the bonds. This will ensure that business, which is benefitting so greatly from my policies of economic revitalization, will do the right thing and give back to the Homeland.[27]"

Kayla knew enough what the Mayor was talking about was nothing more than a scheme for the government to ensure that it always had buyers for its debt. That way, it could keep borrowing and keep spending, with the whole scheme propped up by businesses who were being coerced into doing so.

The *Patriot Bond* scheme was also reflective of just how much the government had inserted itself into the economy. The government was using regulations, laws and now money, to control business and to keep itself propped up. Many businesses were fearful because government kept them all under the threat of force if they didn't comply, so they typically did whatever the government wanted. But many businesses liked what was going on as well. If a business or industry was favored by the government it could find itself on the receiving end of large cash flows from the government. All paid for by high taxes and government debt of course!

Businesses were technically still privately owned, but it was a sham ownership. If they didn't do what the government said or

[27] "No German capitalist or entrepreneur (shop manager) or anyone else is free to spend money on his consumption than the government considers adequate to his rank and position in the service of the nation. The surplus must be deposited with the banks or invested in domestic bonds or in the stock of German corporations wholly controlled by the government." - Excerpt from Omnipotent Government: The Rise of Total State and Total War (1944), chapter 7]
Von Mises, Ludwig. "The Economic Policy of the Nazis." *Foundation for Economic Education*. https://fee.org/resources/the-economic-policy-of-the-nazis/ Posted March 10, 2016. (Retrieved June 7, 2018)

followed its command, they would find themselves in deep trouble. Fines, even jail time were very real possibilities for business owners and managers to face if they didn't do what the government wanted.

Hank must be so happy with all of this, Kayla thought. *It's just what he wanted!*

Kayla shut her TV off and went to bed.

In the days to come Kayla found out she really had no choice but to "buy" *Patriot Bonds* from the government. The Mayor very easily had a law passed commanding businesses to do so. Failure to do so would only result in the owner of the business being locked up, the business getting seized by the government and auctioned off, or both. Kayla and other business owners could no more refuse to buy *Patriot Bonds* than someone could refuse to pay their income tax.

Forcing businesses to buy *Patriot Bonds* ensured the government would have a steady stream of purchasers of its debt. When it came time to pay back the bonds, the government would just issue more bonds. The scary thing was the government was also selling its debt to other governments. What would happen when *they* wanted their money back? Kayla shuddered at the thought.

Reasonable people like Kayla couldn't believe that this whole scheme could work. That people would catch on and put a stop to it.

But the thing is, the scheme did work. On the surface anyway. The first thing the Mayor did with all of this new debt was increase the size and power of the Police Force. As promised, the streets were becoming safer. The Police now had enough officers that the minute a protest started to get out of hand the Police would shut it down. This began to make people feel more confident about opening a business.

The government also used part of its new, debt laden, stash of cash, as the backing of a government financed loan program. The government essentially became the number one banker in town. People who wanted to open a small business went to the government and got a loan at a low interest rate which was set by the government. People used this money to start to open businesses. Main Street became busy again and most of the store fronts found new tenants with new businesses in them. No one seemed to notice, or care, that the whole economy was now built on a house of cards. Only kept standing by government debt.

What was once a natural, vibrant economy, that was strong and secure because it was organic and based on free market principles of a free exchange of goods and services by a free and unhindered citizenry and based on the solid, tangible asset of gold, was now an unnatural economy being directed by the government and based on nothing but debt and a Ponzi[28] scheme which wouldn't be able to last forever.

---

[28] "Ponzi scheme :an investment swindle in which some early investors are paid off with money put up by later ones in order to encourage more and bigger risks." Merriam-Webster. Updated October 13, 2007. https://www.merriam-webster.com/dictionary/Ponzi%20scheme (Retrieved November 21, 2017)

Kayla used to love to go to work at her stores every day. The excitement of growing her business, meeting customers and providing jobs always gave her a thrill. Now, with all the rules and regulations she had to follow it wasn't as much fun anymore. Not to mention the fact that her old employee Jim, the one who now worked at the *Department of Government Syndicates*, always seemed to be in her stores. More than even when he worked for her!

He was there every day with his clipboard and polo shirt and lanyard checking to make that Kayla wasn't "price gouging" and was paying her employees the government dictated wages. One morning Jim walked into the same store that Kayla happened to be at.

She couldn't quite put her finger on why, but all of a sudden, the sight of Jim and his clipboard coming through the door, made Kayla seethe with anger.

"Good morning!" Jim said when he saw Kayla.

Kayla came out from behind the counter and was in front of Jim and in his face in seconds. With all the vitriol she could manage in her voice she said to him, "Back again are you Jim? Here to check the size of the lemons? Or to make sure the ice is cold enough?" She was practically nose to nose with him.

In his haste to back away from Kayla, Jim must not have realized that there was a chair near him. He tripped backwards and landed on his back. His clipboard went flying and went it hit the ground all of his papers on it popped off and skidded across the floor. To Jim's continued misfortune, at the same time he hit the floor one of Kayla's employees pushed the front door open and it hit

Jim on the head. This caused Jim to fall back against the door which must have dislodged the bells that hung on the door to alert the staff when someone came in. The bells came flying down on Jim's head with a loud crashing jingle! All of this happened in seconds.

For a moment Kayla's brain didn't quite register what had happened. Then the bells rolled off Jim's head and hit the floor with another loud crash. In that instant all of the anger she was feeling just drained out of her and was replaced by hysterical laughter. As Jim stumbled to his feet his face turned bright red. The sound of Kayla's laughter must have been too much for him because he turned around and ran out the door.

Kate, Kayla's employee, handed her a napkin to wipe the tears away. She said, "Holy cow! That was the funniest thing I ever saw! Where did he go?"

Kayla finally stopped laughing. "I don't know," she said. "Probably to tell his hero Mayor Franklin what happened! I think what it made it so funny was that Jim thinks he's this big important government official now. We need more of them to fall on their asses! Maybe then they'll leave us alone."

But they didn't. Jim was back later that day and tried very hard to not interact with Kayla. She had a hard time not laughing every time she saw him. But the whole episode did get Kayla thinking that it would be great to embarrass more government people more of the time. She was never much of an activist but she figured it might be a good time to become one. She knew there were a lot of people in town who agreed with her as well. She figured that maybe if they got together and came up with some ideas of how to protest, other people would start to join in as well. If they got big and influential enough she thought that the government would have to listen!

She really wanted nothing more than to wake people up to what was happening to their freedom!

While Kayla was pondering this, she looked out the front window of her store and saw a commotion. She walked outside to see what was going on.

There was a group of union members and others protesting in the small park across the street from the store[29]. They had been there almost every day protesting about "corporate greed" and getting a "living wage" since the days of Mayor Woodrow. They had actually set up a small tent city where many of the people stayed for days on end. Kayla thought the whole area had become kind of disgusting and shouldn't be allowed to exist. What had once been a beautiful park where mothers took their kids to play was now basically a huge outdoor toilet. Mayor Woodrow tolerated them because the people in the park were largely supported by the unions so he left them alone because he did not want to upset a big portion of his voting base[30].

Apparently though Mayor Franklin wasn't as tolerant. Kayla watched as swarms of police vehicles surrounded the park. Scores of cops in riot gear got out of their vehicles and were now wading

---

[29] Occupy Wall Street. http://occupywallst.org/ (Retrieved November 22, 2017)
[30] Kroll, Andy. "Occupied Wall Street, Powered by Big Labor." Motherjones.com. Updated October 5, 2011. http://www.motherjones.com/politics/2011/10/occupy-wall-street-labor-unions/ (Retrieved November 22, 2017)

through the tents in the park, ripping things up and swinging nightsticks. But the protestors weren't going quietly. Cops were literally dragging them kicking and screaming from the park and throwing them into the prison buses they had lined up down the block. But the protesters were fighting back and things were getting ugly. The police were having a hard time containing everything to the park. Groups of masked protesters started to fan out across the street where Kayla's store was. They were chanting and screaming, "Pigs in a blanket, fry 'em like bacon!"[31]

Watching from the front of her store Kayla started to see smoke rising from somewhere in the park. It looked to her like the protesters were turning over garbage pails and using the trash to light fires. She looked to the right and noticed down the street that some hooded and masked people were climbing on top of parked cars and smashing their windows. Kayla saw a cop walking quickly towards her and realized it was her old friend Hank. She always thought he would make a good cop with the way he always followed all the rules. He had his nightstick out and a riot helmet on.

"Kayla! It's not safe out here! Get inside!" he yelled at her. He motioned her back into the store and followed her in. When they were safely inside he took off his helmet. His hair was sweaty and matted to his head and his face was beat red.

"Hank! What's going on out there?" Kayla asked as she went behind the counter to get him some lemonade.

---

[31] Key, Pam. "Black Lives Matter Activist: 'Pigs in a Blanket Fry 'em Like Bacon' Not About Killing Police." Breitbart.com. Posted August 31, 2015.
http://www.breitbart.com/video/2015/08/31/black-lives-matter-activist-pigs-in-a-blanket-fry-em-like-bacon-not-about-killing-police/

Hank put his helmet down on a table and took the lemonade Kayla handed him and drank it down in one long gulp. He handed the cup back to Kayla, "Thank you. I needed that."

"Want any more?" Kayla asked.

"No thanks." He said.

"What's going on Hank?" Kayla asked again. She came out from behind the counter and handed Hank a napkin.

He wiped the sweat from his face. "The Mayor had enough of those people occupying the park and keeping people from using it so he sent us in to clear it out. You should see the place Kayla, it's a pig sty. Garbage everywhere, people using buckets as toilets and just leaving it there. One filthy protester after another."

"I think it's about time the Mayor cleaned out that park," Kayla said. "Those people would come in here trying to use the bathroom and bothering my customers. It's about time it was cleaned out."

"That's not all," Hank said. "There was a lot of subversive stuff in there."

"Subversive?" Kayla asked. "What do you mean?"

"We found all sorts of subversive things in there. Signs and flyers that talk about overthrowing the government and starting a 'workers revolution'. A lot of it seemed to have been financed by the unions," Hank said.

"By the unions? How do you know?" Kayla asked.

"A lot of the signs were all high-quality pre-printed ones. Very professionally done. There was no way a bunch of people living in a park could have afforded to have them made. And at the bottom of most of the flyers and signs were little union logos. See?" He pulled a flyer from his pocket and pointed to a little logo at the bottom of it. Sure enough, Kayla saw there was a little logo from one of the unions there.

"The Mayor is pissed," Hank said as he put his helmet back on. "Word is that he and the Town Council got together behind closed to work out a plan to stop this subversive talk and to curtail the power of the unions." As he turned to walk back outside he said, "Listen Kayla, it's not safe yet out there. Stay inside for now." With that he waved and headed back into the street.

Business was slow all day at her store near the where the riots took place so Kayla closed early. It was dark as she locked up and she saw that there were still a lot of cops near the park, which had been lit up with huge floodlights, across the street. Now the cops seemed to be there only as escorts for the sanitation crews who were seemed to very busy cleaning up the park. They were ripping everything out the protesters had been accumulating there for the past several months and throwing it all into huge rollaway dumpsters. As Kayla walked down the street she saw the destruction that had taken place. There was trash and debris everywhere. She saw two burned out cop cars, one of which had the word "PIG" spray painted all over it in red spray paint, and several smashed up civilian cars. Kayla thought for sure her car was going to be wrecked but she was pleasantly surprised when she got to it and saw it had not been touched.

When she got home, Kayla turned on the news and saw the Mayor was giving a press conference. He was standing outside the park where the riots started this afternoon. Kayla could see her store in the background. Beneath his image it said, "Mayor Announces New Initiative against Subversives." She turned up the volume and heard the Mayor saying, ".... unprecedented levels of violence require a swift and strong response. I have authorized emergency spending for our fine Police Department to get the equipment and tools they need to deal with any threat. I am also working with the Town Council to ensure that we are taking the appropriate measures against subversive groups in our town. We are working hard to ensure our town remains a safe place. Thank you."

When he was done the image cut back to the news anchor. An image of a wheeled armored vehicle, essentially a tank, appeared in the upper right corner of the screen. The news anchor said, "And word of the type of equipment the Mayor wants for the Police Department has leaked out from Homeland Hall and it seems to include new body armor as well as armor of a different kind." The screen then switched to a video of the tank being used by some other Police Department during some other incident[32].

Subversive Groups Kayla thought to herself. *What does that mean? And do they need a tank? What the hell are they expecting to happen here? We are really just a small town with local cops*[33].

---

[32] Lockwood, Brad. "The Militarizing of Local Police." Forbes.com. Posted November 30, 2011. https://www.forbes.com/sites/bradlockwood/2011/11/30/the-militarizing-of-local-police/#4fcaaa35fed1 (Retrieved November 26, 2017)

She didn't like what was going on in the park near her store at all and was glad that the cops finally cleaned it out. She also thought that many of the people in there might actually have been subversives who were intending to cause harm and destruction to people and property. What she didn't like is that the Mayor seemed to be using this incident to go against other groups that *he* thought were subversive. She knew that throughout history some governments and leaders have used emergencies and tragedies as reasons to seize more power for themselves.[34] She was afraid that the Mayor wasn't going to let this incident go to waste as an opportunity[35] for him to take even more control for himself and his government while at the same time allowing him to hurt the people and groups he thought were against him.

In the days after the cops cleared out the park it seemed that the Mayor had identified at least one type of group he thought was subversive...unions. The next day he a "vigorous investigation" into the "nefarious activities" of union leaders and their "subversive" activities.

"During the recent raid on the park our great Police uncovered massive proof of not only a very large subversive movement in our town, but also union support and funding of it." The Mayor said during another press conference. He was speaking

---

[33] Bickel, Carl. "Will the Growing Militarization of Our Police Doom Community Policing?". Community Policing Dispatch. December 2013. https://cops.usdoj.gov/html/dispatch/12-2013/will_the_growing_militarization_of_our_police_doom_community_policing.asp (Retrieved November 26, 2017)

[34] Boissoneault, Lorraine. "The True Story of the Reichstag Fire and the Nazi Rise to Power." Smithsonianmag.com. Posted February 21, 2017. https://www.smithsonianmag.com/history/true-story-reichstag-fire-and-nazis-rise-power-180962240/ (Retrieved March 13, 2018)

[35] Wall Street Journal "Rahm Emanuel on the Opportunities of Crisis." Published on Nov 19, 2008. https://youtu.be/_mzcbXi1Tkk (Retrieved March 13, 2018)

behind a table on which there were several of the signs and flyers that the Police had taken from the park laid out. There were a bunch of blown up images of the small union label that Hank had pointed out to Kayla the day of the riot in her lemonade store hanging on the wall behind him. "This vile type of literature should not, and will not, be tolerated," he said.

A reporter in the audience stood up and asked, "Are you saying that just because they printed things you don't agree with we should crack down on them? What about freedom of speech?"

The mayor looked annoyed. "What I am saying is we need to vigorously go after subversive elements."

The reporter wasn't giving up, "I agree with you. If people are breaking the law, or committing violent acts, or violating the Liberty of someone..." *Liberty?* Kayla thought, *haven't heard much of that word lately.* "...then yes, we should 'vigorously' go after them. But just for saying or writing things you don't agree with? Then no. We shouldn't."

Kayla agreed with the reporter. The government going after people because they wrote or said something that some politician in the government didn't agree with was crazy. It wasn't what their community was built upon. Violence, occupying a public space like a park so others couldn't use it and disrupting others liberty and freedom, all of those things should be policed. But writing flyers or signs? No.

The Mayor apparently didn't like the way the press conference was going so he ended it abruptly by saying, "My job is to protect the people! No further questions!" and walked off.

Walking away, getting emotional, yelling irrationally, all seemed to be a common trait of all these Progressives and Fascists lately. They didn't seem capable of having intelligent, calm and rational discussions with people who disagreed with them. *It's funny*, Kayla thought, *for people who are constantly telling everyone else they need to be 'fair' or 'tolerant', they were the most unfair and intolerant people around.*

In the days after the press conference Kayla started to feel like she had to do something about what was going on in her town. She wanted to offer an alternative voice and opinions to what the Mayor and his cronies saying with the hope that people would start to wake up to the fact that their Liberty was slowly being taken away from them.

Kayla organized some meetings at her house with some other people who were thinking the same way she was and they talked about different ways they could protest and try to get the direction of the town back on the path of Liberty and Freedom. They talked about holding a rally near Homeland Hall, starting a letter writing campaign and collecting money to pay for their activities. They called their group the *Friends of Liberty,* and were one of many different like-minded groups that were starting to get organized around opposition to the government's policies.

Over the course of the next few weeks Kayla's group did that, and more. They were doing a great job of letting the government know they weren't happy and wanted to see things change.

They held rallies outside of Homeland Hall, started a letter writing to the members of the town's government and would appear at the Mayor's press conferences to ask tough questions (which he usually either mocked, ignored, and certainly never gave a straight answer to).

They were doing such a good job that apparently the government noticed...and wasn't too happy.

Kayla received an official letter in the mail from the Jefferson County *Department of Treasury* that both her business and her personal taxes were being audited.[36] This never happened to her before. She knew it was no strange coincidence that these audits only occurred as she was becoming more publicly vocal about her opposition to the Mayor and his policies. But Holy Cow! What a direct example of just how totalitarian her town had become! The government using government agencies to intimidate and punish people who disagreed with their policies was the stuff of dictatorships! Government force being used to silence political dissention was nothing short of tyranny.

Her little protest group also found it harder and harder to get permits to hold their events around town. All of a sudden, they were being delayed over and over again when they requested access to public places to hold an event. When they applied for status as a non-profit organization with the tax department they were denied without any real explanation as to why. Meanwhile Kayla knew for a fact that other groups, those friendlier to the government especially, were granted almost everything they applied for almost

[36] "Judicial Watch: New Documents Show IRS Used Donor Lists to Target Audits." *Judicial Watch*. https://www.judicialwatch.org/press-room/press-releases/judicial-watch-new-irs-documents-used-donor-lists-to-target-audits/ Posted July 22, 2015. (Retrieved May 21, 2018)

every time[37]. *Nothing like people in the government using its power to suppress those who disagreed with them,* Kayla thought to herself. *If that's not a sign of a totalitarian regime, nothing is.*

However, the Mayors efforts to crack down on "subversives" wasn't going as he had planned. At first people were afraid of the Mayor and his newly beefed up Police Force. Groups like Kayla's usually didn't have a problem with the cops because they held peaceful protests and the people who attended them generally respected the Police. At most of the rallies that groups like Kayla's held the people even actually cleaned up after themselves![38]

But then radical groups started to show up in counter protest. Except they weren't just there waving signs and yelling slogans. They came with a clear intention on being violent. Peaceful groups like Kayla's suddenly found themselves being physically assaulted by groups of thugs who would suddenly appear dressed all in black with masks covering their faces to hide their identities and they would assault the peaceful protesters and everyone else who just happened to be nearby.[39]

---

[37] Sekulow, Jay. "VICTORY: In Proposed Settlement, IRS Admits Wrongdoing, Apologizes for Targeting Tea Party and Conservative Groups." *ACLJ*. Posted October 2017. https://aclj.org/free-speech/victory-in-proposed-settlement-irs-admits-wrongdoing-apologizes-for-targeting-tea-party-and-conservative-groups (Retrieved November 27, 2017)
[38] Taylor, Ken. "A Tale Of Two Rallies, Conservative VS Liberal Who Trashed The Mall And The Country." *Redstate.com*. Posted October 3, 2010. https://www.redstate.com/diary/Ken_Taylor/2010/10/03/a-tale-of-two-rallies-conservative-vs-liberal-who-trashed-the-mall-and-the-country/ (Retrieved March 13, 2018)
[39] The ignorance or purposeful deception of these violent Antifa (Anti-Fascist) protesters needs to be recognized. They call themselves "Anti-Fascists" while using violence to shut down who they see as their enemies and opponents. The depth of the hypocrisy of these violent thugs and their useful idiot supporters in society is stunning. Ridiculously, yet not unexpectedly, the author of this particular article blames the violence on the "Trump years" without ever once pointing out the hypocrisy that these so-called "Antifa" thugs are nothing more than the Fascists they claim they are against.-GM
Swenson, Kyle-The Washington Post. "Black-clad antifa members attack peaceful right-wing demonstrators in Berkeley." *Toronto Sun*. http://torontosun.com/2017/08/28/black-clad-antifa-attack-peaceful-right-wing-demonstrators-in-berkeley/wcm/3ff534bd-e758-4a8e-9b21-

It got to the point that groups like Kayla's had to stop organizing in public. It was just too dangerous.[40] And with all of this going on it was election season again. Mayor Franklin was going to have a fight on his hands because all of the violent protesters and anarchists in the streets seemed to have found their man to run for the office of Mayor.

Mr. Barry was a relatively young man who never held a real job in his life. He called himself a "Community Organizer"[41], which essentially meant he was a professional protester and agitator whose whole job seemed to be to get the government to spend money on groups that he agreed with.

His whole campaign seemed to focus on that he wanted to, "spread the wealth around."[42]

---

c5a1cf8b572b Posted August 28, 2017. (Retrieved March 13, 2018)

[40] Even Liberal commentator's like Peter Beinart recognize the hypocrisy and authoritarian make up of Antifa:

"Antifa believes it is pursuing the opposite of authoritarianism. Many of its activists oppose the very notion of a centralized state. But in the name of protecting the vulnerable, antifascists have granted themselves the authority to decide which Americans may publicly assemble and which may not. That authority rests on no democratic foundation. Unlike the politicians they revile, the men and women of antifa cannot be voted out of office. Generally, they don't even disclose their names.

Antifa's perceived legitimacy is inversely correlated with the government's. Which is why, in the Trump era, the movement is growing like never before. As the president derides and subverts liberal-democratic norms, progressives face a choice. They can recommit to the rules of fair play, and try to limit the president's corrosive effect, though they will often fail. Or they can, in revulsion or fear or righteous rage, try to deny racists and Trump supporters their political rights. From Middlebury to Berkeley to Portland, the latter approach is on the rise, especially among young people.

Revulsion, fear, and rage are understandable. But one thing is clear. The people preventing Republicans from safely assembling on the streets of Portland may consider themselves fierce opponents of the authoritarianism growing on the American right. In truth, however, they are its unlikeliest allies."

Beinart, Peter. "The Rise of the Violent Left." *The Atlantic.* https://www.theatlantic.com/magazine/archive/2017/09/the-rise-of-the-violent-left/534192/ Posted September 2017. (Retrieved June 29, 2018)

[41] York, Byron. " What Did Obama Do As A Community Organizer?" National Review. Posted September 8, 2008. http://www.nationalreview.com/article/225564/what-did-obama-do-community-organizer-byron-york (Retrieved November 28, 2017)

[42] Jones, Susan. "'Spread the Wealth Around' Comment Comes Back to Haunt Obama."

A local TV journalist did a story about My Barry. She said, "Mr. Barry is a charming man, clean, articulate and nice-looking. A real story book!"[43] He spoke a lot about how he wanted to "transform" the town and bring about a lot of "change".

Kayla listened to his ideas and didn't like what she heard. For example, he wanted the government to control the health care system. Kayla didn't think there was anything wrong with the town's healthcare system. It wasn't perfect, and had some areas that could be improved, especially the areas where the government was involved, but let the government control the whole thing? That's crazy!

Kayla was nervous though. Over time people had grown very accustomed to having the government control more and more aspects of their life. Things in town were still not great economically. She was worried that what Mr. Barry was saying about government getting even more involved in people's lives was resonating with people. Mr. Barry seemed all too quick to lay blame for the bad things on a need for even more "change".

Kayla did a little research about Mr. Barry and found some things about him that disturbed her. For one, he spent a lot of time as a young person around Communists. In fact, many of his earlier mentors were devout communists and radicals.[44] Kayla was afraid

---

Cnsnews.com. Posted October 15, 2008. https://www.cnsnews.com/news/article/spread-wealth-around-comment-comes-back-haunt-obama (Retrieved March 13, 2018)

[43] http://www.cnn.com/2007/POLITICS/01/31/biden.obama/ (Retrieved February 23, 2018)

Former Senator and Vice President Joe Biden took a lot of heat when, during the 2008 Presidential campaign, he said, "I mean, you got the first mainstream African-American who is articulate and bright and clean and a nice-looking guy. I mean, that's a storybook, man." Many felt the slip exposed his hidden racism.

[44] Kengor, Paul. "Why Obama's Communist Connections Are Not Headlines." *American Thinker*.

this would have a big influence on the way he thought. *How could it not?* She thought.

He also never had a "real" job in the business world. All of his jobs relied on government somehow.[45] *So how can he know what it takes to run a business and create jobs?* Kayla thought.

But the media seemed to love him. She never heard or read any news item, from any of the big main stream news outlets that talked about some of these things. All things which Kayla found out about quite easily by doing a little research, during the whole campaign.

Mr. Barry said he decided to run against Mr. Franklin because he didn't think Mayor Franklin was doing a good job.

Mr. Barry may not have held a real job ever in his life, but boy oh boy did he know how to speak in public! The crowds were mesmerized by what he said. The thing is, he didn't say much. Don't misunderstand. He talked a lot, but all anyone could remember him saying was he was bringing "Hope" and "Change" to the township.

He told everyone that Mr. Franklin was a radical who didn't really care about the people. He said that Mr. Franklin would only look out for the "rich" people in town and not the "middle class" and the workers. Mr. Barry said Mr. Franklin was too "right wing" for the town, that he was "extreme" and "unfit to be Mayor". Mr.

---

https://www.americanthinker.com/articles/2008/10/why_obamas_communist_connectio.html Posted October 10, 2008. (Retrieved May 21, 2018)
[45] "Barack Obama's career path to president." *Boston.com*.
http://archive.boston.com/jobs/galleries/obamasjobs/ (Retrieved May 21, 2018)

Barry, said that he was the only one who understood the people. He also said that the government wasn't doing enough for the people and it needed to do more.

Mr. Barry seemed to believe in making many things "free".

Free college for all...free health insurance...free kindergarten for kids...

It made Kayla think about how her father told her that nothing was ever free.

A reporter asked Mr. Barry how he would be able to provide all of these "free" things to people.

"Why I will tax the rich he said!" he said

"So, then it's not really free," the reporter said.

"It will be free to everyone but the rich!" Mr. Barry said.

"What kind of taxes," asked the reporter?

"With responsible and fair taxes," Mr. Barry said.

"What kind of 'fair' taxes" asked the reporter?

"Well," Mr. Barry said, "I will start by introducing a very modest payroll tax, I call it the 'Responsible Tax', which will be just 2% of everyone's income. There will also be an extra tax that greedy corporations will have to pay. That tax will fund the free healthcare."

"This 'Responsible Tax' will be paid by everyone?" the reporter asked.

"Yes," Mr. Barry said. "It will only be a couple of dollars a week." [46]

"If everyone is paying it, how is it free? And if you start taxing the corporations too much won't they just pick up and move elsewhere? Maybe even out of the township? Won't that cost jobs?" the reporter asked.

Mr. Barry looked at the reporter for a few seconds then said, "Next question!"

But all of this talk of free stuff made a lot of people excited. The people seemed to love him. Kayla was listening to what he said. What she heard him say was that he was going to "transform" the government. She didn't like the way that sounded. She didn't think anything needed to be transformed. Just the opposite in fact. She thought things needed to be *restored*. Restored to what the town charter had intended the township to be, "The Freest Place on Earth".

The funny thing is, Kayla thought, here she was thinking all along that Mr. Woodrow and Mr. Franklin were a little too radical for her tastes because they relied *too much* on government yet Mr. Barry thought just the opposite. He thought Mr. Franklin was a radical because he didn't get the government involved *even more* in people's lives!

---

[46] https://Baracksanders.com/issues/how-Barack-pays-for-his-proposals/

Mr. Barry told everyone that Mr. Franklin was going to take away all of the "benefits" and "entitlements" people received from the government. That was a lie, but people did not seem to care. Even all of the newspapers seemed to love Mr. Barry. Almost every news outlet endorsed him for Mayor. They ignored the lies he told and instead printed bad stories about Mr. Franklin.

Mr. Barry also promised he was there for the workers. He said that 'greedy' bosses would no longer be able to take advantage of them. He also promised to put an end to the repression many said they were feeling under Mayor Franklin. He said if he were elected he would order the Police to immediately stop investigating the unions and to "back off" when the unions were protesting or rallying in the street. Mr. Barry loved labor unions even more than some of the other mayors did. As far as the unions were concerned Mr. Barry was their savior!

The unions responded by gleefully backing Mr. Barry. Large sums of union dues money were spent on campaigning and supporting his candidacy. In fact, it seemed that was the only reason unions collected dues in the first place, that is, to support the politicians they liked.[47]

As Kayla did in the past she invited her old friend Hank over to see what he thought about Mr. Barry. Once again, he showed up on a Friday night with his box of donuts and joined Kayla in her kitchen.

---

[47] "Use of Dues for Politics." Unionfacts.com. https://www.unionfacts.com/article/political-money/ (Retrieved March 13, 2018)

"I don't like him," Hank said emphatically after Kayla asked him what he thought of Mr. Barry. His answer surprised her because Hank typically went for the politicians who believed in bigger and bigger government.

"Wow Hank," Kayla said, "I must say I am surprised." She poured Hank a cup of coffee which had been brewing and sat down across from him at the table. "I thought for sure you would like him."

Hank put some milk and sugar in his cup of coffee and stirred it with the spoon Kayla handed him. He took a sip and set his cup back down. He seemed to be thinking intently about what he wanted to say.

He looked up from his cup of coffee at Kayla. "I always believed the Government should do more to help make thing fair, you know that and I know you don't agree with me," he said in a measured tone. "But this guy Barry scares me a little."

Kayla raised her eyebrows, she was surprised to hear Hank say that.

"Scares you Hank? Why?" she asked.

"Because you and I have always had one thing in common, we love this town and we love the Charter upon which it was founded," he said.

Right away Kayla's first instinct was to put Hank back in his place. She had spent the last few years arguing with him and others like him about just how wrong they were about their interpretation of the town's Charter. She was offended that Hank could even think for one second that she and he thought the same way about it. Hank saw an agitated look cross Kayla's face and that she was about to say something so held up his hand.

"I know, I know, I know!" he said. "Let me explain."

Kayla settled down and said, "OK."

"You and I may have had differences in what we thought freedom looks like for us here in Jefferson Township, and we may have had different ideas about how to interpret the Charter," he said.

"You got that right!" Kayla said to him.

Hank smiled and continued, "But I know that whatever your thoughts about the Government, you truly always have the best interests of the people in town at heart and I think you would say the same about me."

It suddenly struck Kayla that Hank was right. She thought he was way misguided in what he believed about what government should be given the power to do, and she thought his concept of freedom and fairness was completely wrong, but he was right. She thought that in the end he loved their community and wanted what he thought was best for the people.

"I do Hank," she said to him. "I truly believe you have a good heart and have the best of intentions. But I also believe that people like Mayor Woodrow and Mayor Franklin took advantage of your good nature. They used your altruistic spirit for their own pursuits of power. For them, and people like them, people like you were just a means to an end for their own selfish pursuits. And I also believed that they used people like you to support their own ideological agenda. This whole *progressive* ideology of theirs is nothing more than an offshoot of something that has been happening for centuries. The establishment and perpetuation of an elitist ruling class who institute a system of government which they then use to keep us common folk under their thumb! It's a form of tyranny!"

Hank frowned and said, "I'm not here to argue with you Kayla."

"You're right," she said. "I'm sorry. Please go on."

"What scares me the most is all of this talk from Mr. Barry about 'transforming' the town," he said.

Once again Kayla was surprised by what Hank said. She let him know she was thinking the same way.

A small smile crossed Hank's face. "I kind of had the feeling you would agree," he said.

"Can I tell you what scares me about him?" Kayla asked.

"Sure," Hank said.

"The biggest thing for me," Kayla said, "is all of his talk about how we need to break free from the town's Charter because it is filled with 'negative liberties' and we need a Charter with more 'positive liberties'.[48]"

"I've heard him say that before,[49]" Hank said. "What exactly does that mean?"

"Negative liberty is the absence of external control," Kayla said. "Negative liberties are what we *allow* the government *to* do. Positive liberties are the things that people believe the government *can*, *should* or *ought* to do."

"Why does that matter?" Hank asked. Kayla expected as much from him. He might not like Mr. Barry but he certainly liked big government.

She said, "Because enacting so called positive liberties would essentially allow the government to do whatever it wanted to you to. For example, if the Charter said 'the government ought to provide a guaranteed income to everyone', which is a positive

---

[48] "Let's look at an example. Jack's living in New York. He'd like go to California to visit family. Under a negative conception of liberty, Jack is free to go to California if nobody is actively preventing him from doing so. Thus his negative freedom would be violated if his neighbor locked Jack in the basement, or if someone stole his car.
But what if Jack's so poor that he can't afford a car or a plane ticket? What if Jack is sick and so not physically up to the trip? In these instances, no person prevents Jack from going to California, so Jack's negative liberty remains intact. Yet he lacks the capacity to fulfill his desire and so, from a positive liberty standpoint, he is unfree.
Within the context of political philosophy — within the context of what the state is permitted to do and what it ought to do — a government protects Jack's negative liberty by preventing the neighbor from locking Jack up and preventing the thief from stealing Jack's car. If the state is unable to prevent these specific acts, it may punish the perpetrators, thus (we hope) reducing the likelihood of other, similar liberties violations. In addition to — or instead of — punishing violations, the state might force the violator to compensate Jack, striving to make him whole.
On the other hand, a state tasked with directly promoting Jack's positive liberty might tax its citizens in order to buy Jack the car he couldn't otherwise afford. Or it might use that revenue to pay for the medical care Jack needs to get back on his feet so he can travel. A positive liberty focused state would take active steps to assure Jack isn't just free to pursue his desires, but also has the resources to attain them."
Powell, Aaron Ross. "What Are Negative and Positive Liberty? And Why Does It Matter?" *Libertarianism.org.* https://www.libertarianism.org/blog/what-are-negative-positive-liberty-why-does-it-matter Posted December 20, 2012. (Retrieved June 11, 2018)
[49] Walker, Bruce. "Negative Liberties and Obama Newspeak." *American Thinker.* https://www.americanthinker.com/articles/2008/10/negative_liberties_and_obama_n.html Posted October 29, 2008. (Retrieved June 11, 2018)

liberty, then the government would be able to come in and seize your money in order to give it to someone else.[50] Not only is that too much power for the government to have, it sets up a legalized system of plunder at the hands of the government. It's not to say there isn't a place for positive liberty in our lives though. I *ought* to be able to do things like start a business or buy things for my family. We just need to be very, very careful about what type of positive liberty we are allowing the government to have. The government should be restrained from preventing me from starting that business or buying those things and on the same note the government should not be compelled to give me the money to start that business or buy those things."

"I see what you're saying Kayla," Hank said. "Let me tell you why I am scared of him."

"OK," Kayla said.

"Being a cop, I don't like how he says he going to have us 'back off' from going after all of those violent protesters. Is that what he wants to 'transform' the town into? A place where mobs run free? As long as the mobs back him? He seems to have a decidedly anti-police viewpoint and I don't think that's good for any of us."[51] [52]

[50] Gregory, Paul Roderick. "Why the Fuss? Obama Has Long Been On Record In Favor Of Redistribution." *Forbes.* https://www.forbes.com/sites/paulroderickgregory/2012/09/23/why-the-fuss-obama-has-long-been-on-record-in-favor-of-redistribution/#5f88675e593a Posted September 23, 2012. (Retrieved June 11, 2018)

[51] Ocasio, Bianca Padro. "Police group director: Obama caused a 'war on cops'." *Politico.* https://www.politico.com/story/2016/07/obama-war-on-cops-police-advocacy-group-225291 Posted June 8, 2016. (Retrieved June 11, 2018)

[52] Pavlich, Katie. "Katie Pavlich: Obama's anti-police ideology." *The Hill.* http://thehill.com/opinion/katie-pavlich/245049-katie-pavlich-obamas-anti-police-ideology Posted June 15, 2015. (Retrieved June 11, 2018)

"I get it Hank," Kayla said, "I don't like how he seems to be so anti-police either. But as a cop you should be very wary of people like Mayor Franklin who want to use the police to project their own power. The police shouldn't be so eager to carry out the whims of these power-hungry politicians, especially when it involves trampling on the rights of the citizenry. Be careful about following orders that violate the law."[53]

"I will," Hank said.

Kayla wasn't sure though that Hank was really listening to what she was saying. She felt the need to emphasize one important point to him.

"You took an oath Hank"[54], Kayla said, "not to Mayor Franklin or any politician for that matter. You took an oath to protect and defend the town's Charter.[55] Remember that."

With that Hank looked at his watch and said that he had to go. He thanked Kayla for sitting with him and for always being a good friend.

---

[53] Scoville, Dean. "Who Are the Oath Keepers?" *Police The Law Enforcement Magazine.* http://www.policemag.com/channel/patrol/articles/2013/04/who-are-the-oath-keepers.aspx Posted April 4, 2013. (Retrieved June 12, 2018)

[54] "Oath Keepers is a non-partisan association of current and formerly serving military, police, and first responders, who pledge to fulfill the oath all military and police take to "defend the Constitution against all enemies, foreign and domestic." That oath, mandated by Article VI of the Constitution itself, is to the Constitution, not to the politicians, and Oath Keepers declare that they will not obey unconstitutional orders, such as orders to disarm the American people, to conduct warrantless searches, or to detain Americans as "enemy combatants" in violation of their ancient right to jury trial."
"About Oath Keepers." *Oath Keepers.* https://www.oathkeepers.org/about/ (Retrieved June 12, 2018)

[55] "The Senators and Representatives before mentioned, and the members of the several state legislatures, and all executive and judicial officers, both of the United States and of the several states, shall be bound by oath or affirmation, to support this Constitution…" - *U.S. Constitution Article VI*

After Hank left Kayla sat up for a while thinking about what they had talked about. She was more nervous than she ever had been about the direction the town was heading as election neared.

Socialism

(Workers Hall-The Most Equal Place on Earth)

Mayor Barry

It was Election Day again.

The day was dreary. Big dark clouds filled sky. The fading flag was barely lifted by the slight breeze in the air where it hung limply and forgotten from the pole. Kayla noticed it was the same flag that hung there during the last election, and the election before that too.

No one had bothered to change it again. No one seemed to care.

She also noticed there were no festive decorations hanging on Homeland Hall this year. In fact, she didn't see any of the red, white and blue patriotic decorations that were usually hung around town either. This time around there seemed to be a lot more plain old red signs and banners.[1] The red signs Kayla saw hanging around made her feel a little uncomfortable. Probably had something to do with the fact that a lot of those signs and flags had a clenched fist as the symbol in the middle. But the fist symbol made sense to Kayla because everyone seemed just so angry lately.

---

[1] "...the red so prominent in the Russian and Chinese flags today are believed to relate to the blood of the workers – that is, to honor the suffering and sacrifices of the proletariat."
Ghosh, Palash. "Why Is The Color Red Associated With Communism?" *International Business Times.* http://www.ibtimes.com/why-color-red-associated-communism-295185 Posted June 30, 2011. (Retrieved June 29, 2018)

When Election Day was over, Mr. Barry beat Mayor Franklin. It wasn't by a lot, only 50% of the town and a handful more voted for Mr. Barry, but it was enough.

Kayla asked her dad what he thought about everything.

"Well dear," he said, "Mr. Franklin and Mr. Woodrow had policies that made a lot of people depend on the government to survive. The economy started to suffer because of those policies. There just is not enough money available to pay for all of the things that they are promising, so the government had to start borrowing a lot of money. Now all of that borrowed money comes at a price in the form of interest. Remember interest?"

"Yes," Kayla said, "of course. It's what we have to pay to the people who lend us money in order to get them to lend us that money."

"That's right," her father said. "So that money we pay in interest comes right out of the people's pockets. The less money in your pocket means the less you have to spend on things that you need or want. That hurts people who produce the goods and services where you otherwise would have spent your money. That hurts our economy."

"Or we would just borrow more money to pay the interest," Kayla said.

"That's right."

"Unfortunately, Mr. Woodrow's and Mr. Franklin's answer wasn't to let free and independent people find the solutions needed to get the town's economy moving again, no, just the opposite." Kayla's dad said. "They believed it is the government's job to do that. They also believed it's the government's job to provide "relief" to those who needed it. Because he believed the government was the best solution to all of society's woes, Mr. Woodrow created the *Department of Welfare* that has as its main purpose to redistribute the wealth that others have created. He believed that to spread the taxpayer's money around by stealing it from one group of people to give to another was justified.[2] The problem all of that redistribution taught many people a very bad lesson, which is the government will be there to keep paying you no matter what.

"But he also didn't do those things solely because he wanted to help people. In order to get people to depend on him and the government, he abused the very welfare system he was setting up just to increase his grip on power. He did things like give out food stamps to people who didn't really need them, or he would pay people not to work, or he gave away "free" cell phones. Many people support him because they like getting those things so they would vote for him with the hope of getting more 'free' things from the government.

"But sometimes people did need help and now that the government controls welfare and charity they have nowhere else to

---

[2] Former President Barack Obama was quite open in his desire to use government force to take from some to give to others. He spoke openly of his desire to "spread the wealth around". See, for example, (https://youtu.be/OoqI5PSRcXM). Using government to "spread the wealth around" is inherently a form of totalitarianism since people are forced to comply under the threat of government force for failure to do so. For example, if you don't pay your Federal Income Tax (which is a massive wealth redistribution scheme) the Federal Government will seize your property and assets and possibly even jail you. Government "spreading the wealth around" is also a ploy by politicians to amass and keep power. This is accomplished by politicians stealing from some to give to others with the expectation the others will support those same politicians.

turn except to government, so people have become very used to receiving those 'benefits' and 'entitlements' from the government and now are dependent on them.

"Mr. Barry is smart, but in a bad way. He knew that all he had to do was make enough people believe that Mayor Franklin wanted to take those benefits away and it would go a long way to helping him win the election. It worked. Then he simply promised everyone he would keep the existing 'free' benefits in place and then give them even more 'free' things. People who depend on the government to live are more likely to vote for the person who will keep the 'free' things coming than the person they believe will take those 'free' things away."

"Notice," Kayla's dad said, "that he doesn't often talk about how the best way to get people out of poverty is to provide them with the opportunity and freedom to do so. When he does talk about it, it is always tied to some government program."

Kayla said, "I agree Dad. I think that by making it easier for people to create businesses, by reducing silly and unnecessary regulations, by reducing and limiting taxes so people can keep more of their own money, that all goes a long way towards helping people become more prosperous."

"The problem is," her dad said, "that many, many people now have gotten used to getting all of those 'free' things from the government. And sometimes they don't even have to work for it! A lot of the desire to work hard and take chances at being successful has been conditioned out of many people. Why work hard if the government is going to steal money from someone else and give it to you?"

Kayla agreed with her father.

"There is no doubt the economy is suffering as Mr. Barry takes office," Kayla's father said. "But his promise to everyone that he will do what it takes to make things better by getting the government more involved in the economy will not create jobs, it will only further people's suffering.

"Mayor Barry says that there were some things that need to happen though before things will get better. He says that rich people need to pay more in taxes. He says that the government needs this tax revenue in order to 'create jobs'. He says things like, 'We all have to pull together!' and, 'Does it make any sense for one person to make a lot of money and live in a nice house and drive a nice car while others aren't?' He believes things are much better when we spread the wealth around. So now we are going to change the income tax laws. Now, the more money you make the more you will pay! That is a 'fair' progressive income tax according to Mayor Barry!"[3]

Soon Kayla found out exactly what Mayor Barry thought was 'fair'. When it came time to pay her income tax she saw that now she had to give almost 2/3rds of her income to the government so the government could "spread it around"!

---

[3]Marx, Karl. "Manifesto of the Communist Party." Marxists.org.
https://www.marxists.org/archive/marx/works/1848/communist-manifesto/ch02.htm
(Retrieved April 13, 2018)

Mayor Barry said that what he was doing was nothing more than bringing "social justice" to society. He said that it was important to remember that because we all lived in the same community it was important that we share as much as possible.

Kayla didn't mind sharing because she was always a very generous person. What she didn't like was the government *forcing* her to share!

One of the earliest things Mayor Barry did when he took office was to change the name of Homeland Hall. During a speech he said, "In honor of the workers of Jefferson Township, those who toil day in and day out to make this a better community and homeland for us all, we are changing the name of Homeland Hall to Worker's Hall! And yes! We will build the most equal society on earth!"

Then, Mayor Barry announced that he was keeping Police Chief Bernie on the job. He also announced that Police Chief Bernie would be spending even more time and money taking care of the "troublemakers".

The next day a mob of union thugs attacked a bunch of small businesses in town.[4] It seems those businesses recently had

---

[4] "A little over a month ago, in a case that drew national attention, a man was targeted at his home, shot and injured, all because he dared to run union free business. Now, in Buffalo, New York, a case involving outrageous allegations of labor-racketeering and union violence aimed at non-union construction workers and company owners is proceeding through the judicial process. Its outcome, however, may have wide-ranging ramifications on a national level. Forget for a moment that a man was stabbed in the throat, hot coffee thrown on non-union workers, sand put into gas tanks and a woman threatened with sexual assault. Forget the fact that the judge presiding over the federal racketeering case against Operating Engineers, Local 22, in Buffalo, NY ultimately rejected the AFL-CIO's attempt to file a amicus brief, the sheer fact that the national AFL-CIO even attempted to intervene speaks volumes..."
Workplace Report. "The AFL-CIO Defends Union Violence As A 'Legitimate' Union Activity,

union organizing elections which the union lost. This made the unions mad. As they smashed the windows and threw Molotov cocktails into the shattered storefronts, the mob started a chant:

"Hey ho…greedy pigs have got to go!"

A masked demonstrator stood on top of an overturned car and was yelling into a bullhorn, "It's time for a revolution!"

And what did Police Chief Bernie's police force do?

Nothing.

The next day a reporter asked Chief Bernie why he didn't take care of the "troublemakers" who were burning down stores as he had promised.

Chief Bernie replied, "If by 'troublemakers' you mean the protesters, I let them express their freedom of speech!"[5]

Incredulous the reporter asked, "How is violence freedom of speech? You lied when you said you would take care of the troublemakers."

"No, I didn't!" snapped Chief Bernie. "The troublemakers are the greedy business owners. They're the ones who caused trouble

Will The Dept. of Labor Do It Too?" *Red State*. https://www.redstate.com/diary/laborunionreport/2011/09/22/the-afl-cio-defends-union-violence-as-a-legitimate-union-activity-will-the-dept-of-labor-do-it-too/ Posted September 22, 2011. (Retrieved November 16, 2017)
[5] Chuck, Elizabeth. "Baltimore Mayor Stephanie Rawlings-Blake Under Fire For 'Space' to Destroy Comment." *NBC News*. http://www.nbcnews.com/storyline/baltimore-unrest/mayor-stephanie-rawlings-blake-under-fire-giving-space-destroy-baltimore-n349656 Posted April 28, 2015. (Retrieved June 5, 2017)

by their reckless pursuit of selfish profits! They got what was coming to them. The chickens came home to roost!" [6]

The Chief had the complete backing of the Mayor because the Mayor intended on using the unions as one of his tools to gain more power for himself and the government. He saw the unions as a big part of his effort to "transform" society. Mayor Barry intended to use the unions as part of his plans for building his Socialist "Utopia". [7]

Mayor Barry knew that public sector unions especially would be in his back pocket. He knew he could rely on them to support him and his policies because public sector unions needed public money to survive. The more people he could get employed by the government, would mean more public sector union members. More public sector union members who would be earning pay from the public treasury. A portion of that pay would go to pay their union dues. Those union dues overwhelmingly went to support politicians like Mayor Barry. Mayor Barry knew union members, especially public sector union members, would overwhelmingly vote

[6]ABC News. "Reverend Wright Transcript From 'The Day of Jerusalem's Fall' 9/16/2001". *ABC News.* http://abcnews.go.com/Blotter/story?id=4719157 Posted April 25, 2008. (Retrieved June 5, 2017)

[7]"And so there was a whole wave of people, myself included, that went into workplaces, if we weren't already there, as a way of organizing to rebuild a vibrant labor movement and to lay the foundation for a working-class-based radical political movement that would, hopefully, result in the construction of a new political party of the socialist Left." Richman, Shaun and Fletcher, Bill, Jr. "What the Revival of Socialism in America Means for the Labor Movement." Inthesetimes.com. Posted October 9, 2017. http://inthesetimes.com/working/entry/20587/labor-movement-workers-socialism-united-states (Retrieved March 13, 2018)
"About Bill Fletcher Jr." BillFletcherJr.com. "He has worked for several labor unions in addition to serving as a senior staffperson in the national AFL-CIO." http://billfletcherjr.com/ (Retrieved March 13, 2018)
Here we have a great example of how unions in many cases are nothing more than a breeding ground for Socialist radicals. Fletcher is a Socialist who is using the unions to push a Socialist agenda.

for him and people like him because they were the ones who kept the money flowing to them!

It didn't take Mayor Barry long to start his plans for "spreading the wealth around".

He ordered the police to seize all the major means of production and put them under the control and ownership of the government.[8] Going forward the government would run all of the factories.[9] Literally overnight businesses, companies, and people had their property and livelihood stolen from them by the government.[10] When some of the factory owners refused to leave their factories, Mayor Barry had the police drag them out and arrest them. Chief Bernie was more than happy to do it!

One of Mayor Barry's next moves was a further assault on the Free Market and Liberty.

He declared that no longer would the free market or demand and supply determine what is produced and what isn't. Instead, everything, toilet paper, cars, shoes, milk, bread... everything, would now be produced according to a "central plan".

---

[8] Krisher, Tom and Goodman, Joshua. "GM latest U.S. company to have assets seized in Venezuela." Mercurynews.com. www.mercurynews.com/2017/04/20/gm-latest-u-s-company-to-have-assets-seized-in-venezuela/ Posted April 20, 2017 Updated 11:32 AM. (Retrieved April 8, 2018)

[9] Sanchez, Fabiola. "Venezuela's socialist leaders seize bakeries as country's 'bread war' escalates" www.Independent.co.uk. Posted March 21, 201714:07GMT. (Retrieved April 8, 2018) https://www.independent.co.uk/news/world/americas/venezuela-bread-war-socialist-leaders-bakeries-seized-economic-crisis-hyper-inflation-currency-flour-a7641756.html

[10] Wyss, Jim. "Venezuelan government controls more than 500 businesses — and most are losing money" Miami Herald.com. www.miamiherald.com/news/nation-world/world/americas/venezuela/article138402248.html#storylink=cpy. Posted March 14, 2017 Updated 5:43 PM. (Retrieved April 8, 2018)

Mayor Barry said, "Our teams of expert government economists will be able to tell the factories what to produce. This will be exactly what the people need based on very scientific and precise calculations! This will ensure that the necessities of life are available for everyone!"

When Kayla got home, she called her father and asked him how he felt about this whole "planned economy".

"Well," he said, "take your lemonade, how did you know how much to charge for a bottle of lemonade when the government wasn't involved and you could charge whatever you wanted?"

"I charged what people were willing to pay for it," she answered.

"Explain to me how that work," he said.

"OK," Kayla said. "I'll try."

"I have to set a price that I believe will make my bottle of lemonade more valuable than a certain amount of money someone has in their pocket. If a person has five dollars in their pocket, do I believe they will find my bottle of lemonade more valuable to them than the five dollars? Well, it depends. If they were very, very, thirsty they might. But usually they wouldn't."

"And how do you know that", her father asked.

"Because, for one," Kayla said, "I checked to see what similar bottles of beverages cost. That helps me to start to set my price. Most similar beverages cost around $1.50 a bottle. So, I know that chances are they probably wouldn't spend $5 on my bottle of lemonade."

"Keep going," her father said.

"But I market my lemonade as a premium product so I figured I could charge more than the $1.50 everyone else charges, because I think people will be willing to pay more for my premium lemonade. So, I first set my price at $1.75 a bottle."

"And what happened?"

"Oh, it was great!" Kayla said. "I couldn't keep it on the shelf! In fact, it sold so well I started to run out of it. I had empty shelves in my stores which wasn't good!"

"What did you do?"

"I hired more people and began to make more. At first, even with making more, I still had trouble keeping it on the shelf. So, I decided to raise the price to $2 a bottle."

"And then what happened?"

"It still kept flying off the shelf and I still had trouble keeping it in stock!"

"Then what?"

"I couldn't physically produce more based on the capacity of my factory so I raised the price to $2.50 a bottle."

"And what happened?"

"Well, sales slowed down. In fact, they slowed down to the point that I started to accumulate a surplus of the product in my storage rooms."

"Then what did you do?"

"I knew that $2.50 a bottle was too much to charge. Customers decided that their $2.50 was worth more to them than a bottle of lemonade. So, I developed a surplus of the product in my stores. I also knew $2 bottle wasn't enough to charge because I had shortages. So, I set the price at $2.25 a bottle."

"And what happened?"

"Equilibrium."

"What do you mean?"

"I found the best price that people were willing to pay which also kept my factory running at peak performance and enabled me to make the biggest profit I can from a bottle of lemonade."

"So why won't a planned economy work? No matter how smart the people are who are planning it?" her father asked.

"Because how do you know what to produce unless you can kind of figure out what people want to buy? A government planner can say, 'Black shoes were very popular last year. Let's make a million more this year.' But what if no one wants black shoes anymore? Then you made a million extra shoes for nothing. It's wasteful."[11]

---

[11] "Under central planning, there is no profit-and-loss system of accounting to accurately

"That's right," her father said. "That's what's great about a Free Market economy. It allows for the creation of goods and services that people want or desire. Then the people's wants and desires help the producers set prices they can charge for those goods and services. It's impossible for a planned economy to ever do that. Usually in a planned economy, you have chronic shortages of one thing and huge waste of another. It's one of the reasons it's so hard to find any toilet paper nowadays."

"Socialism," her father went on, "is a big lie. And it causes misery for the people existing under its oppressive system. So much misery that people will risk their lives to run away from it."[12]

In another speech Mayor Barry said that it was not right that people were making profits from things that really should belong to everyone. He said that people who made a profit from such essential necessities in life like the railroads or the electric company were selfish and greedy. He said, "...these are things that the community needs and no one should be able to make a profit from them!" He said they belonged to "the people" and from that point on he was taking over those businesses "for the people". "Of course," he said, "the people are represented by the government so in essence the government will be running those businesses in the name of the people."

---

measure the success or failure of various programs. Without profits, there is no way to discipline firms that fail to serve the public interest and no way to reward firms that do. There is no efficient way to determine which programs should be expanded and which ones should be contracted or terminated." See: Perry, Mark J. "Why Socialism Failed". *Foundation for Economic Freedom*. https://fee.org/articles/why-socialism-failed/ Posted May 31, 1995. (Retrieved May 21, 2018)

[12] Knight, Robert. "Socialism's Predictable Outcomes." The Washington Times. https://www.washingtontimes.com/news/2017/nov/19/socialisms-history-shows-it-delivers-misery-murder/. Posted November 19, 2017. (Retrieved May 5, 2018)

Kayla knew this would only end up bad as well. Take the railroad. Jefferson Township's commuter railroad was always a privately owned, for profit business. The trains ran on time, the stations were clean and fares were reasonable. As a for profit business it was in the best interest of the railroad to provide a great service that people would pay to use.

There were other communities that had commuter railroads run by the government. Compared to Jefferson Township's railroad they were a mess. Most of them were in financial trouble because of waste, corruption and huge, very expensive union labor costs. Stations and trains were dirty, service was expensive, but the service people received was poor. There was no incentive to fix the issues because, being a government run entity, the politicians simply raised taxes and fares to cover the never-ending financial shortfalls. And the only ones who suffered were the average citizens who used the railroad. They were the ones who had to bear the burden of increasing fares and taxes.[13]

Now Mayor Barry was going to bring the same misery to the commuters in Jefferson Township.

Then Mayor Barry said that it was not right that some people were making a profit from earth's natural resources. Again, he said these things belonged to everyone and in the name of "the people"; he was going have the government take over those

[13] Gelinas, Nicole. "The MTA's Escalating Cost Crisis." Manhattan-institute.org. https://www.manhattan-institute.org/sites/default/files/IB-NG-0717.pdf . July 26, 2017. (Retrieved May 4, 2018)
Also see from the NY Daily News. A far left newspaper in New York:
Otis, Ginger Adams. "MTA is losing money and headed to financial disaster, despite attempts to find revenue." NYDailyNews.com. http://www.nydailynews.com/new-york/mta-losing-money-headed-financial-ruin-article-1.2202720. Posted April 28, 2015. (Retrieved May 4, 2018)

businesses that "exploited" the earth for profit. Overnight the Spring Water guy who Kayla bought her water from lost his business to the government. The fuel companies which drilled for oil as well.

Kayla knew this was a big problem in the making as well. Take the spring water guy for example. It was in his best interest to make sure that he always had good, clean water to sell to his customers. Because of that he took great pains and spent a lot of money on taking care of the environment around his water sources. He planted forests full of trees and took great care to ensure that his land wasn't polluted. He also supported many different water conservation efforts to ensure the sustainability of having good, clean water available. And not just on his land because he knew if his neighbor polluted the ground it could affect everyone, including his spring water sources. He fought hard to make sure polluters were punished and the environment remained clean. Not to mention the fact that the areas around his spring water sources were areas where animals, plants and people thrived. Yes, he made a profit from the natural resource, but that profit was one of his biggest incentives to spend a lot of money on making sure the environment was kept clean and unpolluted. And that benefitted everyone.

Kayla knew that in a society where individual liberty is treasured, pollution is seen a threat to that liberty. If I am a company that pollutes the air or water around me, that affects others. It causes a potential violation of their life as well as their liberty, and in a free, non-violent society, that is unacceptable. Being free doesn't mean free to pollute and poison the world around you. In Kayla's eyes it is one of the very few times that a government could use force against you. By using the legal system for example. If your neighbor pollutes your land you can sue him in a court of law and the judge can order some form of punishment and fines on the polluter because pollution affects others Life, Liberty and Property.

Kayla had always taken great care of her lemon tree orchard, for example, because she needed the trees to remain healthy and the land to remain unpolluted. The orchard provided her with the resources she needed to run her business which in turn created jobs for people so it was in her best interests that her natural resources thrived. Her profit motive ensured that she would always take care of the things that helped her to create those profits whether it was her lemon trees or her employees.

The system in Jefferson Township gave the government just enough power to force polluters to stop polluting and to force those polluters to pay restitution to those who were negatively impacted by their negligent actions. The system did not however allow the government unchecked power to use "protecting the environment" as a way to interfere with people's freedom and right to the pursuit of happiness.

But what happens when all incentives to maintain a good stewardship of the environment are gone? What if the government owns the land and runs the legal system? What if the government owns the land and pollutes it? Who do you sue in court then?

When government holds all the cards you can't win. And that is what Mayor Barry was doing by seizing all of the companies which sold natural resources to make a profit. Now the government could do whatever it wanted on, or to, that land it seized and the average citizen wouldn't be able to do a thing about it.[14]

Kayla was stunned by what was happening to her community. Freedom and Liberty were dying and she felt helpless to stop it. And her business was dying as well. Not because of anything she had done. It was dying because politicians were using government to interfere in what it was she did best...government was destroying her ability to freely create jobs, and in a broader sense government was destroying everyone's ability to be free. Why were the politicians doing this?

Because they could.

Kayla knew it was human nature to seek to dominate others. Throughout history, man had used government to carry out this desire to dominate. What made Jefferson Township so special was this inherent need to dominate others was kept in check by the rule of law. Government was given only very specific functions and power to exercise over individuals. Everything else was left to the people. It was accepted that people have Natural Rights, and that a government's sole purpose is to secure an individual person's right to Life, Liberty, and Property.[15] Unfortunately, over time people in

---

[14] DiLorenzo, Thomas J. "Why Socialism Causes Pollution." Foundation for Economic Education. https://fee.org/articles/why-socialism-causes-pollution/. Posted March 1, 1992. (Retrieved May 4, 2018)

[15] "A number of times throughout history, tyranny has stimulated breakthrough thinking about liberty. This was certainly the case in England with the mid-seventeenth-century era of repression, rebellion, and civil war. There was a tremendous outpouring of political pamphlets and tracts. By far the most influential writings emerged from the pen of scholar John Locke.
He expressed the radical view that government is morally obliged to serve people, namely by protecting life, liberty, and property. He explained the principle of checks and balances to limit government power. He favored representative government and a rule of law. He denounced tyranny. He insisted that when government violates individual rights, people may legitimately rebel.

Jefferson Township seemed to have lost their faith in themselves as individuals. They had been slowly indoctrinated by politicians in government to believe that they could only be successful, or safe, or prosperous, with the help of the government.

Kayla's father told her, "Many people do not seem to hold the belief anymore that they have the right to alter or rid themselves of any government that no longer protects an individual's Natural Rights. Many people seem to have forgotten that the government gets its just powers from us, the people, and by our consent only. People have become too comfortable with the government simply taking whatever power it wants from us. In fact, most citizens don't even know what Natural Rights are."

Kayla and her family knew truth did not disappear. It is always there waiting to be discovered, but that act of discovery takes work. She was beginning to realize; however, many people had unfortunately become too lazy to seek the truth, or too conditioned not to. Also, many times when people did know the truth, they were too comfortable, or too scared, or too much a part of the system to do the hard work that is necessary to stay free.

Freedom was dying also because politicians were using the government to transform and condition society into one in which people no longer thought and fought for themselves, or what was right. In fact, "right" and "wrong" were now terms whose meanings were irrelevant. Their definitions were left up to whoever had the power to say what they meant. Right and wrong, good and evil,

These views were most fully developed in Locke's famous Second Treatise Concerning Civil Government..." Powell. Jim. "John Locke: Natural Rights to Life, Liberty, and Property." *Foundation for Economic Education.* https://fee.org/articles/john-locke-natural-rights-to-life-liberty-and-property/ Posted August 1 1996. (Retrieved May 21, 2018) were at one time based in a spiritual faith in which an individual believed in a higher moral being who helped a person determine how to act towards others. Mostly rooted in a philosophy of, "do to others as you would have them do to you"[16]. Now for many, particularly the Progressives, Socialists and Fascists, the State, or the government, had become that higher moral being.

And what is the State? Kayla thought. "The State" is nothing more than a limited earth-bound entity born out of the minds of men; it is not of a higher being. Kayla also knew that when a State enacts laws that curtail a person's Natural Rights, those laws are immoral and wrong, and one should ultimately feel empowered to resist them. With the form of resistance depending on the situation.

For example, if during a time of war, a President decides that a group of people cannot be trusted solely because of their race, and then decides to illegally confiscate their property and forcibly drive them from their homes to be relocated in an internment camp,[17] do not those people have the right to resist? Forcibly if necessary?

Or, what if the government decides a group of people living together in peace are a threat, although they have shown no signs of being one? What if the government then says that they are "religious fanatics", (as if the government has the right to decide that)? What then if the government seeks to forcibly deny some of those people of their Life, Liberty or Property, based on trumped up charges? What then if the government uses extreme and

---

[16] "Luke 6:31 NIV." biblestudytools.com. https://www.biblestudytools.com/luke/6-31.html (Retrieved May 1, 2018)
[17] "Japanese Relocation During World War II." www.archives.gov. https://www.archives.gov/education/lessons/japanese-relocation (Retrieved May 1, 2018)

unnecessary violent force against those people which results in the deaths of many, including children?[18] Shouldn't the government be held accountable?

But that is what Kayla saw happening to her beloved Jefferson Township. It was becoming a place of unchecked power in the hands of a politician, with the consent and appeasement of those being ruled.

It was once a town where the people lived by the creed that respect for Life, Liberty and Property allowed people to pursue their own happiness. They had now become a society based on War, Oppression and Plunder.

The government was constantly "at war" with something...drugs, poverty, social injustice...you name it. If the politicians thought they could get something out of it for themselves, rest assure they would "declare war" against it. And during those "wars" they invariably needed to take special emergency actions to fight that "war". Typically, these emergency powers and action the government took led to a further suppression of Liberty and oppression of the people. And how did they fund all of this? By plundering the property of others of course. Whether through heavy taxation or the printing of more debt, which was essentially a plundering of the wealth and economic security of future generations.

Kayla thought about her lemon tree grove. The place which she bought with her hard-earned money to supply the lemons for

---

[18] Steigerwald, Lucy. "Paramount's 'Waco' Finally Gives The Branch Davidians Their Due." The Federalist. http://thefederalist.com/2018/02/26/paramounts-waco-finally-gives-branch-davidians-due/. Posted February 26, 2018. (Retrieved May 4, 2018)

her lemonade. Weren't lemons a "natural resource"? She wondered how long it would be before someone from the government came for her lemon trees.

It wasn't long at all.

One morning soon after the election Kayla was down in her lemon tree grove. She loved to go there a lot. Not just because it smelled so great with all of those lemons around, but because she was proud of it. Proud of the fact that she was able to have bought this land with her own money. Money that she had earned fairly and legally. She was also proud of the fact that she was able to employ so many people in her lemon grove.

When Kayla drove through the gates of her lemon grove the people who worked there all waved and smiled at her. She waved and smiled back and said "hello" to everyone by name. To her, this place was like home, the people who worked there were like family.

Kayla drove through the gate and parked her car alongside the barn which was built by a local construction company which created jobs for that construction company. The barn was used to store and process the lemons which were gathered from the fields. A barn, by the way, which also created a bunch of jobs for the people in the town because it had to be maintained on a regular basis. Kayla hired a local cleaning company who would come and clean it every night. Kayla also hired a local construction company to keep up the maintenance on the building. They would do things like paint the walls, fix things that broke and clear the debris in the winter. All of these things were jobs created for people because of Kayla's lemonade business.

No sooner had Kayla gotten out of her car when she looked towards the gate and noticed a big dust cloud approaching her. She hadn't even seen the other car follow her in.

Suddenly a big black SUV appeared coming at her at a pretty quick speed. For a second she thought for sure the thing was going to hit her. Instead in it swerved over next to her car, shooting up dust and pebbles as it came to a stop.

The windows on it were tinted so black she couldn't see in. Its clean black paint job glimmered in the sun and was a stark contrast to her own dusty pick-up truck. She could see through its windshield a stone-faced man sitting behind the steering wheel. He had sunglasses on and barely seemed to acknowledge that Kayla was standing right in front of him. Not knowing what else to do she gave a tentative half wave to know one in particular in the car.

For a few seconds nothing happened. Kayla stood there trying to figure out what was going on. One of her employees, a man named Rafael, noticed the commotion, and came over to her side.

"What is this Ms. Kayla?" he asked in a thick Spanish accent.

"I don't know," she said.

Instinctively the hair on the back of Rafael's neck stood up. He didn't want to say anything to alarm Ms. Kayla but he could guess exactly what was going on. The town had just elected a Socialist as the Mayor, much to Rafael's dismay. He had seen this before in his homeland when he was a just a boy. When his homeland had decided to embrace the lies of Socialism.

His home country had once been a vibrant, bustling, rich country. The people there enjoyed one of the highest standards of living in the area, fueled by immense income generated from crude oil production. But all of that went away once the Socialists took over. Now people back home eat garbage to survive.[19]

He thought back to the day when the government in his homeland came to his father's small piece of land that his family had farmed for generations. He remembered how they too got out of their big government vehicles.

He remembered how they had told his father that his land, the land he owned...the land he worked...the land he provided for his family with.... that that land was no longer his. That the land now belonged to the *State*.

Rafael remembers that his father was a proud man. That his father said to these strangers that they could not take his land. That they had no right. The rest was blurry for Rafael after that. He remembered flashes of his father pushing the government man and another government man hitting his father in the face with the butt of his rifle. He remembered the blood.

He remembers his father falling to his knees.

---

[19] Martell. Frances. "Venezuela: Over 15% of People Eat Garbage to Survive." *Breitbart*. http://www.breitbart.com/national-security/2016/09/18/venezuela-15-percent-eat-garbage-survival/ Posted September 18, 2016. (Retrieved May 21, 2018)

He remembers the government man with the gun going over to his father, who was still on his knees on the ground, on HIS ground, on MY ground...

How the man with the gun bent over and put his arm around his father's shoulder and started to whisper something in his ear. How his father grew silent as both him and the government man with the gun looked over at young Rafael. How his father slowly nodded his head and was slowly helped up by the man with the gun.

Then the government men got in their truck and drove away.

Rafael remembered how his father came over to him and told him that everything was OK. That it was just a misunderstanding. Rafael's' father told him that from now on he wouldn't have to worry so much about keeping up with his family's farm. That the government was going to help him run things. That from now on he would be a "partner" with the government and instead of worrying all the time about making a profit to support his family, that now, his father would work for the government as an employee.

Rafael didn't quite understand at the time what was going on, he was so young, but he did know that from that day forward things were different. He father was not so proud anymore. His father seemed broken after that. Not too long after that his father died. He had taken to drinking a lot and was known to wander around town late at night complaining about how the government had stolen his farm. How the government had taken everything from him.

One morning they found his father dead in the gutter. He had been shot and had bled out in the gutter among the trash and sewer water. No one helped him. And of course, no one saw who did it. But since the government had taken away everyone's guns and the only people who could own a gun was members of the government, Rafael had a pretty good idea of who had killed his father.

Rafael's' uncle, his father's brother, came by his house late one night and took him and his sister away to Jefferson County where they have lived ever since.

Now, standing here in the driveway of Ms. Kayla's farm all of these years later, Rafael felt like he was living a nightmare all over again.

Before Rafael could finish that thought the doors of the SUV opened up and three men got out. A chill ran down his spine.

"Ms. Kayla Alexander? Are you Ms. Kayla Alexander?" one of them asked.

"Yes, I am," she said.

"Why hello Ms. Alexander!" the man who got out from the passenger's side of the SUV said with all of the happiness and smiles he could muster in a phrase. "It's a great day today!" he said.

Kayla tried her best to remain calm and smiled back at the pasty-skinned man in khaki pants, and red polo shirt. But she was only half looking at him. Over the pasty skinned man's shoulder the two other guys who got out of the SUV took up a position just behind him. They weren't visibly carrying guns but their jackets had bulges in them and both of them had their hands up and just inside their zippers.

"And why is that?" she asked.

"Because today is the day you get to be true patriot and give back to your community!" Pasty man said.

"Because now this lemon tree grove and all of its natural beauty and splendor gets to be used not for evil profits...but for the good of the people! Because Lemon trees are a natural resource and no one should be able to own a natural resource!"

Kayla felt something she had never felt before take hold in her stomach and make its way up her chest and into her heart...and her throat. It was a burning, choking feeling. It made her face turn red and her hands shake. It made her eyes narrow into slits and teeth clench down. It was rage.

But Kayla felt a hand grab hers. She looked over into the eyes of Rafael and knew she could not do that. She knew she had to stay in control.

"Of course," Kayla said, "a patriot."

The pasty skinned man hesitated for a second. For a split second he felt a flash of abject terror. He saw a look splash across the eyes of this girl in front of him that caused his heart to skip a beat. At that moment he was very grateful for the two, armed men with him. He was also grateful that a few years ago all of the guns had been taken from the people. After all, it's the government's job to defend and protect people. People cannot be trusted, only the government can.

"So..." Pasty skinned man continued, "...here is a letter from the government that says this land now belongs to the people." He handed Kayla the letter.

"Going forward anyone who works here is now an employee of the government," Pasty skinned man said.

"As for you Ms. Alexander, you may continue to purchase lemons from the farm at a price set by the government," he said. "This will ensure that profiteering does not occur."

"The government also needs access to all of your business records. From here we will head to your main office and collect whatever material we need." Pasty skinned man and his bodyguards turned to get back into the SUV.

"But..." Kayla said, "...this will destroy my business."

Pasty skinned man stopped and looked back at Kayla.

"Probably," he said. "But let's face it, you had it coming. All of that greedy profit you made, all of that selfishness. It was only a matter of time. Now the people will control your lemon tree grove through the government because, after all, the government represents the people."

With that he got in the SUV and drove away.

Kayla could do nothing but cry.

Rafael tried to console her. He took her by her hand and led her just inside the big barn where the lemons were brought after being harvested. Kayla loved coming in here. The smell of lemon in the air made her always feel happy. She sat down on a stack of wooden crates.

"Listen Ms. Kayla," Rafael said ", everyone who works here loves you. You gave us all jobs that helped us to provide for our families. You treated us with dignity and respect, paid us fairly, and helped us all to value ourselves as people. Because of you and your business, you changed many people's lives for the better. But things are going to be different now. What happened today was just the beginning. You need to understand that and you need to be prepared for it. Once the will of the people to be free has been broken, the chains wrapped around them by the powerful begin to get pulled tighter and tighter."

Kayla knew that what Rafael said was right. Little by little, the people of Jefferson Township have been changing. Incredibly, being free seemed to be just too hard for some people. Blaming others was easy. Taking from others became acceptable. The opportunity to be as successful as you could be had always been a key part of what Jefferson Township was all about. Self-reliance, independence...Liberty, was the soul of the town. But the people let their guard down. They allowed others to teach them that being dependent on government was o.k. They allowed others to teach them that someone else knew what was better for them and their family. That they weren't smart enough to think for themselves. That they *needed* things from others. That any success they had wasn't because of their own hard work, dedication and brains. No, they were told that their success was only possible because of others. And the sad thing is, many actually believed it.

Kayla then took the time to walk around what was until a few minutes ago, her lemon tree grove. She wanted to talk to as many of her employees as she could. She wanted them to hear from her what happened.

The whole time Kayla walked around Rafael was by her side. He would translate what Kayla was saying to those who didn't understand her English too well. People cried, people grabbed her hand and looked into her eyes and said thank you. Kayla did her best to be strong but by the time she was speaking to the last few people she was in tears as well.

At the end she hugged Rafael and got in her truck and drove away. She knew he was right. Things were going to get much worse and she needed to be ready. She didn't want to leave Jefferson Township, it was the only home she ever knew. But she knew if she was going to stay she needed to be strong, and smart.

The next day Kayla went for a walk to try to gather her thoughts. She wound up walking all the way into town. She couldn't believe what had become of her beloved Jefferson Township. All up and down Main Street once again there were closed and boarded up stores. Many were damaged when the unions were causing trouble against union free businesses. The business owners either couldn't afford to fix things up anymore, or they simply had given up. Deciding it just wasn't worth the hard work anymore.

It was shocking because not so long-ago business had started to make a comeback in the town. It was a government-debt fueled comeback built on a foundation of wet mud, but businesses had started to open again and the streets were getting cleaned up. Kayla was startled by the fact that she actually started to feel a longing to have the previous Mayor back! He was a tyrant but at least the streets were clean and people had jobs! She quickly shook these thoughts from head, and forced herself to think even further back, to when she had opened her very first lemonade stand in front of City Hall as a kid. She felt a warmness in her mind as she remembered just how free they all were. Then she felt a pit in her stomach when she realized that even for just a brief few seconds she actually thought fondly of the last Mayor. She felt a sense of hopelessness because if someone like her, someone who was keenly aware of just how bad things had gotten, that if someone like her whose entire life was systematically being destroyed by the government, if someone like her could think fondly of the government, even for a second, then all may very well be lost. Because if she could think that way, someone who lived to experience all that Freedom and Liberty provided, just imagine how lost the people are who never knew what Kayla lived and experienced. Those people who never saw true freedom.

It would take a miracle to change things now.

As Kayla continued walking, lost in thought, she noticed there were people out and about. Most were on foot or riding bikes, owning a car had become a luxury not many could afford anymore.[20]

No one looked happy. Quite a few were pushing shopping carts piled high with scrap metal, bags of empty bottles. What bothered Kayla the most was when she saw two people fighting over some scraps one of them had pulled from a garbage can.

As she was pondering what she was seeing she was almost knocked down by a man running down the street carrying a big box. The young man bumped into her and spun to a stop.

"Hey lady I'm sorry, I didn't see you!"

Kayla shook it off, "It's ok."

At that moment a few more people ran by carrying boxes. "What's going on?" She asked the young man.

The guy smiled and said, "Mayor Barry said that the electronics store was charging too high prices that no one can afford to buy anything from them anymore. He ordered the store to start giving stuff away for almost nothing!"[21]

"Nothing?"

---

[20] "Private car ownership has been limited in Cuba since the 1959 revolution…"
"Cuba's treasure trove of 1950s U.S. cars." *USA Today*. https://www.usatoday.com/picture-gallery/money/cars/2014/12/18/cubas-treasure-trove-of-1950s-us-cars/20548357/ (Retrieved June 19, 2017)
[21] "Venezuela's President Nicolás Maduro intensified his perceived fight Monday against 'bourgeois parasites' he accuses of an economic war against the socialist country by threatening to force more stores to sell their merchandise at cut-rate prices.
National guardsmen, some of whom had assault rifles, were positioned around outlets of an electronics chain that Maduro has ordered to lower prices or face prosecution. Thousands of people lined up at the Daka stores hoping for a bargain after the government forced the companies to charge 'fair' prices."
Gupta, Girish. "Venezuela vows to take other stores in attack on retailers: Venezuela vows to take other stores in attack on retailers." *USA Today*. https://www.usatoday.com/story/news/world/2013/11/11/venezuela-seizes-stores/3497003/ Posted November 11, 2013. (Retrieved June 13, 2018)

"Almost nothing," he corrected her. He said, "You better get yours while you can!"

"But what about the store owner?" Kayla asked.

The young man looked confused.

"What happened to the store owner?" Kayla asked.

A smile crossed the man's face, "Who cares?" he said and turned to start running away again.

At that moment, Kayla knew that *Grandmas Old-Fashioned Lemonade* was essentially dead.

****

In the months after Pasty Skinned Man had shown up at the lemon tree grove representatives of the government were sent to Kayla's business to help manage it "in the name of the people". None of them seemed to know what they were doing. Many of them were given the job simply because they knew someone in government or were closely connected to Mr. Barry's political party.

Technically, Kayla still owned her retail stores, the few she had left, but she couldn't do anything in them without permission from the government. Just about every business decision she wanted to make had to have approval from one of the khaki pants-polo shirt wearing government agents who continued to visit her frequently.

She made what the government told her to make and sold it for what price the government said to sell it for. Inflation was out of control and people had a hard time buying anything because they simply weren't making enough money anymore to pay the inflated prices.[22] Mayor Barry responded by doubling and then tripling the minimum wage. But prices kept rising and this did nothing but make the currency even more worthless. The government's actions destroyed Kayla's business and she finally wound up closing all of her stores but one.

As far as her factory was concerned, being it was a "means of production", it had been seized by Mayor Barry's government at the start of his reign like all other manufacturing business.

At home things weren't much better. She managed to hang on to her house up to this point, but it was getting harder and harder to do so. At one point in the distant past she had managed to save a lot of money. She had a nice retirement nest egg and was even able to have a pretty sizeable portfolio of investments. Now, all of that was gone. Inflation had decimated her personal finances. She had to liquidate her retirement account and investment portfolio to keep her house. When that wasn't enough she had to start selling her personal belongings. Furniture, clothes, jewelry, almost everything. Who did she sell most of it to? People connected to the government of course. They seemed to be doing just fine.

Things got steadily worse in Jefferson County as well.

---

[22] Zerpa, Fabiola. "Venezuelan Hyper Inflation Explodes, Soaring Over 440,000 Percent." *Bloomberg*. https://www.bloomberg.com/news/articles/2018-01-18/venezuelan-hyperinflation-explodes-soaring-over-440-000-percent Posted January 18, 2018. (Retrieved May 21, 2018)

It seemed like every week Mayor Barry accelerated his policy of having the government assume control over the businesses in town. First starting with the large ones. The big supermarket in town was his first target. Mayor Barry said the owner of the supermarket was "price gouging" people and that from this day forward the government would be running the supermarket. When the owner of the supermarket protested, he was locked up by Chief Bernie's police for being an "agitator" and a "parasite".

At one time, the supermarket had been a great place to be. You could find almost every food you wanted there. The shelves were always stocked with items, the food was always fresh, and the prices were reasonable. Kayla used to be so proud every time she walked into that store because right up front was always a big display of *Grandma's Old-Fashioned Lemonade*.

Not too long after the government took over the market Kayla went there to buy some things she needed. Just some milk and toilet paper.

When she got there, she saw a huge line waiting outside the store waiting to get in. Most of the people waiting on line looked tired and hungry. Some were pushing old shopping carts and some people were just pulling little kiddie wagons.

The store itself didn't look anything like it used look. It used to be well lit and clean. The parking lot was always full of nice cars. There used to be aisle after aisle of stocked shelves and happy people. Every register had someone working it, ringing up the lines of people who waited there with shopping carts overflowing with goods.

Now the parking lot had hardly any cars in it at all. Except the big black SUV that sat with its engine running far off in the corner, the lot was mostly empty. Most people had walked here being that owning a car was now beyond the reach of owning for most people now.

The store itself was in bad shape. Half the letters on the sign on top of the building weren't lit anymore and most of them lost their fronts so all you saw were the dead light bulbs inside.

Kayla could not see inside the store anymore because all of the windows were covered up with brown paper. She asked a hunched over old woman at the back of the line what was going on. "We heard they got toilet paper in," she said. "They haven't had it for weeks so I figured I better get here to get some."

Since the government had taken over all of the means of production and had started taking over businesses in town, shortages seemed to be common. It was becoming harder and harder to find the necessities of life. Not just toilet paper...soap, bread, shoes...everything that was needed seemed to be in short supply.[23]

Mayor Barry didn't blame his "centrally planned economy". He would never acknowledge the fact that an economy is too big and too dynamic of a thing to be planned. He would never admit that supply and demand and the free exchange of goods and

---

[23] "Socialism is the Big Lie of the Twentieth century. While it promised prosperity, equality, and security, it delivered poverty, misery, and tyranny. Equality was achieved only in the sense that everyone was equal in his or her misery."
Perry, Mark J. "Why Socialism Failed." *Foundation for Economic Education.*
https://fee.org/articles/why-socialism-failed/ Posted May 31, 1995. (Retrieved June 13, 2018)

services in a free society is the best way to determine what gets produced and what doesn't and for how much.[24]

Mayor Barry blamed the shortages on everyone else. Especially "hoarders". He said anyone who "hoards" food and other essentials is a traitor and the police will deal with them.[25] Kayla had heard that one of her neighbors had some friends over one night. One of the guests had gone to the bathroom and saw that the homeowner had an extra roll of toilet paper under the sink in the bathroom.

The next day the police showed up and arrested the homeowner for "hoarding". She hadn't seen that neighbor since. And now his wife and kids wander the streets, in filthy clothes, begging for scraps to eat. The wife carries a picture of her husband around and asks everyone she sees if they had seen him. Most

[24] "Fabians believed in gradual nationalization of the economy through manipulation of the democratic process. Breaking away from the violent revolutionary socialists of their day, they thought that the only real way to effect "fundamental change" and "social justice" was through a mass movement of the working classes presided over by intellectual and cultural elites."
Bowyer, Jerry. "Barack Obama, Fabian Socialist." *Forbes.* https://www.forbes.com/2008/11/03/obama-fabian-socialist-oped-cx_jb_1103bowyer.html#671686f4317c Posted November 3, 2008. (Retrieved May 21, 2018)
[25] "During the decades of continuing price controls, the profits of farmers and other processors were eliminated through the artificially low state-mandated prices. What happened to the coffee-roasting companies beginning in 2006 is a typical scenario. First, some coffee producers simply held supplies off of the market in hopes the government would agree to price increases that covered their costs. The government countered with military force, authorizing the National Guard to 'find every last kilogram of coffee' being 'hoarded.' By 2009 the Venezuelan government seized control of two of the largest coffee-processing plants, claiming that the private companies were engaged in hoarding and smuggling coffee and therefore being disloyal to the state. Shortly thereafter, Chavez nationalized the two largest coffee enterprises. However, the government running the plants produced no benefits for the consumers. Today, market analyst Luis Vicente Leon sums it up this way. "They [the government] expropriates the sugar companies, and you cannot find sugar ... They expropriate the coffee companies ... and you cannot find coffee. They expropriate Owen-Illinois, and we cannot find packages."
Sparks, John A. "The Truth About Socialism: The Venezuelan Disaster." *The Center for Vision and Values. Grove City* College. http://www.visionandvalues.org/2016/06/the-truth-about-socialism-the-venezuelan-disaster/ Posted June 21, 2016. (Retrieved May 21, 2018)

people just ignore her, some don't have the heart to tell her that her husband is probably gone for good.

The line moved slowly into the supermarket. While Kayla stood there waiting she watched people come out of the store. None of them had full carts or bags of groceries. In fact, most only had one or two items.

When Kayla finally made it into the store, she could not believe her eyes. Gone was the once vibrant, bustling place of business. Now the store was mostly dark. The rows after row of stocked shelves were now mostly empty. Only the middle aisle seemed to have anything in it and that was the only aisle that had lights on. At the end of the aisle, where Kayla's lemonade display once stood, was just a stack of empty shelves. One lone cashier stood at her register. Her old store apron was dirty and torn. Kayla saw the stitching of her name "Emily" had started to unravel. Behind her stood one of the government people in his clean khakis and red polo shirt, watching Emily's every move.

Kayla started to walk to the back of the store where the milk case was.

"Where are you going?" the government guy called out.

"I need milk," Kayla said. "I was going to the milk aisle."

"There is no milk," the government guy said. "There was a problem at the dairy farm."

"Problem?"

"Don't you worry about that," the man said, trying to sound authoritative. "Our great Mayor Barry has the problem under control."

"When will we get the milk?" Kayla asked.

"Soon."

Kayla headed into the middle aisle. There wasn't much there. A couple of cans of beans and assorted vegetables, a bag of rice, not much else. She looked for toilet paper and didn't see any.[26]

"Do you have any toilet paper?" Kayla asked Emily.

Emily started to answer when the government guy cut her off. "No toilet paper either! The great Mayor has that under control too. It seems selfish greedy people have been hoarding toilet paper! The anti-hoarding division of the police is going door to door right now enforcing the anti-hoarding law. As they collect the illegally hoarded items from the selfish and greedy people they will bring the items to the store and stock the shelves."

Realizing that she had to take what she could get Kayla grabbed the last bag of rice and a couple of cans of vegetables...beets and lima beans.

She took them to the register and Emily rang her up.

---

[26] Simons, Jack Wallace. "EXCLUSIVE - 'Why shouldn't we enjoy ourselves just because the country is burning?' Super-rich Socialists quaff champagne in Venezuela country club while middle class mothers scavenge for scraps in the gutter... and even the DOGS are starving." *Dailymail.com*. http://www.dailymail.co.uk/news/article-3640941/Super-rich-quaff-champagne-Venezuela-country-club-middle-classes-scavenge-food-rubbish-dumps-DOGS-starving.html Updated February 7, 2017. (Retrieved July 2, 2018)

"They killed the cows," she heard Emily say in a very quiet voice without looking up.

"What?" Kayla whispered.

"The government, they killed the cows so the politicians could eat," Emily said.[27]

"There's no milk because the government killed the cows for themselves? That's why there's no milk?" Kayla asked.

Emily nodded her head slightly.

"How do you know that?" Kayla asked Emily.

In a whisper still Emily said, "I was in the bathroom in the back. They didn't know I was there. I heard the manager joking about it with the guy from the government."

Emily stopped talking when she saw the government guy start to walk over.

"What's the hold up?" he said loudly to Emily.

Kayla took her things and headed quickly out of the store.

When she made it outside she heard, "Miss! Miss!"

She stopped and turned around and saw the government agent who had been inside at the front of the store waving her over.

[27] Hayes, Christal. "Venezuelan President Eats Empanada on Live TV While Addressing Starving Nation." *Newsweek*. http://www.newsweek.com/venezuelan-president-eats-empanada-live-tv-while-addressing-starving-nation-701050 Posted November 3, 2017. (Retrieved July 2, 2018)

"Miss, can I speak to you?" he said.

Kayla held her ground. "What about?" Thinking for a second that maybe he thought she didn't pay for her items she quickly said, "I paid for these. Ask Emily, she'll tell you."

A look of puzzlement crossed his face. He stepped closer to Kayla and looked left and right to see if anyone was nearby. He was close enough that she could hear him when he whispered, "You want milk?"

"Milk?" Kayla said out loud.

A look of panic crossed his face. "SHHHH!" he said, waving his clipboard at her for emphasis. He stepped even closer to her. "I know you were looking for milk. If you want some I know where you can get it."

"Really?" she asked. "How? And why did you pick me to ask?"

"Well you don't look like the others who come around," he said. "I mean, you still are dressed pretty nice and I noticed you are wearing a watch."

Kayla looked at her watch. It wasn't anything special. Something she had worn for years. The fact is though that not a lot of people had watches or jewelry anymore. Most people had to sell those things to pay for other things like their rent, or bread, or milk.

"Yeah, and?" she asked.

"I know someone who would be interested in trading you some milk, or other things you can't get in the store, for your watch." He casually looked in the direction of the government SUV parked in the back of the lot.

Kayla realized what was going on but made pretend she didn't.

"I thought all the milk, and 'other things' weren't available right now. I thought there was a problem at the dairy farm?"

The government guy got annoyed. "Listen lady, you interested or not?"

Kayla felt like she had to see what would happen next.

"Sure," she said.

Government guy said, "Follow me," and started walking towards the government SUV. About ten feet from it he said, "Wait right here," and walked over the passenger side of the SUV. Kayla saw the window roll down a little and the guy inside said something to the government guy. She saw the window roll up and the door opened. Whoever was in the passenger seat got out and walked to the back of the SUV. Kayla couldn't see who it was. As she watched she saw the hatch go up on the back of the SUV. Government guy waved her over.

When Kayla got to the back of the SUV she couldn't believe her eyes. It was her old friend Hank. She hadn't seen him a while and saw that he was still a cop.

Hank gave a big smile and said, "Kayla! When I saw you go into the store I radioed Philip here," he pointed at government guy, "to make sure he brought you to me when you left." He walked over to Kayla and gave her an awkward hug. She didn't hug him back.

Hank stepped back and looked confused.

Kayla tried to muster a half smile and said, "It's good to see you Hank. How are you?"

Kayla didn't know what to think. The sight of Hank in his police uniform unnerved her for some reason. Hank had always been good to her and treated her with respect, but, like most people nowadays, she was always wary when interacting with the police. A result of them over the past several years having become more like enforcers of government policy than protectors of the law. Kayla always respected the police in the past because they were always neutral and always respected the rule of law. She still respected them, however now she was very cautious of what she said or did when she was around them.

Hank's face lit up when Kayla spoke to him.

"I'm doing great! This government work suits me well! I get paid a good salary and even get to be driven around by someone!"

Kayla looked inside the SUV and saw a big, stone faced, guy with dark sunglasses on sitting in the driver's seat. He made Kayla nervous. His police uniform was very tight on him and his huge bulging arm muscles looked like they would rip the fabric of his shirt. She wondered where the guy was from, he didn't look like he was from around here....

Hank's voice brought Kayla's thoughts back to the current situation. "And by the way," Hank continued, "there are a lot of good perks that come with the job!"

"Perk's?" Kayla asked.

"That's why I wanted to see you!" Hank exclaimed, grabbing Kayla's arm. "Well...not the only reason...we're old friends and all...but, come here! Let me show you!"

He pulled Kayla to the back of the truck and she couldn't believe her eyes. There were all sorts of goods back there! Even toilet paper!

"Perks!" Hank said.

Philip said, "She was looking for milk."

"That's great!" Hank said. "I can help you with that!"

He pushed some of the other stuff out of the way a pulled a big cooler forward. When he took the top off Kayla looked inside and saw quite a few containers of milk sticking out of a layer of ice. He pulled a quart of milk out of the ice and pushed it into Kayla's hands.

"This is for you!" he said. "A gift!"

Philip said, "She has on a nice watch she can trade."

Kayla saw a wave of anger cross Hank's face. He turned sharply around and walked over to Philip. Kayla saw Philip's eyes go wide with fright.

"I mean...I thought..."

WHACK!

Kayla couldn't believe her eyes. Hank punched Philip in the face and Philip reeled back in shock and pain. Hank hit him again and Philip went down.

"JUST SHUT THE FUCK UP!" He yelled at Philip. "SHE'S MY FRIEND!"

"Hank!" Kayla yelled. "Don't!"

She threw the milk into the back of the SUV and ran over and grabbed Hank. He was breathing heavy and sweating. His fists were still clenched. Kayla saw the driver had gotten out and was walking towards Kayla. He was even bigger than she thought. Hank bent over to catch his breath and waved the driver off.

"It's ok," he said through pants of breath.

Philip was slowly getting to his feet.

"Why Hank?" Kayla implored. She was utterly flabbergasted by what was going on.

"Why what?" Hank asked.

Kayla was taken aback for a split second. Everything happened so fast. Everything was so confusing. Just started to spurt out single words.

"Milk...how...hitting...stuff...Why?"

275

She took a deep breath.

"All of this stuff! How did you get it? I thought everything was gone yet you are driving around with a trunk full of stuff people need? Why Hank? How?"

Hank stood up straight. "How?" he asked. "I just take it from the hoarders. I give some back to the government but I keep some for myself. To sell. And why not? Who's going to stop me? The government? Hah! I am the government! I give some to Philip and my driver so they keep their mouths shut and sell the rest."

"You run a black market!" Kayla said. It was a statement, not a question.

"I don't like that term," Hank said. "I like to think of it as a service."

Kayla was very upset now. "But the people!"

"Fuck them!" Hank said. "Every man for himself."

Kayla turned and ran away.

"Kayla! Wait! Your milk!"

Kayla needed to try to clear her head. She ran as fast and as far away from Hank as she could. When she couldn't run anymore she decided to just keep walking. Without even realizing it, Kayla found herself in front of the entrance to her lemon tree grove.

Except it wasn't hers anymore and now it didn't look anything like it did when she owned it. The once open entranceway now had a huge, closed, Iron Gate across it. She always had a fence around the property but now that fence was probably twenty feet high and topped with razor wire. New, huge guard towers stood at various spots around the perimeter and she could see shadowy men up in them staring down at her.

The lemon trees were mostly bare. Most looked dead. Through the fence, she could see people shuffling around, moving things, digging things, under the watchful eyes of the guards. In the background where her barn sat she could see work being done on it. Workers were building huge smoke stacks up through the middle of the barn, and a she noticed that the train tracks, which ran through town, now had a second line running off them that disappeared into the lemon tree grove and ran towards the barn.

As she peered through the tight wired of the fence she noticed a familiar figure..." Rafael!" she yelled. "Rafael is that you?!?"

The sullen figure looked in her direction when he heard her name and raised his arm in a half acknowledgement. He then looked up at the guards and immediately dropped his arm and turned away. He picked something up off the ground and slowly disappeared into the distance.

Kayla started to cry.

What was happening to her town?

Kayla continued to look through the fence trying to catch another glimpse of Rafael. As she scanned the property, she noticed the people inside all looked very sick. Their clothes were dirty, shabby, and torn.

Kayla turned and started to walk home. She found herself walking past City Hall. Except now the sign out front read *Workers Hall: The Most Equal Place on Earth*. Kayla laughed.

She turned and looked down Main Street. In the fading light of approaching darkness she could still see the boarded-up windows on most of the shops that lined both sides of Main Street. In the twilight most of the street was dark because the most of the streetlights were out. There weren't enough light bulbs around to keep them all lit.

In some of the doorways of the closed-up shops she could make out figures, huddled up against the chill night air. She could see one figure rummaging through a garbage pail on the side of a building. Another figure was trying to start a fire in another garbage pail.

Kayla was in a daze.

But then something started to penetrate her thoughts. At first, she thought it was coming from inside her own brain...music. Thumping, muffled dance music. When she realized that it wasn't coming from inside her own head, she shook herself out of her daze and looked around.

"What is that? Where is it coming from" she thought out loud?

She started to walk in the direction of the music which took her around the back of Town Hall. When she rounded the corner, she couldn't believe her eyes.

Light.

The whole area was lit up. The neighborhood behind *Workers Hall* at one point was the newest residential development in Jefferson Township. When Mayor Ronald was Mayor lots of new families moved into the neighborhood. Now the area was where all the people in the government lived. A huge fence had been erected around the neighborhood and a guard booth where you had to show your government ID to enter stood next to a big iron gate. Kayla noticed that every streetlight in that area worked.

As Kayla walked closer to the fence the music became louder and clearer. Kayla walked up to the fence and could see into the neighborhood. There were a lot of cars parked around one house in particular, the Mayor's. There seemed to be some kind of party going on. Kayla peered intently through a large window that was on the front of the Mayor's house. Through the window, she could see people dancing. Two people stood out the most, the Mayor's daughters. Kayla could see them laughing and dancing, drinking and having fun.[28]

Kayla didn't see the big cop walking towards her. He was dressed in black body armor, helmet and carried a huge AR-15 rifle.

---

[28] Martel, Francis. "Report: Hugo Chavez's Favorite Daughter Is Richest Person in Venezuela." Breitbart. http://www.breitbart.com/national-security/2015/08/11/report-hugo-chavezs-favorite-daughter-is-the-richest-person-in-venezuela/. Posted August 11, 2015. (Retrieved May 4, 2018)

"You there! Step away from the fence!"

Kayla did as she was told. "I'm sorry officer. I heard the music and was just wondering what was going on."

The big cop came next to her. Through all the gear she could see he was a young guy. He had bright blue eyes and not a trace of facial hair. The radio attached to his uniform was squawking some chatter between some other cops. The volume was turned down low so Kayla couldn't hear what was being said.

"It's o.k. miss. But you really shouldn't be here. My Sergeant will be back soon and you should be gone before he gets here." The cop was staring at Kayla as if he knew her.

"Hey, aren't you the lemonade lady?" He asked.

Kayla managed a smile. She had never been called that before. "Yes I am. Do you like it? Grandma's Old-Fashioned Lemonade?"

The cop smiled back. "Yeah, I do. Great stuff. Haven't had it in a while though. The store near where I lived closed up. What happened?"

Kayla didn't know if he was joking or not. Or was he just trying to get her to say something bad so he could then lock her up. Was he trying to provoke her? She didn't know. Could he really be so naïve or out of touch that he didn't know what was going on in the town? Could he be that blind to the slow collapse that was happening all around him?

"Well," she said, "business has been better. Now I'm just trying to make a living."

"Hmmph," the cop uttered. "That's too bad. I liked it a lot."

"Thanks," Kayla said. "It is too bad." She looked at him for another few seconds and realized that there was nothing else there. This guy really seemed to have no clue as to what was happening. And why should he? She thought. He's got a steady job. Probably a decent place to live. His government paycheck, pension and other perks were secure. The politicians needed guys like him on their side so they paid handsomely from the taxes they took from others to ensure guys like him were kept happy. They kept the peace...better yet, they kept ORDER...and the politicians rewarded them for that and they paid it back to the politicians by being a solid source of votes for them come election time. That was the mindset of most unionized government workers. It was in their own self-interest to keep voting for the people who kept them employed. The politicians knew that and kept them happy with rich contracts that paid them salaries far above what an average non-government worker makes.[29]

"I better be going," Kayla said.

"Good luck!" the cop said to her as she turned to walk away. "I hope things get better for you!"

Kayla walked back through the darkened streets of Jefferson Township to her house on the other side of town. As she

[29] Schwartz, David M. and Candice Ferrette. "Nearly 1,000 workers for Suffolk County made $200,000 in 2017." *Newsday*. https://www.newsday.com/long-island/politics/suffolk-county-salary-200-000-nassau-1.17655983 Posted March 25, 2018. (Retrieved May 21, 2018)

opened the door to step inside she saw a flyer sticking out of her mailbox. It was a campaign flyer.

She had almost forgotten Election Day again was coming up again soon.

Kayla didn't know why it even mattered since Mayor Barry was running unopposed. He had become so powerful he simply banned his opponents from running.[30] [31] She didn't know why he did that since the town was ruled by one party anyway... his.[32] And if one party rules, you essentially have a dictatorship. Even in a "free" society. One party rule in Jefferson Township ensured that there would be no effective opposition to the ruling party probably ever again. The ruling party would create a system that perpetuated its existence forever. Whatever opposition to the ruling party existed would be easily suppressed by changing laws, creating regulations that targeted that resistance and by simply using the machinery of government to block any actions or activity that the opposition tried to mount. As the one party ruling government solidified its existence by rewarding its friends and punishing its enemies, the opposition would simply give up.

---

[30] Kew, Ben. "Venezuela's Maduro Bans Opposition Parties from 2018 Election." *Breitbart*. http://www.breitbart.com/national-security/2017/12/11/venezuelas-maduro-bans-opposition-parties-2018-election/ Posted December 11, 2017. (Retrieved June 13, 2018)
[31] Reuters. "No Surprise in Iraqi Vote." *The New York Times*. https://www.nytimes.com/1995/10/17/world/no-surprise-in-iraqi-vote.html Posted October 17, 1995. (Retrieved June 13, 2018)
[32] "Democrats in California hold every statewide office and dominate both chambers of the Legislature, while counting a 3.6-million edge in voter registrations and a 39-14 advantage in U.S. House seats."
Blood, Michael R. "One-party rule? California Democrats look to expand power." *The Press Democrat*. http://www.pressdemocrat.com/news/8397429-181/one-party-rule-california-democrats-look Posted June 4, 2018. (Retrieved June 13, 2018)

Kayla figured the Mayor wanted the election simply for the spectacle of it. This way he could claim another "victory" and use the attention to further his own agenda.

Communism

(People's Hall-The Freest, Fairest, Most Secure, and Most Equal Place on Earth)

Comrade Bernie

Election Day came and it was a gray, cold day.

Only this time there wasn't going to be an election.

Kayla woke up the next morning and got ready to head out to vote. As she normally does every morning, she went into her bathroom to brush her teeth. When she flicked the light switch, nothing happened. Half asleep still she flicked the switch up and down a few more times. Still nothing.[1]

She walked through her cold living room and thought to herself that the heat wasn't on either. Unlocking her front door and stepping onto her porch Kayla looked up and down the street at her neighbor's houses. In the gray half-light of dawn, she didn't see one porch light on anywhere and all of the street lights, which would still normally be on at this hour, were all out as well.[2]

Power is out again, she thought to herself. This was a regular occurrence now in Jefferson Township ever since Mayor Barry had the government take over all of the utility and energy companies. He instituted planned power outages, he called them

[1] Sunil, W.A. "Massive power outage in Bangladesh." World Socialist Website. https://www.wsws.org/en/articles/2014/11/05/bang-n05.html. Posted November 5, 2014. (Retrieved May 6, 2018)
[2] Armas, Mayala and Juan Forero. "Venezuela Plans Electricity Outages to Save Energy." The Wall Street Journal. https://www.wsj.com/articles/venezuela-plans-electricity-outages-to-save-energy-1461276840. Posted April 21, 2016. (Retrieved May 6, 2018)

Patriotic Downtimes, during the overnight and sporadically throughout the day.

The Mayor had said these power outages were being done to "protect the environment". But it was pretty common knowledge among the people of Jefferson Township that the power generating plants had all fallen into such a state of neglect that the government had to limit the time they could operate just to prevent them from collapsing permanently. They had fallen into disrepair for one, the government couldn't afford to buy the parts to fix it anymore, and two, all of the qualified workers at the plant had long ago been replaced by unqualified supporters and cronies of the government.

Kayla went back into her bathroom and looked at herself in the mirror. Even though still a young woman the face that looked back at her looked much older, and tired. The stresses of what had been happening in her beloved township as well as to her business had taken its toll on her. Also, ever since the government had taken over the healthcare industry things had gotten worse as well.[3]

---

[3] "But the opponents of health-care socialism also have in their minds a vision of what life would be like under socialism. Mostly these visions are drawn from experiences under socialist countries that have been driven into poverty by state ownership of the means of production. The state in these cases does not have much money. There is no private store of wealth to speak of, and no private business that has the motivation or the means to provide customer service.

What happened in these countries is entirely predictable. There was an undersupply of medical services just as there was an undersupply of everything else. Yuri Maltsev tells harrowing stories of how people would suffer relentlessly in the USSR. When the death rate per hospital would grow so as to embarrass the state, the state would simply order the rate to be lowered, just as they ordered grain production to be higher.

The hospitals would respond in perverse ways. Instead of providing better care, they started rolling people out the door if the personnel suspected that the patient was near death. The result was a decline in per-hospital death rates, but an overall increase in deaths.

One thing that the state has not been able to lie about is vital statistics. The Soviet state did its best to keep them from being revealed. But once the data were collected, the truth came out. Between 1971 and 1986, the Soviet state faced a calamity. Life expectancy decreased. Infant mortality increased. In fact, the Soviet state stopped collecting data again. But later, once the

Incentive to innovate new medicines and treatments had all but disappeared. There was no reason to do it anymore because the government bureaucrats in charge of health care didn't have a profit motive to improve things in the health care industry. The government kept pumping borrowed money into the system but it only disappeared into an ocean of corruption and incompetence. Health clinics and hospitals, when they were open, were nothing more than a place to go to get pain medicines...or to die.

The pain medicines served another purpose as well. When people got hooked on them they became dependent on the government for their "fix". They were willing to do, or vote, for anything the government wanted in order to keep their meds flowing.

Kayla also knew that malnutrition was having a negative impact on her overall health. You couldn't buy vitamins anymore, and things like fresh fruit and vegetables were rare.[4] Just the other day she had heard that one of neighbors had a small child who died because of malnutrition.[5]

---

truth was revealed again, it turned out that infant mortality was on the increase, in some cases as much as 58 percent between 1971 and 1986.

A similar experience was repeated in every socialized state. Health declined. Vital statistics did not keep up with capitalistic standards."

Rockwell, Llewellyn H. Jr. "Socialized Medicine in a Wealthy Country." Lewrockwell.com. https://www.lewrockwell.com/2006/12/lew-rockwell/socialized-medicine-in-a-wealthy-country/. Posted December 15, 2006. (Retrieved May 6, 2018).

[4] Kohut, Meridith and Isayen Herrera. "For five months, The New York Times tracked 21 public hospitals in Venezuela. Doctors are seeing record numbers of children with severe malnutrition. Hundreds have died." New York Times. https://www.nytimes.com/interactive/2017/12/17/world/americas/venezuela-children-starving.html Posted December 17, 2017. (Retrieved May 6, 2018)

[5] Ellis, Mark. "Socialism's bitter fruit in Venezuela: Hundreds of children dying of malnutrition." Godreports.com. http://blog.godreports.com/2017/12/socialisms-bitter-fruit-in-venezuela-hundreds-of-children-dying-of-malnutrition/ Posted December 20, 2017. (Retrieved May 6, 2018)

All of a sudden, the lights came back on. Kayla turned on the small TV in kitchen, the only one she has left because she had to sell all of her other ones to buy food.

There seemed to be a lot of action going on at the news station. There were a bunch of reporters running around and then the screen switched to a shot of the Mayor's podium, which was empty at the moment. Kayla turned up the volume on the TV and heard a reporter say, "...tragedy like this to occur on election day. We are waiting to hear from Chief Bernie...oh hear he comes now. Let's listen."

Chief Bernie took the podium. He looked grim. He said, "Good morning citizens of Jefferson Township. It is with a heavy heart that I can confirm that the rumors of Mayor Barrack's death are true."

"What! Dead?" Kayla said out loud.

Chief Bernie kept talking. "This morning I called Mayor Barry to wish him luck in the election and became worried when the Mayor wouldn't answer his phone." He paused to wipe away tears. "I had a feeling something was wrong. So, I grabbed a couple of officers and proceeded to drive over to the Mayor's office." Another pause and more tears. "That was when we found him."

What Kayla and everyone else didn't know was that much earlier that morning, Police Chief Bernie and a few of his loyal thugs simply walked into Mayor Barry's office and shot him dead in his chair.

The Chief then lied when he said the Mayor left a suicide note in which he confessed to stealing from the town's treasury. In the note, Chief Bernie said, the Mayor had written he had become so wracked with guilt he couldn't go on living anymore knowing what he had done. Chief Bernie also said the note instructed that his loyal friend, Chief Bernie, should run the town until a suitable replacement was found.

Bernie then said, "In the meantime, because of this tragedy, we will not be holding the election today in order to mourn this great loss". He said he would let the town know what happens next "in a little while".

The townspeople started to get nervous. Right after the announcement there were many of Chief Bernie's "friends" roaming the streets, carrying weapons, pushing people around, telling people to go home, asking people who the "troublemakers" were. This went on for a few days. But Chief Bernie was nowhere to be seen during this time.

Then, a few days later Mayor Bernie resurfaced. He invited the townspeople to a meeting at the Town Hall. There were cameras there to broadcast the meeting on TV. Kayla didn't go to the meeting but was watching with her parents at their house.

The cameras showed the outside of the building with townsfolk starting to arrive. As they entered the building the camera focused in on the sign out front. The sign where Kayla had once set up her first lemonade stand in front of. Now it was changed to read People's Hall - The Freest, Fairest, Most Secure, and Most Equal Place on Earth.

That was fast Kayla thought.

Inside, in the auditorium there was a podium set up in the middle of the stage. The podium, covered in a red cloth, had a strange symbol on it. Watching on her TV Kayla saw that the symbol was a combination of a Hammer and Sickle. There were several red flags on the stage as well each that had the same symbols on them.

Also, on the stage were several heavily armed men who stood with arms folded, eyes gazing out at the gathering crowd. When the lawn was finally full of townspeople Chief Bernie appeared and walked up on the stage and over to the podium.

He wasted no time, "The Town Charter is dead", he said, "It was a document of oppression and negative liberties; therefore, I am tearing it up and from now on I will rule in the name of the people as first Comrade".

A buzz went through the crowd. Someone in the audience yelled out, "What gives you the right to do such a thing?" A camera swung around to view the person in the audience who asked the question. Kayla saw it was the guy who used to own the water delivery company. She also saw one of Comrade Bernie's men grab him and start to pull him towards the exit. No one ever saw him again.[6]

Comrade Bernie went on, "We have too long lived under an oppressive capitalist system where evil profits were put ahead of

---

[6] "Saddam's 1979 Baath Party purge." *BBC.* http://www.bbc.com/news/av/world-middle-east-25363857/saddam-s-1979-baath-party-purge Posted December 13, 2013. (Retrieved May 21, 2018)

the people. The capitalist class is a racist, despicable, amoral enemy who have stolen, embezzled, and extorted the wealth of millions of working people for decades. All at the behest of evil corporations who have been controlling the levers of power for the sole purpose of exploiting the natural resources of the earth and oppressing the working people of this land! The revolution has begun!"

Capitalist? Kayla thought, *Is he nuts? We haven't been a Capitalist society in years!*

Comrade Bernie went on, "From now on there will be no private businesses in our great town. Businesses will now be organized into great, worker controlled, cooperatives. All overseen by government experts of course. The anarchy and destructive competition of the last vestiges of capitalism will be replaced by a fully planned economy. Free market? Bah! There is nothing free about a market that exploits people. Workers will each produce according to their ability and consume according to their needs. No more, no less. That is fair!"

He then said, "The working class and all who work for a living – the vast majority of the people – face a relentless, vicious, and amoral enemy: the capitalist class. Our country is oppressed by one of the most controlling, despicable, entrenched capitalist ruling classes ever."[7]

Kayla shut the television off and started to cry. She could not believe that it had come to this. That everything she had built

---

[7] "The Road to Socialism USA: Unity for Peace, Democracy, Jobs and Equality." *Communist Party USA*. http://www.cpusa.org/party_info/party-program/ Posted May 19, 2006. (Retrieved May 21, 2018)

was gone. That some years ago, when she created her first lemonade stand she had been hailed in the community as an outstanding citizen who was providing good jobs for people and was helping everyone in town because her business was good for the overall economy. She had been fair and honest in her dealings and had been rewarded for this with a growing business. Sure, she made profits. Lots of them, and she had become richer than she had ever dreamed she could be. However, it was all through honest, hard work. Now, she was considered a criminal, an exploiter and evil person for those very things that she was once praised for.

For the next few days Kayla stayed home. There was no reason to leave anymore. Her business was gone, Comrade Bernie's thugs were roaming the streets beating on people and taking them away and she was simply too depressed to do anything other than sleep the day away.[8]

A few nights later, while at home, Kayla heard a knock on her door. She opened it to see another one of those khakis and polo shirt wearing agents of the government standing there. This was a woman. On her shirt was a patch that read "District Housing Department". She was middle aged and her thinning hair was pulled back tight into a pony tail. Her polo shirt and khakis were way too small for her and her belly flowed over her waist band. Kayla noticed she barely got the zipper on her pants all the way up and the button looked like it would fly off at any second and could take her eye out.

[8] Norrholm, Seth Davin PhD. "Anxiety, Depression and Other Mental Health Issues in North Korea." *Anxiety.org*. https://www.anxiety.org/anxiety-and-mental-health-in-north-korea-past-and-present Posted July 29, 2016. (Retrieved July 2, 2018)

Behind her on the street was parked another one of those government SUV's. Kayla could see it was still running and saw shadows moving around in it.

"Are you Kayla Alexander?" she asked.

"Yes I am. What is this about?" she asked.

Ignoring the question, the agent said, "You live alone here?"

Before Kayla could answer the agent said, "No need to answer. We know you do. The government declared that all homes with extra living space are now required to forfeit said extra living space to provide for the housing of those who do not have a place to live. You may continue to live here in one of the smaller rooms as the larger rooms may be used to house families. As per regulations you will be granted the standard 29.6 feet of personal living space."

It took a second for Kayla to understand what was going on.

The agent continued, "Excess rooms as an entirety are subject to requisition from tenants by administrative order and will be placed at the exclusive disposition of district communal departments for the settlement of productively employed citizens. Tenants are granted their choice of rooms remaining to them within the limits specified by regulation, as well as the right within three weeks to settle in the requisitioned rooms tenants of their choice, on the condition that said tenants surrender to the district communal department any rooms occupied by them or some other rooms suitable for habitation in exchange for those subject to requisition."[9]

"But...what? I own this house," Kayla said. "You don't have the right..."

The agent cut her off, "Ms. Alexander you do not 'own' this house. The bank does because you were paying a mortgage on it. With the 'Fairness in Banking Act' the government has assumed control of the banking system and all of the banks. To stop greedy profit taking of course. Now the Government owns the banking system so it is now the true owner of this property and it can...and will...exercise its rights as the property owner. As the regulation says, you can find people to live with you, like your family. They will of course have to surrender their property to the government. If you don't, you can expect your new housemates as chosen by the government to arrive soon after the expiration of the three-week time limit." The agent then turned and walked away. Kayla watched her walk across the lawn to her neighbor's house. No doubt to let her neighbors know they are no longer property owners either.

Kayla closed the door and walked upstairs to her bedroom. At that moment the power went out again as it did every night. She packed a bag with some clothes and filled a backpack with some personal items. Photographs, family keepsakes and such. She knew right away she could never live here with strangers. If she was going to live with anyone it would be family.

She went back downstairs, opened her front door and headed out into the cool, dark night. She didn't bother closing the

[9] Utekhin, Ilya and Alice Nakhimovsky, Slava Paperno, Nancy Ries. "Translation of the Russian Transcript: Compulsory Apartment Consolidation." Communal Living in Russia A Virtual Museum of Soviet Everyday Life. National Endowment for the Humanities. http://kommunalka.colgate.edu/cfm/documents.cfm?ClipID=734&TourID=1000 Posted 2006-2008. (Retrieved May 9, 2018)

door and she didn't look back as she walked across the grass and headed off to her parents' house.

A few doors down she noticed the government SUV idling in front of one her neighbor's house. She crossed to the opposite side of the street and kept walking. As she walked she noticed that the same government agent who was at her house, was standing near the open front door of the house and seemed to be arguing with whoever was inside, Kayla couldn't see who it was she was yelling at because all of the lights were out and it was very dark inside the house. She stopped near a tree to see what was going on and was confident that no one could see her.

Then it all happened so fast.

Kayla heard a man's voice inside the house get very loud and the agent yell, "WHAT ARE YOU DOING?!?" The agent turned to run but was too fat to move quickly.

A blinding light like an explosion and a loud BANG! made Kayla instinctively duck.

From the light of the explosion Kayla saw the side of the agent's face disappear in a haze of blood and brain matter. Her body collapsed instantly down the front steps.

She saw the homeowner emerge from the shadows inside the house carrying a shotgun which he immediately racked to load another round. She heard the empty shell casing hit the walkway. Kayla immediately hit the ground and curled up behind the big tree she was standing near for protection. Having been around guns all her life she knew the homeowner didn't have many rounds left in his pump action shotgun so she knew if she could just stay down and not be noticed she would probably be OK.

Besides, the homeowner had his sights set on something else, the government SUV and whoever was inside it. He jumped over the dead agent lady and started to head for the SUV. As he did so Kayla saw the doors facing her open and two agents rolled out and hit the ground. Each was holding a handgun. One of the agents from the car peeked around the front of the SUV and took a shot at the homeowner but missed him. Mostly because the homeowner seemed to know what he was doing and was zig-zagging as he ran towards the SUV. The agent must have been terrified because he didn't do anything else but curl up next to the SUV's tire and cover his head with his hands.

Kayla saw the homeowner come around the front of the SUV and shoot the agent point blank. The agent's body jumped from the force of the blast and didn't move again. Kayla knew he was dead. The other agent managed to work his way to the back of the SUV and took a wild shot at the homeowner. Kayla heard the bullet hit the branches above her. The Homeowner shot at the agent but missed, blowing out the rear window of the SUV. While the homeowner reloaded the shotgun, Kayla saw a third agent, who was still in the SUV, lean out of the car and shoot the homeowner several times in the back. The homeowner collapsed dead on the spot.

Kayla didn't wait, she got up and ran. She had only one thought, get to her parents.

Cold rain started to fall.

As she ran, everywhere she looked all she saw were empty houses and shuttered stores and businesses.

A thought crossed her mind... *Where was everyone?*

She hadn't been out of her house much since Comrade Bernie had seized power. Afraid to venture outside she had felt safest just staying home. But as she ran past all of the dark and empty homes she realized she may have missed something.

Panic started to set in and she ran even harder towards her parent's house. The rain started to soak her hair and was running into her eyes. A feeling of dread was overcoming her. She tried to force it down, but it was persistent. Her mind was swimming.

She could see her parents' house in the distance. Getting closer as she pounded her way through the rain towards it.

Finally, she was there.

Her heart sank.

The front door was wide open.

She walked up the walkway and climbed the stairs to the porch. Her heart ached. She started to sob. She looked through the door but didn't go in. In a small voice she called, "Mom? Dad?"

No answer came but the whistling wind.

Kayla had never felt such sorrow in her life. She tried to convince herself that maybe they just ran. That like her, when they heard they no longer owned their house, they set out to find her!

YES! She thought! That was it! They knew they needed to get to her so they set out to find her. At this very moment they could be wandering the streets calling her name. Kayla was determined to find her parents.

She started walking back towards her house thinking that maybe she would find them along the way.

She didn't.

Kayla didn't know what to do. She continued to walk until she found herself approaching the edge of town where there was a park that had been there for years. She remembered learning that at one point, a long, long time ago, on the land where the park now stood, there was a huge estate of one of the original founders of the town. Over the years the park became a place where during happier times families would come to play in the playground or fish in the small pond. Kayla loved the park because it was filled big, old trees and was surrounded by a huge, old fashioned, iron fence. She always felt safe when she was there.

The entrance to the park was through a huge iron gate above which an iron arch read *Jefferson Park.* As she approached the entrance she froze. There were people there.

In the darkness she couldn't make out what they were doing, but there were definitely two people right by the entrance. For a few seconds she stood as still as she could force herself to be while her heart was pounding in her chest, afraid that whoever it was would all of a sudden see her and come after her.

The realization that the figures she was looking at weren't moving either dawned on her. She slowly started walking again. Being careful to use the trees along the sidewalk to shield her from the view of whoever it was.

As she got closer she realized something wasn't right. The figures seemed too still. As she moved closer and her eyes adjusted to the darkness around the figures she could see that their feet weren't touching the ground. She moved a few inches closer and then saw why. Both figures had a rope around their necks and they were hanging from the side of the fence. Both figures were dead.

Kayla gasped.

Horrified she moved closer, carefully looking around to make sure no one was around. Her heart was pounding. Now she could see that both figures had on uniforms. They were cops. They looked familiar.

Oh my God! Kayla thought. She closed her eyes. "It can't be," she whispered to herself. When she opened her eyes again she saw, staring lifelessly back at her, her old friend Hank. Tied to the front of him was a sign that simply read: *Hoarders. Executed by order of Comrade Bernie.* Kayla glanced at the person hanging next to Hank and saw it was Philip, the same guy Hank had punched in the face back in the supermarket parking lot when Hank had tried to give Kayla some milk. Apparently, Comrade Bernie wanted to be the only hoarder in town.

Kayla said a small prayer and then walked away.

She kept walking along the road that led out of Jefferson Township. Going further and further past the edge of town. Her mind was numb.

Through the blowing rain and darkness, she kept walking until she noticed a faint light in the distance. Clutching her coat tightly around her she put her head down against the wind and walked off the road towards the light. She was now and crossing the big field that lay behind the town. The light was coming from between the trees of the small forest that sat way out on the outskirts. Kayla heard what sounded like heavy equipment moving around. She heard voices shouting but couldn't make out what they were saying.

Kayla knew this area well because it was near where her lemon tree grove had been. She also used to play in the woods with her friends when she was a kid. The rain had caused the ground to become very muddy. Kayla stumbled through it, falling to her knees a few times.

As she approached the tree line the ground became a little firmer. Not wanting to be seen she crawled on her hands and knees to a bush. She peered through the branches to a clearing that had been made in the middle of the trees. A huge ditch had been dug and there was a very tall mound of dirt from the hole piled up behind the ditch. Bulldozers were pushing dirt back into the ditch. The spot where she was hiding was a little higher up than the rest of the area around her. By craning her neck, she was able to see just over the edge of the ditch.

With horror she finally realized where everyone in town had gone. She knew why the town seemed so empty. Because they were all here, and they all were being buried in that ditch. [10] [11] She raised her body up a little higher to get a better view into the huge hole. She could see arms, legs, torsos...protruding out from the dirt. She focused on one hand in particular. The red nail polish on its fingernails stood out under the harsh lights. It was reaching towards the sky as if imploring the heavens to pull it out.

Kayla collapsed onto her back. She wanted to vomit. She rolled over onto her side and retched into the ground next to her. She made a lot of noise but she didn't care. She wanted it to all be over. She wiped her mouth onto her sleeve and rolled onto her back again. She could see the night sky through the trees with twinkling stars and the bright moon looking down on the horror that was only a few yards from where Kayla lay. The rain had stopped.

She didn't know how long she lay there staring into the sky, the cold ground to her back, listening to the sound of the bulldozers going back and forth when off to her side she heard branches crack and whispered voices. *It's all over now* she thought. *I'll be joining red fingernails soon enough.* She was exhausted. She didn't move other than to turn her head in the direction of the noises she heard.

[10] Somin, Ilya. "Lessons from a century of communism." Washingtonpost.com. https://www.washingtonpost.com/news/volokh-conspiracy/wp/2017/11/07/lessons-from-a-century-of-communism/?noredirect=on&utm_term=.98fc32336899 Posted November 7, 2017. (Retrieved May 10, 2018)

[11] Edwards, Lee. "The Legacy of Mao Zedong is Mass Murder." Heritage.org. https://www.heritage.org/asia/commentary/the-legacy-mao-zedong-mass-murder Posted February 2, 2010. (Retrieved May 10, 2018)

Through the branches she could see a couple of figures crouched around a tree. One was pointing towards the ditch. They both were holding long things in their hands. One of the figures nodded and started to move towards Kayla. She could see him clearly now. It was a young man dressed in dark clothes. He had a bandana or scarf covering his nose and mouth so all that was exposed was his eyes. He kept glancing towards the ditch as he moved forward.

He kept getting closer. Kayla closed her eyes. She started to pray. She wasn't afraid to die for she knew she would soon be with the Lord. Her Christian faith taught her that. She knew that Jesus would come for her and she asked Him to watch over her in her last few moments of life on earth. She asked Him to just make it quick, no pain. She felt peace. She thought of her parents. She didn't know where they were, if they were in that ditch or not, but the images of them in her mind made her feel at peace as well.

The masked man was over her now. Her heart was racing. She closed her eyes and thought *Lord please make it quick.*

She could smell him now. He smelled like cut grass and gun oil. She sensed him over her. Her body tensed...

And then he grabbed her wrist with one of his and put his other hand over her mouth. Her eyes snapped open wide with fright...

Oh God! She thought, *He's going to take me and do God knows what!*

She made an instant decision that she wasn't going to just go quietly. It was as if all of her anger, fear and even hatred gave her a sudden burst of clarity. She was no longer afraid, no longer willing to lay there and die. She was going to fight until her last breath! Adrenaline surged through her body she tried to roll away from the masked man but he was strong. He kept one hand over her mouth but let go of her wrist.

Then he did something unexpected.

He raised his free hand to his mouth and made the *Shhhhhh* gesture with his index finger.

In this split-second Kayla became confused and stopped struggling. He then let go of her mouth as well and whispered, "I am not going to hurt you but you have to be quiet."

Now free of his grasp, Kayla scrambled to an upright position. She shook dead leaves and small sticks out of her hair.

The man pulled the mask off his face, apparently to ease her fears a little. She saw a very young face looking back at her. He backed up from Kayla and squatted down.

"Who are you?" she demanded.

"My name is Philip. Please, you have to be quiet," he shifted his AR 15 so it lay across his lap. "I am a member of the *Forest Brotherhood*[12]. I can tell you're not with them," he gestured with his

---

[12] Kaszeta, Daniel J. "LITHUANIAN RESISTANCE TO FOREIGN OCCUPATION 1940-1952." Lituanas: Lithuanian Quarterly Journal of Arts and Sciences Volume 34, No. 3. http://www.lituanus.org/1988/88_3_01.htm Fall 1988. (Retrieved May 11, 2018)

head towards the ditch, "but for both our sakes you have to be quiet."

"Ok," Kayla said in a whisper. She didn't know what to think of this guy. She did know that if he did mean to do her harm he probably would have done it already. It freaked her out his name was Philip when she just saw the only other Philip she knew hanging by his neck from the park fence.

"What are you doing?" she asked him.

"Fighting back," he said.

"Fighting back?"

"Yeah," he said. "Me and a bunch of others figured we were all dead men anyway, so why not go down swinging?"

"How?" Kayla asked.

"Anyway we can." He said with a smile. "Starting with these assholes here." He gestured towards the ditch with his rifle. "We're about to make them pay."

As soon as he said that Kayla saw a bottle with a flaming rag in it come flying out of the tree line about fifty feet away. It hit one of the several bulldozers right in the cage where the operator was sitting and exploded in flames. The man in the bulldozer screamed and fell out of the cage to the ground, covered in flames.

Philip yelled at Kayla, "GET DOWN! THAT'S THE SIGNAL!" and all of a sudden the tree line erupted in gun fire. Philip raised his rifle up and started shooting towards the bulldozers as well. More Molotov cocktails[13] found their mark on the various other pieces of equipment, and people, in the clearing.

It was loud with gunfire. Kayla covered her head and ears with her hands. To her left she saw Philip get up and start moving forward. As Kayla peered through the branches she saw fifteen or so other people emerge from the trees, all firing their weapons at the equipment and people who were operating them. They didn't stand a chance. It was over in less than two minutes.

Kayla heard someone yell, "CEASE FIRE! CEASE FIRE!" and the rifle fire slowed to a stop. The only noise left was the sound of the flames consuming the equipment. It hissed and popped as the fire burned.

A few seconds later Kayla heard Philip yell, "You can come out now! It's all over."

Kayla got up slowly from the bush. When she stood up she had a better view of the scene. There were dead workers laying all over the place. She saw the first guy, the one who got hit with the first Molotov cocktail, laying on the ground where he fell. The flames were out but his charred body was still smoking. His arms and kegs twisted in grotesque agony towards the sky.

She could Philip standing near a group of people and he was waving her over. "It's OK," he said. "It's safe now."

---

[13] "Molotov cocktail: a simple bomb made from a bottle filled with gasoline and stuffed with a piece of cloth that is lit just before the bottle is thrown." *Merriam-Webster.com* . https://www.merriam-webster.com/dictionary/Molotov%20cocktail (Retrieved May 11, 2018)

Kayla walked down the embankment and approached the group. There were a handful of men and a couple of young girls standing around. All armed with various types of firearms.

Philip said to the group, "I found her lying in a bush up there," he said to Kayla, "I never got your name."

"Kayla. Kayla Alexander."

One of the girls asked, "What were you doing up there?" Her dark hair was pulled back in a tight ponytail. She was holding a Ruger Mini 14 in one hand and wiped her dirt stained face with the other. She eyed Kayla suspiciously.

"Looking for my parents," Kayla said.

The girl's expression softened immediately. She said, "Oh, are they...." As she motioned with her rifle towards the ditch.

Kayla said, "I don't know. I went to their house and they were gone..."

"Hmmph. Gone," Philip said. "A lot of that going on."

"Yeah," Kayla said. "Gone."

There was a moment of silence while everyone seemed to consider that one word...Gone.

Philip then said, "Well Kayla Alexander, you are more than welcome to join us. Can't promise you it will be fun, but I can promise you we will fight."

Kayla's parents had always taught her that there were things worth fighting for, and things worth fighting against, in life. That you couldn't always let others do the fighting for you because sooner or later there would be no one left to do it.

She decided right there, on the soil of her beloved Jefferson Township, in front of these strangers she just met and on top of where so many of her neighbors now lay buried, she decided right then and there that she would never stop fighting until Freedom and Liberty reigned once again. And she knew, that no matter where her parents were, they would agree.

-END-

Afterword

We have become a society where children opening a lemonade stand has become a matter of government concern. Little kids as young as four years old have had the cops come and shut down their innocent foray into free market capitalism.[1]

Why?

I believe it's actually a pretty deep and involved answer to that question.

For one, it's about money. Permit fees, fines, licensing fees, are all big bucks to a government. And in government's eyes no one...not even a four-year-old, ought to be immune from feeding the cash hungry, financially overstretched government.

It's also about power. Who does that four-year-old think she is selling lemonade without government's permission? We'll show her!

It's also about a war on capitalism. How dare that four-year-old want to make 25 cents on a cup of lemonade! What a greedy Capitalist pig! What a robber baron!

And most chillingly it's about efforts by the ruling class to condition people from a very early age to accept that they can't do anything the government doesn't want them too or *allows* them to

---

[1] Kain, Eric. "The Inexplicable War on Lemonade Stands." *Forbes.* https://www.forbes.com/sites/erikkain/2011/08/03/the-inexplicable-war-on-lemonade-stands/#35e94f8f2a52 Posted August 3, 2011. (Retrieved May 23, 2018)

do. All that four-year-old will think for the rest of her life is that the government can tell her what to do.

How does that conditioning manifest itself when those kids become adults?

Well, how about the lady who threatened to call the cops on an eight-year-old who was trying to sell bottles of water to help her mom, who lost her job, pay for a trip to Disney? Apparently, she demanded the eight-year-old show the permit she obtained (from the government) to sell the water. That is what we have become. A society where adults demand that four and eight-year old obey their government masters just to make a few, innocent bucks.[2]

Is that freedom?

Lately, one of the most disturbing trends in America is the growing acceptance of socialism, and even communism, among many people in this country. Particularly the youth who have been taught in a public education system that has become the ideological training ground for totalitarian (i.e. Progressive, Socialist, Communist, and Fascist) thought. Just search "millennials and socialism" and you will find scores of articles and research documenting how socialism is finding acceptance by vast numbers of youth in this country.

---

[2] Seely, Taylor. "Woman dubbed '#PermitPatty' appears to call cops on 8-year-old girl selling water in viral video." *USA Today.* https://www.usatoday.com/story/life/allthemoms/2018/06/23/permitpatty-video-woman-appear-call-cops-girl-selling-water-bottles/728682002/ Posted June 24, 2018. (Retrieved June 27, 2018)

I would argue this acceptance has come about mainly through deception, sheer ignorance and a glossing over, even denial, of socialism's murderous history.

According to the Victims of Communism Memorial Foundation, 40% of millennials (typically someone born in the 1980's or 1990's) have never heard of Chinese Communist Leader Mao ZeDong and that he was responsible for the deaths of 40 million people. One fifth of millennials do not know that the Communist Soviet Union's Josef Stalin killed over 30 million people. In spite of that horrific history, the likes of outward Socialists like Bernie Sanders have found a great amount of support among the people, again, particularly the youth, of America, for his totalitarian views. People are not ashamed or afraid to be called a Socialist anymore. And that's scary.

To highlight this an avowed Socialist just beat an entrenched, establishment Democrat Party leader in a New York State Primary for the 14th Congressional District in New York. [3] Now in the People's Republic of New York this may be par for the course, but Socialists have been winning elsewhere in the country as well.

The Democratic Socialists of America website points out that in the November 2017 elections, "...its membership now includes

---

[3] "Alexandria Ocasio-Cortez, a former campaign organizer for Bernie Sanders, pulled off a stunning upset in New York City on Tuesday by defeating U.S. Rep. Joseph Crowley, D-N.Y., who was considered a kingmaker and an all but shoo-in... Ocasio-Cortez, 28, who is from the Bronx, is a member of the Democratic Socialists of America.."
DeMarche, Edmund. "Alexandria Ocasio-Cortez win stuns Democrats, puts new attention on Pelosi." *Fox News.* http://www.msn.com/en-us/news/politics/alexandria-ocasio-cortez-win-stuns-democrats-puts-new-attention-on-pelosi/ar-AAze5mr?ocid=ientp Posted June 27, 2018. (Retrieved June 27, 2018)

15 new elected officials. This is in addition to 20 elected already in offices around the United States."[4]

As for the murders committed by Socialist and Communist rulers, I am not a gambler, but I would bet that if you asked a bunch of random people on the street, of all ages, race and gender, if they believed that could happen here, the majority would say "Of course not!"

One of the hardest things for people to accept is the notion that "it can happen here". The denial of the fact that yes, it most certainly CAN happen here, has led not only to the slow yet inexorable degradation of our freedoms here in the United States, it has also contributed to the torture, death and oppression of millions upon millions of people throughout the world as demonstrated above.

That's not hyperbole.

And America is not immune to the fact that "it can happen here" ...if we let it.

Ask those same people on the street if they have heard of Bill Ayers and Bernadine Dohrn, friends of Barack Obama, by the way, and I bet the overwhelming majority would say "no".

Why are Bill and Bernadine relevant?

[4] "15 DSA Members Elected!, 2017 election." *Democratic Socialists of America.* https://www.dsausa.org/15_dsa_members_elected Posted November 9, 2017. (Retrieved June 27, 2018)

Because if they had had their way it *would have* happened here. Their violently radical Communist terrorist group, *The Weather Underground*, planned on *eliminating* 25 million Americans in "reeducation camps" after seizing power. [5]

Sure, it never came to pass. But that was back when being called a "Socialist" was still an insult. Nowadays, as I point out above, it's not. Bill and Bernadine may have just come on the scene a little too early to fulfill their dreams. What about today's "Bill" and "Bernadine"? Maybe they're just waiting for all those millennials to start voting (where apparently in the NY 14th Congressional District they have). That's scary too, given their apparent propensity to socialism and glaring ignorance of the horrors caused by it.

But it's not just all about the Socialists.

Fascists too are having their day in the sun. But no one calls themselves a Fascist as quickly as someone will call themselves a Socialist. Why is that?

Because the mistake that many seem to make is to associate fascism with genocide as if they go hand in hand. They don't. Genocide is just evil, it has existed under many kinds of systems. Fascism is about economics. It's about power and control.

Tell people America has many symptoms of being a Fascist State and you probably get laughed at, yelled at, or both.

---

[5] Lifson, Thomas. "Eliminating 25 million Americans." *American Thinker.* https://www.americanthinker.com/blog/2008/10/eliminating_25_million_america.html Posted October 23, 2008. (Retrieved May 22, 2018)

Then ask them if they think we have government apparatus in this country that overburdens society with regulations and directives; or ask them if they think we have a financial system that is regulated by the government where the government controls the flow of money and is effectively the chief banker of society; or even ask them if they believe this country is addicted to deficit spending and the resultant accumulation of massive government debts; and most people would say "yes", we do have those thing in America, without realizing those are some of the key attributes of a fascist system.

The American people over the past several generations have been duped into believing and accepting that we are still the "home of the free". The change to the contrary has come about so gradually, we didn't even realize we have been cooked alive like the proverbial frog in a pot of water. Yes, we are still freer than say, North Korea. But compared to our own history, which is the gold-standard of freedom, we most certainly are not.

I got the idea to write *The Lemonade Stand* a long time ago. I did it mostly for my kids. I wanted to teach them that not only can it happen here, but, in fact, it is *happening* here. The signs of it are everywhere. All you have to do is look...and understand.

Every single day you can find an example in the news about just how unfree we have become. Just like the examples I cited above. Those examples happened as I was writing this. And when I am done writing this, examples will continue to happen every single day. If I waited for the examples to stop so I could stop writing, I would never stop writing. But there are not enough people looking and understanding anymore so I wanted to bring it to people, especially young people like my kids, in a way that was easy to understand. The writing of this story may stop but the understanding of what is happening around us must continue. Hopefully I have contributed to that in some small way with this book.

As my kids read the story, I wanted it to be that almost every time something happens in the story to the main character, Kayla, or an event occurs in her town, and my kids say to themselves *that couldn't or wouldn't happen,* there would be proof that yes it can, or did. The reason I put so many footnotes and references in the story is to point them to that proof.

And because the story is fiction based on fact, because it is based on actual historical and current events, it is a story that can go on forever writing itself as headlines change. I tried to reflect that in the story by not giving it a final ending. Because in real life, this is a story that does not end as well.

There are several big questions that come out of *The Lemonade Stand*:

- Do we wind up like "red fingernails"? Dead in a ditch?
- Or maybe we continue hobbling on as we have been for decades now, blissfully unaware that the walls of tyranny are slowly closing in?
- Or maybe, just maybe, enough of us wake up and start fighting to take back our freedom?

In the end, if I can use this story just to convince my two kids that Freedom and Liberty are worth fighting for, it was worth it.